Praise for
The *Love, California* Series

"A captivating world of glamour, romance, and intrigue."
— Melissa Foster, *NYT* & *USA Today* Bestselling Author

"Jan Moran is the new queen of the epic romance."
— Rebecca Forster, *USA Today* Bestselling Author

"Jan rivals Danielle Steel at her romantic best.
— Allegra Jordan, author of *The End of Innocence.*

The Winemakers (St. Martin's Griffin)

"Beautifully layered and utterly compelling." — Jane Porter, *New York Times* & *USA Today* Bestselling Author

"Readers will devour this page-turner as the mystery and passions spin out." – *The Library Journal*

"Moran weaves knowledge of wine and winemaking into this intense family drama." – *Booklist*

"Spellbound by the thread of deception."
– *The Mercury News*

Scent of Triumph (St. Martin's Griffin)

"A gripping story of poignant love. Perfumes are so beautifully described."
— Gill Paul, Author of *The Secret Wife*

"A sweeping saga of one woman's journey through WWII. A heartbreaking, evocative read!"
— Anita Hughes, Author of *Lake Como*

"Courageous heroine, star-crossed lovers, an HEA."
– *Heroes and Heartbreakers*

Beauty Mark

A Love, California Novel

Book Number 2

by

Jan Moran

SUNNY PALMS

PRESS

Library of Congress Cataloging-in-Publication Data
Moran, Jan.
/ by Jan Moran

ISBN 978-1-942073-00-0 (softcover)
ISBN 978-1-942073-02-4 (epub ebooks)

Disclaimer: In this book we have relied on information provided by third parties
and have performed reasonable verification of facts. We assume no responsibility
or liability for the accuracy of information contained in this book. No
representations or warranties, expressed or implied, as to the accuracy or
completeness of this book or its contents are made. The information in this
book is intended for entertainment purposes only, and the characters are entirely
fictional. Every effort has been made to locate the copyright holders of materials
used in this book. Should there be any errors or omissions, we shall be pleased
to make acknowledgements in future editions.

Printed in the U.S.A.
Cover design by Silver Starlight Designs
Cover images copyright 123RF

For Inquiries Contact:
Sunny Palms Press
9663 Santa Monica Blvd, STE 1158, Beverly Hills, CA, USA
www.sunnypalmspress.com
www.JanMoran.com

Books by Jan Moran

Contemporary Fiction
The Love, California Series
Flawless
Beauty Mark
Runway
Essence
Style
Sparkle

20th Century Historical Fiction
The Winemakers: A Novel of Wine and Secrets
Scent of Triumph: A Novel of Perfume and Passion
Life is a Cabernet: A Companion Wine Novella to The Winemakers

Nonfiction
Vintage Perfumes

Browse her entire collection at www.JanMoran.com.
Get a free read when you join Jan's VIP list.

1

London, England

"WHERE IS SHE?" Scarlett Sandoval sat in the tea room at Brown's Hotel in Mayfair waiting for her client to arrive. She was annoyed, as usual, at Fleur's perpetual tardiness. She ordered a second pot of tea and checked her watch. Even though they were traveling on a private jet to Los Angeles, they did have a schedule, something that frequently escaped the fashion designer's notice.

"I'll take a car to the airport," David said, rising from his chair and slipping a button through a buttonhole on his crisply tailored bespoke suit. "I don't want to get stuck in traffic. You're the best one on the team at handling her anyway."

"We'll see you there. Soon, I hope." Scarlett made a face. David Baylor was on the partner track at the same high profile law firm, Marsh & Gold, in Los Angeles. Years ago, when she'd been in the firm's New York office, and he'd been in Los Angeles, they'd threatened a cross-country affair, but now that she'd relocated and they were in the same city, they were glad they hadn't crossed the line. David was a good work friend, and had recently become engaged.

Her mother was right. At this rate she might never get married. Polite conversation bubbled across the room. Scarlett nibbled on a scone, and then checked her watch again. She glanced around the stylish room, which had been renovated in recent years. Antique fireplaces flickered in the corner, while contemporary art splashed color across the walls. Silver gleamed against white tablecloths, and VIPs of London filled every tapestry covered chair.

A flurry of activity erupted at the entry way to the Georgian townhouse in which Brown's had been established since 1837. The venerable old hotel was the law firm partner's preferred hotel in London. As the story went, Alexander Graham Bell made the first telephone call from the lobby at Brown's. Couldn't Fleur have managed a call on the gold-plated mobile phone usually glued to her ear?

Speak of the devil, thought Scarlett, dropping her buttered scone in shock. Fleur strutted into the room, and Scarlett realized what the commotion at the front door was about. Her client struck a defiant pose at the door, while a murmur rose across the room and the tea room manager hurried to speak to her. Waist-length purple hair matched her six-inch platform shoes, but it was the attire in between—or rather, the lack of it—that had the manager in a dither. Her sliver of a dress was definitely against the dress code at

Brown's Tea Room. Why then had Fleur insisted on meeting her here instead of at the airport?

"Put this on my corporate account, please," Scarlett whispered to the tea sommelier. Hastily grabbing her briefcase, she slid from the booth. She covered the room in long strides and hooked her arm in Fleur's, whisking her from the room.

"Hey, wait a minute," Fleur said, struggling to keep up in her platform shoes. "We need to get some shots."

That's when Scarlett saw the billionaire shipping magnate with whom Fleur had been pictured in the tabloids. The impeccable Vladimir Ivanov was having tea in a booth near the entrance with another woman. She sighed and checked her anger against her client. "The plane is waiting."

Scarlett nodded to the doorman, who was attired in a formal top hat and three-quarter length coat. He signaled for a black town car that had been idling on the quiet block. Out of nowhere appeared several paparazzi; they began snapping photos like mad. Fleur placed her hands on her hips and angled a shoulder in a provocative pose for them.

"Let's go, Fleur." Scarlett gave her a minute, and then grabbed her hand. This was not the brilliant legal career Scarlett had imagined while she was pulling all-nighter study sessions in law school. She slid into the backseat and let out a sigh of relief as the driver steered his way through London.

"Did you call them?" Scarlett had traveled with Gina "Fleur" Georgopoulos long enough to know that she often called paparazzi to keep herself in the headlines. A Greek native from the Bronx, she'd moved to London, adopted an accent, and took the world by surprise when she had one of her boyfriends buy billboards over Sunset Boulevard in Los Angeles. Soon everyone was asking, *who is Fleur of London?* On some level—a low one, Scarlett thought—it was brilliant.

"If I'd just had the chance to speak to Vladimir, they could've gotten some great shots. Cover page stuff." Fleur sniffed. "I'll be lucky if those make it into print at all."

Fleur was known for her outlandish costumes. "Chin up, Fleur," Scarlett said. "I'm sure that outfit is print-worthy. Besides, you should be celebrating. This new cosmetics trademark deal is nearly complete. You're about to be one very wealthy woman." One of the top makeup companies in the world, High Gloss Cosmetics, was licensing the Fleur of London trademark for a new line of brilliantly colored products, including lipstick, eyeshadow, eyeliner, and mascara.

"Pour me a couple of shots of vodka then." Fleur smiled coyly and shoved on oversized sunglasses, her signal that she was through talking.

"I have a call to make," Scarlett replied, matching Fleur's smile. A bartender she was not.

Scarlett punched in a number on her phone. "We're on our way," she said, and clicked off. She had already had a long day of negotiations regarding the intellectual property uses, and now they were in route to Los Angeles for Fleur to meet with the company in person. It was the final phase in the deal. Fleur was a master of self-promotion who had, surprisingly, few other talents. She hired other fashion designers to create her line, dressed outlandishly, wore makeup more suited for Kabuki theatre, and dated billionaires. This got her a multimillion dollar deal that others worked a lifetime for and never realized.

When they arrived at the airport, Fleur gravitated toward the partner, which was fine with Scarlett. In her mauve silk blouse and chic grey wool suit, she could hardly compare to the peacock style of Fleur. Not that she wanted to, though. Scarlett preferred being an advisor to her famous clients.

Most fashion designers and actors she worked with were creative and accomplished, and they worked well together with mutual respect, but occasionally an eccentric client like Fleur came along, and usually landed in her lap at the firm. Scarlett was one of Marsh & Gold's top intellectual property attorneys, and made the firm a fortune every year.

"Welcome aboard." Lucan Blackstone was her fifty-something boss from Los Angeles. Originally from London, Lucan seemed to be going through a permanent mid-life crisis. Fast cars, fast women, fast money—that was his motto. He traded in Teslas, Lamborghinis, yachts, and long-legged European models. Both men and women were attracted to his charm, his intelligence, and his silver-haired, movie-star good looks. He was the consummate rainmaker. Marsh & Gold partners often overlooked his missteps to keep his deals flowing.

Scarlett stepped into the cabin of a newly outfitted Boeing jet, which had replaced the Gulfstream 550 Lucan had deemed too small. The crew closed the door behind her, ready for wheels up.

She cocooned herself in a large white leather recliner, surrounded by creamy white and beige leather, polished burl wood trim, and every amenity one could want at fifty thousand feet. With a touch to a digital screen, she lowered the shade and adjusted her light. Her sparkling water and crudité vegetable plate had already been set out for her.

She might be cruising in luxury, but Scarlett had plenty of work to do on the twelve-hour flight. She'd learned to tune out whatever went on in the bar, or the stateroom behind her. She placed her laptop on the workspace in front of her and opened her briefcase, ignoring the blaring television, Fleur's incessant chatter, and Lucan's barking guffaws.

"Working the entire flight?" David asked. He'd already stretched out his large frame in the reclining chair. His hands were cupped behind his head.

"Some of it. We need to get this deal done. Just received the red-lined agreement back."

"Don't those High Gloss corporate attorneys have anything better to do? You'd think they were billing by the hour."

She felt the rumble of the jet engines as they prepared for take-off.

She shrugged. "Keeps us in business."

Lucan walked by on his way to the galley. "David, don't let us keep you up. Late night of partying with our English clients?"

"Sure, you know me, sir." David winked and Lucan playfully punched him on the shoulder.

"That's my boy," Lucan said.

Scarlett grinned. She happened to know David had worked much of the night, too. He'd called her to discuss points several times.

Lucan skirted the curved divans that followed the lines of the plane. No telling how many models had lined those seats, Scarlett thought. She was the only female in the firm who'd ever flown on this corporate jet, which was reserved for partners and their handpicked team, but there were plenty of women's things in the stateroom. Scarlett didn't want to know any more than she did. She kept her head down and kept working. "You've sure got him fooled."

"Lucan just wants to relive his misspent youth," David said with a chuckle. "Hey, thanks for your help last night. Couldn't have done it without you. Now, I've got to get some shut-eye," He snapped open a prescription bottle and poured out a couple of tablets. "Need an Ambien to sleep?"

Scarlett shook her head. "Not for me." A lot of consultants, attorneys, corporate finance pros, models, and entertainers who crisscrossed the globe on a weekly basis wolfed down Ambiens like they were Altoids. Shifting time zones could cause people to do that, Scarlett knew. In the old days it was alcohol, and she knew all about that from her father. She squeezed lime in her bubbly mineral water and took a drink.

"G'night, Scarlett." David pulled a sleep mask over his

eyes.

"Night, David. I'll wake you when we arrive." Scarlett flicked a few keys on her keyboard and hooked up to the wireless service onboard. One advantage to flying private was that there were no annoying announcements asking flyers to turn off their electronic equipment on departure and take-off. Coupled with long security lines and layovers, private jets were massive time-savers that allowed the firm to squeeze maximum time from valuable employees to serve high-paying clients. The deals they worked on were often staggering in value, especially in the Mergers and Acquisitions practice. The airplane began taxiing, gaining speed as it hurtled down the runway.

A minute later the wheels lifted from the ground and Scarlett felt the pressure of her body heavy in the seat as the plane climbed through clouds to blue skies above.

Once airborne, Scarlett gazed out the window and watched London recede from sight. When she was young she had dreamed of traveling like this, but it wasn't as glamorous as she'd imagined. As a first year attorney, she'd taken red-eye flights, arriving at client's offices after spending the night on an airplane. Or the corporate limousine would shuttle her home at five in the morning, just long enough to shower and return for another demanding day, while she napped in the back seat in route.

But she'd committed her life willingly. Scarlett loved the law and had a strong sense of justice. Even as a little girl, she'd wanted to protect the good kids and stick it to the bullies.

The intellectual stimulation never bored her, and she met fascinating, creative people in her beauty trademark work. She smiled. Instead of *trademarks*, her friend Johnny often teased her, shortening it to *beauty marks*.

She stifled a yawn, and made a mental note to call her mother when she landed. She'd missed her mother's birthday in London, but she promised to make it up to her.

Her family had moved to Los Angeles from Spain when she was a young girl. A few years later, after her father died of liver failure, and her brother Franco died in an ambush in the war in Afghanistan, Scarlett became her mother's sole support. She worked throughout school, received scholarships, took student loans, and lived frugally.

Scarlett's eyes welled as she thought of Franco. She and her brother had been so close. She missed his quick smile and sharp wit. Everyone loved him, and hardly a day went by that she didn't think of him. He was the bravest soul she'd ever known, and the best tribute she could give him was to emulate him and his approach to life.

As soon as Scarlett graduated from law school, she'd moved her mother from the barrio to the west side of Los Angeles, where she lived in a lovely little condominium and spent her time making baby clothes for children Scarlett might never have time to have.

Still, Isabel Sandoval didn't give up easily. Every time Scarlett visited her, she seemed to have another *nice young man* to introduce her to.

Somehow time had slipped away from Scarlett. It

seemed that one minute she was twenty-four and graduating from law school, and the next minute she was thirty-two with a ticking clock. She'd been a bridesmaid so many times she'd lost count. Even if she met someone today, she'd probably be thirty-five before she had children. She'd always thought she'd have a family by now. And so did her old-school mother. She adored her mother, but the world was different today.

One of the problems was that she wanted to get to know a man well before she married. As an attorney, she'd heard far too many horror stories to jump into a relationship. Maybe that's what held her back, she thought, suppressing another yawn.

Scarlett put on headphones to focus on the detailed task at hand. Dinner came and Scarlett ate while she worked, anxious to finish the agreement during the flight. They crossed the Atlantic and the eastern seaboard. Judging from the time they'd been in the air, they were somewhere over the Midwest United States, Scarlett figured. Finally, she hit save, closed her laptop, and got up to stretch.

She took off her jacket, and then wandered to the flight deck to say hello to the pilot and crew. "Hi, Jeffrey."

"Hi, Scarlett," the pilot replied with a grin, touching a finger to his forehead. The aircraft was on autopilot.

She chatted with Jeffrey and the crew about upcoming flight plans, which included the next European rugby match, snow skiing in the southern hemisphere, a fly fishing junket in Scotland, and Formula One and Grand Prix races. Lucan spent a fortune on entertaining clients, but it certainly paid off.

Scarlett was booked for Fashion Week in Paris, and the Cannes Film Festival, where she often negotiated licensing deals for many of her clients. She went to all the glamorous parties, but she was not there to play. Marsh & Gold partners expected her to bring in new business, and she did.

In truth, her manic work pace and extensive travel didn't allow for much of a personal life. She envied her friends who managed to balance their lives.

As she walked to the galley for tea, she thought of her good friend and client, Verena Valent, who, after having lost her family's legendary skincare salon to an unscrupulous investor, created another skincare line. Verena managed to blend work, the care of her twin sisters and her grandmother, and a new relationship. How did she do it?

But Scarlett knew the answer. It was the flexibility Verena had as an entrepreneur. She was always busy, but on a time schedule of her own making. It was the same with their other friends, such as Dahlia, whose family ran a perfume business, and Fianna, who was a fashion designer and owned a boutique.

For eight years Scarlett had been focused on working her plan, investing her life into her career, and making partner. After graduation, she had sat for two of the toughest bar exams in the country—California and New York—and passed them both on the first try.

She'd had several competing offers, but she'd accepted a

generous one from Marsh & Gold. Now, she was next in line on the partner track. The decision would be made next week. A satisfied smile curved her lips. Soon it would be worth the years of struggle.

Scarlett picked up the green tea she'd brewed and sat down on the divan. She kicked off her shoes, took a few sips, and leaned her head back. She closed her eyes. It felt so good to relax. They still had a couple of hours before landing at the Van Nuys airport in Los Angeles, where the corporate plane was kept. She felt herself drift off.

Her dreams were quite realistic sometimes. "Mmm," she murmured, as someone stroked her shoulders and arms, which felt so good. She couldn't remember who he was, this man in her dreams, she couldn't see his face. If she opened her eyes... but her eyelids were heavy.

"Just relax," he whispered. He ran a firm hand down her throat and chest, pausing on her breast.

She smiled in her sleep. Who was this virile dream man who seemed so real? One of her old boyfriends, or someone she was yet to meet? She had to know. Straining against her slumber, she fluttered her eyes, trying to capture him.

As she did, she gasped, and shot bolt upright on the divan. "What are you doing?"

"Relax," Lucan repeated. He hovered over her, and his white dress shirt was unbuttoned. "You work so hard, Scarlett. A beautiful woman like you needs a break."

"Lucan, stop it." Scarlett glared at him. "We're not doing this. Get away from me."

"Come on, Scarlett." He twirled a lock of her coppery blond hair around his finger. "Who's to know? David's zoned out on Ambien. Fleur passed out in the stateroom from too much vodka." A smile curved his perfectly tanned face. "And the crew won't talk. So let's have fun."

"Absolutely not." Scarlett stood up, weaving a little on her feet from a mixture of exhaustion and air turbulence.

"Scarlett, Scarlett. So naïve in so many ways." Lucan patted the spot next to him. "Sit down. I'll have a couple of nightcaps made for us." He pressed a button and spoke to the crew. "I won't bite."

She touched the cabin wall for support and glanced around. Where could she go? The stateroom door was closed. David was snoring in the front of the cabin. But a crew member would be here any minute. She perched on the bench, leaving space between them.

"So, is there someone else in your life?" His voice was warm and amicable. "You can tell me. After all, you're going to be a partner soon."

"Lucan, I don't want to talk about my personal life." Of which I have none, she thought. And then, partner? Did he really say that? She scooted to the edge of the seat. "And I'm awfully tired."

He stared at her, his brilliant blue eyes crinkling with laughter at the corners. He was a virile, handsome man, and he knew it. His irresistible charm had made a fortune for the firm. "I have a little pick-me-up if you need it." He brought out a tiny vial filled with white powder. "Come on, loosen up, Scarlett."

"Look, I'm not into that. Please leave me alone so I can take a nap before landing."

"Let me help you relax," Lucan said.

She started to rise, but he pounced, knocking her against the back of the sofa. In a flash, he was all over her. Scarlett flailed, but he was a muscular man, and he pinned her down. She glanced over his shoulder and saw a female crew member delivering the two snifters of cognac Lucan asked for.

"Help me," Scarlett cried.

The petite dark-haired woman looked shocked, then angry. Scarlett reached out to her, pleading with her as she struggled under Lucan's weight. Suddenly, the crew member dropped the drink tray on purpose, and the glasses shattered on the table. "Sir, I'm so sorry!" she exclaimed. "Watch out for the glass."

Startled, Lucan rolled off her and jumped to his feet. "You idiot! What's wrong with you? Clean this up and get out." Lucan buttoned his shirt and fussed with his hair.

Scarlett sprang up and threw a grateful look to the woman, who scurried away to get cleaning supplies.

"Don't you ever do that again," Scarlett snapped.

"What? You're overreacting." Lucan spread his hands out in an innocent gesture. "Your honor, I'm innocent."

The crew member rushed back, but she took her time cleaning. "Need to clean this mess up," she said calmly, brushing her dark hair over her shoulder. Her name tag read Lavender. She flicked on a small vacuum cleaner.

Scarlett turned on her heel and marched to the flight deck. She was so livid she couldn't stay in the same cabin with him.

"David, we're almost home." Scarlett spoke loudly to wake her colleague.

"Huh? Oh, Scarlett, what'd I miss?" David lifted his eye mask and rubbed his eyes.

"Not a thing." She shot a look at Lucan, and he suppressed a grin. "It was the best kind of flight. Unremarkable." She wished she could slap that grin off Lucan's face. What on earth was he thinking? She was still fuming.

Fleur came stumbling from the stateroom, her purple hair and makeup in disarray, her gold-plated phone already pressed to her ear.

"Have a good sleep?" Lucan asked when she hung up.

Fleur yawned. "Yeah."

Lucan's eyes roamed over her. "I assume you want to swing by the hotel and freshen up before we go out."

"Sure. Whatever."

Scarlett bit back a reply. The man was indefatigable. Then she remembered she'd gone straight from a meeting in Studio City to catch the outbound flight for London. Her car was still at the office in Century City, near her townhouse in Beverly Hills.

"I've got a car waiting for us here," Lucan said, as if reading her mind.

"Thanks, but I'm meeting a friend," she said cordially. Why had he ruined their professional relationship? What a jerk.

When they scudded down the runway in Van Nuys, Scarlett breathed a sigh of relief, glad to be home. As they taxied, he gazed out the window at palm trees swaying against a mountain backdrop.

Lucan and Fleur got off the plane first. Scarlett gathered her laptop and exited the plane with David.

"Wait right here," Lucan said to Fleur. "I forgot something."

Lucan pushed his way past Scarlett, and she nearly dropped her laptop. She clucked her tongue. The man was an oaf.

Once inside the airport, Scarlett ducked into the women's bathroom to avoid Lucan pressuring her into joining them in the car. She was washing her hands when the petite, dark-haired crew member who'd come to her aid opened the door. Scarlett raised her eyes and met her gaze in the mirror.

"Hi." The woman drew her brows together. "Are you okay?"

"I guess so." Scarlett lifted a shoulder and let it fall. "That was fast thinking. I really appreciate what you did." She smiled. "My name is Scarlett."

"And I'm Lavender. Hey, we're a colorful pair," the young woman said with a grin. "My mother was a hippie."

"I have no excuse. My real name is Escarlata."

Lavender laughed. "Look," she said, turning serious, "I've been in situations like that myself, but you're a big attorney, right?"

"Not immune to idiots, though." She turned off the faucet and dried her hands.

"And he's your boss?" Lavender looked sorry for her.

Scarlett nodded.

"I left my last job because of sexual harassment." Lavender shuddered. "I don't need that in my life."

"No woman does." Scarlett was still furious. She was smart, but she was street smart, too. She was angry with herself for missing the signs. But Lucan was the one to blame.

They spoke a little more before Scarlett left to retrieve her luggage.

As Scarlett walked out, she saw Lucan ahead of her, so she hung back to avoid him. He glanced around and then tossed a package into the trash. She stopped, hoping he hadn't seen her.

Lavender caught up with her. "It's okay, I've got your back," she said. "He's gone."

Scarlett grinned at her new friend. "Thanks." As she was wheeling her luggage toward the taxi line, her phone rang.

"Hi chica, are you back from London?" It was Johnny Silva, her childhood friend from the barrio, who'd been best friends with her brother Franco. He was the maître d' at the Polo Lounge now.

"Just landed, and waiting for a taxi." She was glad to hear from him.

"You, in a taxi line? It's almost eleven at night. Thought Marsh & Gold always called a limo for you. Are they having budget cuts?"

"No, it just worked out that way." Scarlett didn't want to tell Johnny about Lucan. Ever since they'd been children, he'd always sprang to her defense. She'd never hear the end of it.

"I'm nearby. I'll come get you. Wait there."

When Johnny wheeled into the airport fifteen minutes later, Scarlett greeted him with a hug. "So glad to see you, Johnny. Thanks for the ride."

"Anything for my chica. Things were awfully quiet without you." Johnny lifted her luggage into the trunk of his vintage red Mustang convertible. He'd bought it years ago, and had restored it one piece at a time.

It was a warm evening, and he had the top down. As he opened the door for her, his glossy black hair shimmered in the evening lights. "Are you hungry?"

"A little. Dinner was somewhere over the Atlantic." Scarlett slid into the car.

"Want to head over to the hotel? Lance is working on some new dishes tonight."

"I'd like that," Scarlett said, finally relaxing after the long flight. She never had to be anyone other than who she was with Johnny. Why can't romantic relationships be like this?

As Johnny drove, they talked about their friends, Verena and Lance, who had been dating for a while. Lance was the executive chef at the Beverly Hills Hotel, the legendary pink palace on Sunset Boulevard in Beverly Hills, a favorite hotel of Hollywood stars throughout the decades. Johnny was the maître d' at the Polo Lounge, where the beautiful people still gathered and felt at home.

To the people who'd lived in Beverly Hills for many years, like some of Scarlett's friends and their families, the five-square-mile community would always be a little village, where doctors still made house calls, shops had private house accounts, and restaurants and delicatessens let regular customers run a monthly tab.

Today, Van Cleef & Arpels and Cartier glittered on Rodeo Drive, and tour buses lumbered along pristine residential streets, but the city still maintained its charm among residents, who could walk almost anywhere in the city—a rarity in the car-dependent culture of Los Angeles.

Not that many of them did, of course.

Johnny parked and they threaded their way through the back entrance of the luxury hotel. Outside, under pink archways, the open air terrace dining area was ablaze with red bougainvillea, green garden chairs, and white tablecloths.

They reached the front of the Polo Lounge, where Johnny showed Scarlett to a booth in the bar area. Dark green walls created a clubby ambiance, mirrors reflected the dazzling array of guests, and polo pictures and a green-and-white striped ceiling harkened to the hotel's early days. Strains of jazz floated in the air.

"Scarlett, welcome home," said a slender blond woman who was already seated in the booth. She wore a creamy silk sheath dress and pearls.

"Verena, it's so good to see you." Scarlett hugged her friend and scooted in beside her. "I feel like I've been gone forever." She loosened the collar of her blouse and smoothed her hair back.

"Seems like it. A month, wasn't it?" Verena's fair porcelain skin seemed to glow in the low lights. Whether it was from happiness or her new skincare line, Scarlett couldn't tell, but she was glad Verena was doing better. After all she'd been through with her business and her family, she deserved it.

"That's right. Milan, Florence, Paris, London." It sounded exciting, but she'd often worked sixteen hour days. Still, she had to admit she met amazing people and dined in all the best restaurants. Working at the firm was like having velvet shackles.

"Has Johnny told you the news?" Verena could hardly contain herself.

"No, what's going on?"

Verena looked like she was going to burst with happiness. "I'll let him tell you."

Johnny winked at her. "I'll get Lance." He disappeared into the kitchen.

"Did Lance propose?" Scarlett touched Verena's left hand, which was bare.

"No, not that. Too soon for us." Verena's blue eyes were as brilliant as sapphires, and they glowed with excitement.

"When you're ready, we should talk about prenuptial

agreements."

"I lost everything, remember?" Verena laughed. "But we're happy."

"You're creating new intellectual property now, trademarks, copyrights, service marks." Scarlett started to launch into a legal discourse, and then she caught Verena's amused expression. It was late, and she was being overzealous again. She couldn't help it; it was in her blood.

"Relax, Scarlett. Everything in time, Mia says."

At the mention of Verena's grandmother, Scarlett pressed a hand to her heart. "How is she?"

"Much better now. She's been released from the hospital. She's a real fighter. In fact, she and Camille went shopping today. You can't keep a fashionista down when Neiman Marcus has its Last Call sale."

Scarlett smiled, imagining the two doyennes of beauty together. Camille was their friend Dahlia's grandmother; Camille had founded a perfume empire decades ago. Originally from Switzerland, Mia had established a skincare salon in Beverly Hills in the 1940s. After Verena's parents died in a tragic accident, Mia raised Verena and her two younger twin sisters.

Johnny appeared at the table, and with him was Lance Martel, the executive chef. They all greeted one another and sat down.

"I told Scarlett that you've been experimenting with some new dishes."

A half smile tugged at Lance's mouth. "Salmon or pork?"

"Salmon," Scarlett said.

"Good choice. I'll whip one up for you. Did Johnny tell you?"

Scarlett shook her head. "No, and I wish someone would. You're all killing me. What's going on?"

Johnny and Lance traded a look. "We're starting our own restaurant," Johnny said. "We'll finally be in a place of our own."

"Why, that's wonderful." Scarlett was truly happy for Johnny. Both men were talented, and had devoted followings. The restaurant business was tough, but if anyone could do it, these two could. "Congratulations. When, where, and what's the name?"

"Scarlett, slow down," Johnny said. "We just decided. As usual, you're several steps ahead of us."

Scarlett felt her cheeks grow warm and she laughed. "Occupational hazard."

Lance excused himself and went to prepare Scarlett's meal while the three friends caught up. When Lance returned with the salmon dish, it was one of the best preparations she thought she'd ever had. It was perfectly moist, and seasoned with fresh herbs. A citrus reduction sauce was just the right accent, and a bed of spaghetti squash and spinach balanced the fish. Scarlett realized she was starving.

After she'd finished eating, Verena and Lance left. Scarlett watched them go. She was elated for them, but she also wondered where the magic was that had brought the two of them together. Where was her magic?

"Would you like to have hot chocolate by the pool before I take you home?" Johnny asked.

Johnny knew her well. She'd almost forgotten how they used to drink hot chocolate together. "I'd like that."

They strolled through the hotel, past the old soda fountain shop and out to the pool. A server delivered the hot chocolate he'd asked for. They were seated at a table when Scarlett said, "You know what I'd like to do?"

"No telling," Johnny said, watching her with dancing eyes, dark as mahogany.

Scarlett slipped her feet from her high heels and rolled up her trousers. Johnny laughed and followed suit. Soon the two of them were sitting at the pool, dangling their legs in the cool water, and cupping hot chocolate in their hands.

Scarlett tilted her head back and gazed up at the full moon, which cast shimmering shadows on the rippling water.

Johnny touched her chin. "Hold it right there. You have cat's eyes in this light, a gorgeous golden green. Simply beautiful."

As was Johnny. Lots of women adored him. Scarlett noted a dimple in one of his cheeks when he grinned. "What a funny thing to say, Johnny."

He shrugged. "I'm noticing the little things more." He waved a hand around. "Look at us. Good friends, a good place in our lives. We've come so far, chica. Let's savor our success."

"Who has time?" The partner track had sapped her energy. The memory of Lucan assailed her thoughts.

"What a sad comment." Johnny slid his hand over hers and held it. "We have to make time. Think about it. Life doesn't get much better than this."

Scarlett gazed into his eyes. Johnny always spoke with such passion. That's what attracted her to him. Where, oh where, is a man like this in my love life?

Still, it was good to have friends like Johnny. If only Franco were here with them now, the three of them laughing and teasing each other like they used to, so long ago. Maybe he was looking down on them.

She rested her head on Johnny's shoulder and sipped her hot chocolate.

2

"HAPPY BIRTHDAY, DAHLIA," Scarlett said, hugging her friend before she sat down at the table for lunch at Crustacean in Beverly Hills. "Sorry I'm late." Her heels tapped along a plexiglass covered stream in the floor that curved through the upscale restaurant, which was beautifully decorated with Vietnamese antiques and fresh flowers.

"Just glad you could make it," Dahlia said, greeting her with warmth. "I know you're busy."

"Aren't we all?" Fianna swung her wavy red mane over the shimmering, one-shoulder aquamarine blouse she wore, a stark contrast to the black suit Scarlett had on. "I barely beat you here."

"Hi Fianna," Scarlett said, embracing her. "Love your outfit. One of your designs?"

"Of course. And it would look great on you. We need to update your image. Honestly, how many dark conservative suits do you need? Even if they are Armani. Come by the shop and I'll choose some fresh styles for you."

"Wish I had time," Scarlett said. "But my days are booked solid." And she'd been up half the night thinking about Lucan. His behavior was so disturbing. She could report it to Human Resources, but since Lucan was a partner, it could impact her partnership. Or, he might become overly solicitous, causing other partners to take a harder look at her. Not that she had anything to hide, and her work was outstanding. She stifled a yawn.

Fianna said, "Then let's meet after hours. I'll bring in Chinese food and you can play dress up."

"Promise me fresh coffee, too, and I'll be there." Scarlett loved the idea. It had been so long since she'd taken time for herself. Fianna Fitzgerald was the gregarious, outgoing one of their group. With wild red tresses, one blue eye, one brown eye, and a soft Irish lilt, she turned heads wherever she went. A graduate of FIDM, the Fashion Institute of Design and Merchandising in Los Angeles, Fianna was struggling to make her way as a fashion designer. "And I owe you a plan for your licensing strategy, too."

"If you're busy, Scarlett, I could look at it for Fianna." Dahlia ran her family's perfumery, Parfums Dubois, which had been established by her grandmother, Camille Dubois. "We've done so many celebrity licensing deals for perfume. Fianna, you should brand a fragrance, too." Dahlia was a petite powerhouse who regularly commuted between Paris, New York, and Los Angeles.

"This is why I love my friends," Fianna said. "You're all so smart and generous."

"And don't forget gorgeous." Verena slid into a plush chair beside Scarlett. "Every man in the place is sneaking glances at this table." She placed an oversized Chanel bag beside her chair, and took out two gift boxes. "Happy birthday, Dahlia. The small one is from all of us."

Dahlia unwrapped the first item and held up a pair of gold chandelier earrings embellished with faceted amethyst drops. "These are absolutely stunning. Thank you all." Dahlia put the earrings on. "I love them."

Scarlett said, "We thought they'd be beautiful on you."

"Elena Eaton made them especially for you." Verena said, smiling. "Now open the next one."

"Is this what I think it is?" Dahlia picked up the box wrapped in shiny white paper with a silver bow and wax emblem and unwrapped it. "Your new line! Congratulations, Verena. You've worked so hard on this." She removed several skincare items and opened the serum, which was based on Verena's grandmother's formula. "This smells wonderful," she said. "And the new packaging is so chic. Are you ready to launch?"

"We're close," Verena said. Her friends had been testing the line. This was the first time they'd seen the actual packaging. "Dab a little on the back of your hand. I think you'll love the new consistency. It's still incredibly effective." She reached into her purse again. "Actually, I have goodie bags for everyone."

While they all exclaimed and began sampling the new line, Scarlett inclined her head. "How is your partnership with Wilhelmina Jones working out for the infomercial production and fulfillment?"

"Excellent. She's a professional, and a welcome change from Herringbone Capital."

"Enough business for a minute. Am I the only one who's famished?" said Fianna. As a server sailed past them with a platter of hot dishes, she raised her nose and inhaled. "The scent of garlic is making me hungry." The friends decided to share appetizers, as well as the garlic crab and garlic noodles, famous An Family specialties from the secret kitchen-within-a-kitchen at the upscale Vietnamese restaurant.

After ordering, Scarlett handed her menu to the server and went on. "When are you filming the infomercial?"

"Soon." Verena glanced around the table. "And I'd love for you all to be in it. Wilhelmina thought it was a great idea."

Fianna and Dahlia immediately agreed. Verena told them that another friend, Penelope Plessen, a renowned model, had also agreed to be in the shoot as a special favor. "What about you, Scarlett?"

She shook her head. "I'd love to, but I'm afraid it might be a conflict of interest for other clients I represent."

Lunch was served and the friends continued to talk as they exclaimed over the crab and noodles. Scarlett was thinking about the episode on the plane again when Fianna snapped her fingers. "Earth to Scarlett. Are you still with us?"

Scarlett passed a hand over her forehead. "Oh, sure, I'm

here." She hadn't caught a word. "Say again?"

"We were talking about the premiere in Westwood this weekend," Fianna said. "Several of the stars are wearing my designs, so I can bring all of you. Do you have a date, or can you make it? Could be good for business."

Fianna was right. "No date, but I'll come," Scarlett said. How long had it been since she'd been on a date?

"Bring Johnny," Verena said. "Lance is going, too."

"I'll check." Johnny had been Scarlett's stand-by date for years. Many people even thought they were a couple. Scarlett had always laughed about that, but if she really examined their relationship, she'd have to admit he was the best date she'd ever had. She'd had some spectacularly bad dates. Hollywood attracted its share of strange characters.

After they ate, Scarlett checked her watch and gulped her jasmine tea. She had to go back to work. "Do you have a date, Fianna?"

"No time for one, I'm afraid. I'll be working beforehand to make sure my gowns fit the actresses perfectly. I have a seamstress standing by for any accidents. Remember the Golden Globes fashion disaster last year? At least that wasn't one of my gowns that split open."

"Thank goodness it wasn't on stage," Dahlia added. "The poor girl." They all remembered the actress who'd literally split her seams laughing at an after party.

"I hate to break this up," Scarlett said. "But I have a full afternoon of meetings." And her first one was with Lucan Blackstone. She dreaded seeing him again.

Scarlett stepped into the elevator in a high-rise building in Century City, a community adjacent to Beverly Hills, where Marsh & Gold's west coast offices were located. She was whisked to the top floor without a stop. Behind the reception area was a wall of glass. On a clear day, even the Hollywood sign in the hills was visible from this high vantage point.

The décor was at once classic and modern. Hunter green walls and sleek ebony furniture met plush burgundy carpet that masked footfalls in the busy office. Scarlett hurried to a glass conference room. She was always early.

Scarlett grabbed a bottle of water and eased into a leather chair at the oblong table. She was organizing her notes when Lucan Blackstone sauntered in.

"Well, if it isn't Miss Scarlett," Lucan said with a drawl, mimicking a *Gone with the Wind* southern accent.

The hair on the back of Scarlett's neck bristled. She hated the nickname Lucan called her when he wanted to annoy her. Clearly he hadn't forgotten she'd snubbed his advances.

"Lucan." Scarlett nodded pleasantly, acting as if nothing had occurred between them. Other partners and David would be here any moment. In addition, she'd once heard a rumor that the main conference room had a recording device, though she doubted if meetings were seldom, if ever, recorded anymore. It had to be a holdover from the last decade.

"You missed a good talk with Fleur yesterday evening," Lucan said, leaning back in his chair. "You should've come with us. We met some of her colleagues over dinner. Good thing I was there. We have an opportunity for substantial new business on the table."

Scarlett stared at him. She seriously doubted that Fleur or her friends had been in any shape to discuss business last night. "That was sure lucky, Lucan. You know, David and I have been pulling all-nighters. Glad you saw to it." She was fuming under her calm exterior. She consulted her notes. When she looked up, she saw Lucan's eyes locked on her blouse. She cleared her throat, and he grinned.

Scarlett was appalled. She'd never had this treatment in the New York office. Some of her colleagues there had referred to the Los Angeles office as the "wild west," but she'd had no idea what they meant by that. She had a sinking feeling that she was discovering their meaning.

In New York, she commanded respect. Her clients were major cosmetic companies and international fashion designers. She'd been transferred to Los Angeles to work with Hollywood clients on licensing agreements. As her mother was here, she'd been pleased when the firm made it permanent, though now she was beginning to regret it. Had Lucan waited until the paperwork was complete to make his move?

David rushed in. His hair was mussed, and his shirt was partly untucked. He plopped down a large cup of coffee. "Scarlett, Lucan, good to see you."

Lucan slapped him on the back. "David, my man. We've got a new piece of business with Grier Pharmaceuticals I'd like you to handle."

David shot a look at Scarlett. "Uh, sure, Lucan. But Scarlett's got the lead on that account, right?" He shifted uncomfortably in his chair.

"What do you need, Lucan? I've got room on my calendar." She didn't, but she'd find the hours somewhere.

Lucan grinned and waved her off. "Not to worry, Scarlett. David's got this one, right buddy?"

Scarlett opened her mouth to protest, but the other partners filed in and took their seats. As the meeting progressed, Scarlett contributed to the dialog and Lucan demonstrated his usual ebullience. No one would have suspected a thing.

Afterward, Scarlett had an off-site meeting scheduled to introduce Fleur to High Gloss Cosmetics. She passed an imposing cherry wood reception desk on her way out. A vase with at least three dozen red roses sat on the edge.

The young blond receptionist called to her. "Ms. Sandoval, these flowers arrived for you. Here's the card. Shall I put them in your office?"

Scarlett opened the little envelope. *For last night. LB.* Scarlett stuffed it into her pocket. "I'm going to be out for a while. Why don't you take those flowers home and enjoy them?"

The receptionist beamed, gushing about how gorgeous the flowers were.

Scarlett stalked through the front door. *The nerve of that man.* Was he teasing her, or was he a threat?

A sleek black limousine was idling in the parking garage. Scarlett got in and rested her eyes until they reached the Chateau Marmont, which was built high on Sunset Boulevard. Like the Rolling Stones, Fleur had taken up residence in suite sixty-four, the two bedroom penthouse suite with a wraparound terrace.

Chateau Marmont was designed after a royal villa in the Loire Valley. For decades it had been the favorite of rock stars and actors. Its reputation as a hedonistic west coast retreat was well deserved.

Scarlett called Fleur, who said she'd be right down.

An hour later, purple hair piled high on her head, Fleur made a dramatic exit, pausing again for paparazzi and angling her face to the side just so, and then swung into the car.

Fleur wore a silver metallic, skintight body suit with a belt slung low on her hips. Circular pieces were cut from each side, and the V-neckline dipped to her navel. One wrong move and she'd have a shocking wardrobe malfunction.

"These are business people, Fleur, we should be mindful of their schedule."

Fleur gave her smug smile. "I'm the star. They'll wait for me."

"My goodness, what happened to your lip?" Fleur's lip was cut and swollen, and it hadn't been like that when she'd left her at the airport.

Fleur mumbled something about slipping in the shower.

"It hurts. I need a drink. And I hope they shot me from my good side."

"Looks like you need stitches."

Fifteen minutes and two vodkas for Fleur later, they arrived at High Gloss Cosmetics on trendy Melrose Avenue in the heart of the fashion district. The corporate office was on nearby Wilshire Boulevard. The design group was still housed in the original shop, where they could keep abreast of fashions and trends.

Scarlett had completed other deals with High Gloss in the past. She'd handled the licensing for a glamorous Academy Award-winning actress and a French couturier. Both deals had been enormously profitable for everyone involved. Scarlett enjoyed representing her clients and handling the legal process. High Gloss wanted an edgy line to appeal to a younger clientele now.

"Good afternoon. Sorry to have kept you waiting," Scarlett said. She introduced Fleur to Olga Kaminsky, the chic, seemingly ageless granddaughter of the original founder.

"Not at all," Olga said, as gracious as ever. "Although I'm afraid we won't have as much time as I'd hoped."

Scarlett knew Olga ran a fast-paced company, and everyone was expected to keep up with her. High Gloss Cosmetics, Inc. was a Fortune 500 company listed on the New York Stock Exchange.

Olga's eyes fell to Fleur's lip. "Oh, dear, you've had quite an accident."

Fleur dropped her gaze and her cheeks flushed. "It's okay. It was nothing."

As they walked through the creative studio, Olga turned to Fleur. "My grandfather was a makeup artist who began in Vaudeville. After moving to Los Angeles in the 1920s, he established High Gloss Cosmetics for silent motion picture stars. Actors needed special makeup to withstand the intense heat of the lights used. Now, a century later, High Gloss still maintains its prestige position in the world of color cosmetics."

Scarlett knew their long affiliation with famous faces kept them in the forefront of fashion. Not a week went by that *Fashion News Daily*, the industry trade newspaper, didn't report on High Gloss products and deals. Fleur was lucky to be here. Scarlett hoped she realized it.

Scarlett glanced at Fleur, who was quiet and glassy-eyed. Scarlett made a mental note to have the bar removed from the limousine while Fleur was in town.

Olga stepped into a brightly painted open room that was a funky Mecca for makeup. Products of all colors lined the shelves, zebra-covered slipper chairs and leopard sofas were gathered in the middle of the room, and painted chandeliers brightened a pink ceiling.

"Makeup should be fun," Olga said. "That's the feeling we like to convey. Have a seat," she said to Fleur, who plopped onto a chair. "I look forward to sharing our creative visions and bringing a great new line to market."

Fleur glanced around. "I've changed my mind on the

deal."

Scarlett nearly flew out of her chair. "Olga, I'm sure what Fleur means is that she has some questions. We can discuss those and circle back to you. This is a get-to-know-one-another meeting today."

Fleur scowled. "I think I'm worth more. That's all I'm saying."

"You have quite a following, and that's why we're interested." Olga was blessedly levelheaded. "And we'll bring the full force of our creative, marketing, and distribution to the table."

"Let's look at the line," Scarlett said, diverting Fleur's attention. She wanted to throttle her client. Her behavior was wrong on so many levels. The deal had already been struck. Negotiation took place between the attorneys. If they couldn't work it out, the parties might meet again, but in this case, terms had already been agreed to. Only the final signatures remained outstanding. Since High Gloss was a public company, the licensing agreement was a carefully detailed document that had taken tremendous time to create.

Olga gestured to an array of lipstick, eyeshadow, eyeliner, and mascara on the table. "I had my creative team put together our proposed vision for you."

Fleur leaned over and began gouging color with her fingernail from tiny purple cases.

Olga quickly moved cleanser and cotton balls toward Fleur. Scarlett wished she could kick her client under the table, but the table top was glass.

"Such vibrant colors, aren't they?" Olga adjusted a makeup mirror for her.

"Awfully bright," Fleur said, scrunching her face.

"We welcome your input," Olga said. "You'll work with our creative team, who—"

Fleur cut in. "Black and white."

"You mean colors to go with neutrals?" Scarlett hoped it wasn't what she thought.

"Makeup in black and white," Fleur said, waving her hands. "To balance bright colors. The fashion is the focus. Black eyes, black lips, white cheeks. That's it. Revolutionary. Write that down, Scarlett." She slung her purse over her shoulder and got up, meandering to the door.

Her lips parted in astonishment, Olga stared at Scarlett.

"I imagine we'll be in touch later," Scarlett said. She rose and grabbed Fleur's arm. "We're going now," she said.

Once the car door was closed, Scarlett dropped her bag. "What the hell was *that* all about? Unless you come to your senses fast, you just lost the deal."

Fleur hiked her upper lip in disdain. "Lucan said I should make my own line."

"He *what?*" Scarlett couldn't believe what she'd just heard.

"He said I could make a lot more money." Fleur reached for the bottle of vodka.

"That's enough." Scarlett grabbed the bottle and put it back. Fleur's eyes widened.

The tiny hairs on the back of Scarlett's neck bristled, as

they always did when something wasn't right. One of her law professors once said she seemed to have a sixth sense for ferreting out the truth. "When did Lucan tell you that?"

"Last night."

"On the plane, or after we arrived?" Scarlett automatically switched gears and went into a line of questioning.

"After. You know, last *night*."

"Where did he tell you this?"

"In bed."

That wasn't exactly what she'd meant, but she'd take it. "And where was this bed?"

Fleur looked amused. "Uh, in my room?"

"At the Marmont?"

"Yeah, so?" She crossed her arms indignantly.

"So I'd appreciate it if you told me the truth from now on. I'm actually on your side, Fleur." As they crept along Sunset Boulevard in traffic, Scarlett gazed out the window.

Was Lucan harassing her because of her denial of his advances, or was there something more to this? She rubbed her neck. *What was Lucan up to?*

3

"READY TO GO?" Johnny leaned against the doorjamb and straightened his printed bow-tie. Scents of garlic, oregano, and rosemary swirled in the kitchen.

"Sure, just a minute." Lance finished his recipe calculations. When he looked up from his desk, he started to laugh. "Is that what I think it is? Come closer."

Johnny grinned and stepped into Lance's office.

"Bacon, I love it. I have to have one," Lance said. "And I don't even wear bow-ties."

Johnny's bow-tie had bacon silk-screened onto it. He'd collected more than a hundred bow-ties, but now he was making his own. "This one took a long time to get just right." Crisp-looking bacon strips flared from the center, and the knot appeared to be another strip wrapped around the bunch.

Bow-ties were a sort of trademark for Johnny, who started wearing them when he went to work for the Beverly

Hills Hotel. Once he ascended to the position of maître d', regular clients began recognizing him by his bow-ties. They even surprised him with ties, and he'd wear those gifts when he saw their reservation in the book. Dahlia's grandmother, Camille Dubois, was particularly keen on giving him exotic bow-ties she found in her travels.

Lance removed his white chef jacket. He wore a black T-shirt, checked chef pants, and rubber-soled clogs. "Where's this restaurant we're looking at?"

"Beverly Hills."

"Can we afford it?"

"It's a small place." Johnny kept a close eye on expenses. They could always grow into a larger space, and a small restaurant was intimate and easier to run. He didn't want to risk the mistakes he'd seen other restaurateurs make.

He and Lance had looked at a lot of restaurants, but something was always missing.

"Good location? That's the most important thing." Lance ran his hands through his thick hair.

"Great location. Come on, let's go." Johnny punched him in the arm, and the two men left through the back door.

They took Johnny's vintage Mustang convertible and cruised south from the Beverly Hills Hotel across Sunset Boulevard, past Will Rogers Park to a six-way intersection, where cars bolted from stop signs into the chaotic center.

"Whoa, there," Lance said, as a determined blond in a Bentley nearly side-swiped the car. "This is madness. You need the skill of a French cabbie negotiating the Arc de

Triomphe roundabout in Paris."

"Was that the scene of the crime?" Johnny swerved again, and then continued through a sunny, tree-lined residential neighborhood known as *the flats*, or the blocks between Sunset and Santa Monica Boulevards. Each street featured a different type of tree. Towering palms lined one, overarching maples grew together on another, and jacarandas blazed springtime purple on still another.

Lance grinned. "Verena's sly grandmother, Mia, orchestrated our meeting there, and we wandered the streets of Paris late one night. It was romantic, but nothing happened. Not until we returned to L.A., that is." He nodded at Johnny. "We have a special bungalow at the hotel."

"You're one lucky guy," Johnny said.

"Verena is great," Lance said. "That's one reason I'm determined to make this restaurant of ours a success. I want to build something for our future."

Johnny grew silent, thinking about Scarlett. He'd known her for years, ever since they were kids in the barrio. Their lives had traversed such different paths. She had gone to college and law school, graduated top of her class, and left for New York. He had gone to work, washing dishes and moving up the ranks. Some men were intimidated by Scarlett, but he knew her well. Did he know her too well?

"Lance, do you think Verena is *the one*?"

Lance stared from the window, and then nodded slowly. "If we keep on like this, I think so."

"How did you know?" Johnny wheeled into a parking

place in the commercial village of Beverly Hills. "I mean, was it like a lightning bolt from the sky?"

"Sure, at first. She's pretty hot. But then there's this feeling that grows. It's like you know you're home, but it's still exciting. Does that make sense?"

"Actually, it does."

"Verena's grandmother calls it kismet." Lance raised a brow. "Why do you ask?"

Johnny got out and slammed the door, dodging his friend's question. "Here we are." He waved his hand toward a small stone cottage, a solitary holdout from the shops that lined the street. The front yard was been turned into an outdoor dining patio.

"I've always wondered about this place," Lance said. "Looks like the owner held out against progress."

"That's exactly what happened. It was built in the 1920s. They sold the surrounding land and kept their house." Johnny strolled along a stone path that wove through the patio. Ivy climbed a low rock wall. Hummingbirds zipped past, and white tablecloths fluttered in the light breeze. Johnny walked inside.

"What a great place," Lance said. "We could do a lot with this." The hardwood floors needed refinishing, and the fireplaces needed a good cleaning, but he was most concerned about the kitchen.

The owner met them at the bar and explained the restaurateurs renting it were relocating to a larger place. They were closed, and cleaning out their furnishings and fixtures.

"May I see the kitchen?" asked Lance.

Johnny and Lance followed the owner to the kitchen, which was situated in the center of the cottage. Gleaming stainless steel equipment shone under bright lights. There was plenty of workspace for the staff they'd need.

Johnny walked around, but this was really Lance's domain. "What do you think, buddy?"

Lance ran a hand over the cool counters and grinned. "I think it's kismet."

"So what's kismet?"

"Mia says that's when something is meant to be."

After they left, they walked down the street for coffee. It was sunny, so they sat outside. Johnny whipped out a notepad. "Let's figure out what we'll need to open the doors, and to survive until we break even."

Lance started ticking off items he'd need in the kitchen. They put in costs for professional services such as accounting and legal work, though Johnny thought Scarlett could help them some, or at least advise them. They mapped out a plan to renovate and open the restaurant, and worked out a time table to do it all in. They'd have a lot more to do, but it was a beginning.

Johnny scribbled estimates for signage, advertising, a launch party, press, and kitchen and wait staff.

"Now pad those by at least thirty percent," Lance said.

"For what?"

"I don't want any surprises. When you're starting a business, everything seems to cost more than anticipated.

Let's plan on it from the beginning."

They continued working on their business plan. When they finished their coffee, Lance got up to get refills for them. Johnny added a few more items to the list, and then he tallied the numbers again. He leaned back in his chair and pushed a hand through his hair.

"What's the damage?" Lance placed a steaming cup in front of Johnny.

"More than we've got."

"It usually is. We'll need investors," Lance said. "I've got a couple of clients from the hotel who expressed interest in backing us." Lance grinned. "Between my food and your good looks at the door, they think we've got a winning combination."

"How much are they willing to invest?"

Lance named a figure. "I know it's not enough, but we'll raise the money. How about you? Anyone you know?" He sipped his coffee.

Johnny stirred his coffee and grew thoughtful. "I'll make a few calls. You know how it is, people talk and promise things, but when you actually call them on it, usually turns out few of them were serious."

"I've noticed that here in L.A. Not so much when I worked in New York and Europe."

"Maybe it's the sunshine." Johnny chuckled. He met hundreds of people a day, and sorting out the genuine from the flaky was always a challenge. Though his aim was to provide excellent service for all who visited the Polo Lounge, he made sure the regulars were given extra special care. Regular customers kept the restaurant full. They brought their friends and referred new people to him. Word of mouth could make or break a restaurant fast, particularly in the village of Beverly Hills. They weren't in a large city like New York or London, and their reputation was paramount.

"Well, my friend, I think we've found our location." Lance gulped his coffee and studied the numbers Johnny had written down. "But there's one huge item missing."

Johnny frowned. "What's that?" They'd covered of all the major items and needs.

"What's the name of our restaurant going to be?"

As he'd promised Lance, Johnny immediately began making phone calls to people he thought might invest in their restaurant. They were the usual sort of exuberant people who expressed interest: the trust fund babies who needed a profession to satisfy their parents, the retirees who longed to stay in the game, the Hollywood producers and stars who wanted a personal playground.

After a few hours on the phone at his kitchen table, Johnny was dejected. Everyone wished him well, but no one was willing to invest.

He drummed his fingers on the plan he and Lance had drawn up. Johnny had transferred the numbers to a spreadsheet and prepared a summary of their business plan for investors to review.

Someday he'd be in a position to write a check. He knew

many people thought he was a playboy, but he'd learned a great deal by observing people at the Polo Lounge, a destination for the power lunch crew. Every day he overhead business conversations, including negotiations, investment strategies, startup issues, fundraising, and so much more.

Whenever Johnny heard a new business term, he jotted it down and looked it up later online. He started reading the *Wall Street Journal* and the *Harvard Business Review*. What he lacked in education, he was determined to acquire through independent learning. He had the confidence to speak to anyone, and wanted to converse on their level, understanding what they did and how they thought. *And I want Scarlett to be proud of me.*

Whoa, where did that come from? He corralled his thoughts. He really hadn't seen Scarlett that much since she'd left for New York. When she visited Los Angeles, she spent most of her time with her mother and friends. But now that she'd returned for work, he discovered how much he'd missed her. There was no one else quite like Scarlett.

He thought of all the people who came into his restaurant, and mentally sorted through them, discarding the flakes and the unscrupulous, and those he didn't know well enough.

One name kept popping into his mind. Maude Magillicutty. She had been a girl-next-door child actress who blossomed into a blonde bombshell in the early 1960s. She was proud of saying she'd been the highest selling pinup poster girl for soldiers during the Vietnam War.

Maude had given Johnny a couple of bow-ties from famous leading men she'd known. One from Gregory Peck, and another from Cary Grant. He didn't ask how she came by them, but Maude was a collector of many things. Real estate, stocks, artwork, businesses, and men. She was on her fifth husband, Patrick, but only because the last two died, she always said.

Though she seldom appeared on screen anymore, except for the occasional highly acclaimed cameo role, he knew Maude had a keen appetite for deals. He'd overheard a few of her lunch meetings, and he's been impressed with her business acumen.

Johnny picked up his phone and dialed.

"Hello, Maude?" Johnny clutched the phone and mentally rehearsed his pitch for the restaurant. "It's Johnny from the Polo Lounge. Do you have a moment to talk?

"Why, Johnny, darling," Maude exclaimed, her deep voice still as vigorous and sensual as it had been years ago. "It's truly my lucky day. To what do I owe the pleasure of this call?"

Johnny quickly told her about his idea. "And Lance, the executive chef at the Beverly Hills Hotel, is an equal partner."

"It will be sad to lose you both there, but sounds like you'll have a marvelous new restaurant to visit. I sent my husband to Shanghai to visit his son, but I'd like to hear more. Unfortunately, I'm down with a sprained ankle. My doctor tells me that if I have any thought of walking across the stage and accepting an Oscar for Best Supporting Actress,

I should stay off this ankle now." She gave a throaty laugh. "At my age, it might be the last little golden statue I'll see."

"Nonsense," Johnny said. "Lance can make dinner, and we'll come to you."

"Johnny, you always have the best ideas. I'd love that. How's tonight? My cook is off, and the housekeeper burns water. I'll provide the wine."

They agreed to meet, and Johnny hung up the phone. He punched in Lance's number. "Hey buddy, I've got a VIP order tonight. To go."

Later that evening, Johnny parked in front of Maude's mid-century modern home above Sunset Boulevard in Beverly Hills. He straightened his Cary Grant bow-tie and stepped from his car. He carried two large insulated bags to her front door. Unlike some celebrities who fenced themselves off from the public and their neighbors, Maude's home was accessible from the street.

Out of habit, he glanced around. Beverly Hills was a far cry from the barrios of East Los Angeles, but Johnny's routines were long-ingrained. A dark car across the street caught his eye. He pegged it as a security guard vehicle. The neighborhood was full of A-List industry moguls.

Maude's cheerful housekeeper greeted him at the door, and then ushered him inside. "Right this way. Madam is waiting for you. I understand you brought dinner."

"I did. Can you lead me to the kitchen?" As they made their way through the sprawling one-story home decorated entirely in white, Johnny caught glimpses of floor-to-ceiling windows overlooking the Los Angeles basin. Twinkling lights below sparkled like diamonds in the night.

"The view is spectacular isn't it?" Maude limped into the kitchen. Despite her injury, she carried herself with grace. She kept herself in impeccable shape, easily passing for a generation younger than she was. Johnny always saw heads turn whenever she entered the Polo Lounge.

"I've lived here since the sixties, and I never tire of this panorama." She pecked him on the cheek. "I see you're wearing Cary's favorite tie." A wistful smile crossed her face. "I must say, you wear it as well as he did."

Johnny thanked her for her invitation. "Lance couldn't join us due to a private party at the hotel, but he sent some of his best dishes for you." Johnny knew her tastes. He unpacked appetizers, entrees, salads, cheeses, and dessert. After quickly plating the first course, he sat down with Maude at the table.

Maude had uncorked a Château Rothschild from her cellar. "Whenever we shot on location in Europe, we shipped back cases and cases of wine. This one is an excellent vintage. I wanted to share it with you."

Johnny poured the fleshy red wine into crystal goblets and they toasted. It was indeed one of the finest wines he'd ever tasted. He appreciated Maude's time and knew she'd be honest with him. She was as smart as she was stunning. In that way, she reminded him of Scarlett.

Maude's vivid blue eyes sparkled. "Your idea for a new restaurant is interesting. I want to hear all about it over dinner."

As they ate, Johnny shared their plans. Maude listened, and when he was finished, she began asking questions. Because he'd been in the restaurant business for years, he handled most of them with ease, but there were some points he told her he'd have to research more. He made notes as they spoke.

As they were having coffee and dessert, the phone rang. The housekeeper appeared at the table. "Madam, it's your husband calling from Shanghai. Would you like to take his call?"

"Yes, bring the phone in here please. I'd like to put Patrick on the speaker phone with Johnny."

Johnny outlined their plans again, and her husband asked more pointed questions. Finally Patrick asked, "What's the name of this restaurant going to be?"

Johnny laughed. "That's the one thing we haven't thought of yet."

After Maude hung up the phone, she turned to Johnny. "We're very interested in backing this endeavor. Many good ideas pass our desks, but we like to invest in people of integrity who will run a business like we would, only better, of course. What do I know about cooking? But I do know about food and ambience and making guests feel welcome. You and Lance have strong followings. I think this might be a huge success."

They talked about the investment required and the percentages of ownership. "We're patient money," Maude said. "We'll be there for advice and introductions, but we expect you to run your business. Be honest and proactive when you encounter problems. There's nothing that can't be solved. All we ask is a fair return on our money. And a nice table when we come in."

Johnny gave her his business plan summary and spreadsheets for their financial and business advisers to review. Their accountant and attorney would handle the due diligence. The documents he and Lance would need to produce would be the usual ones, such as a lease and their personal financial statements and resumes.

"My husband and I will be back in touch soon," Maude said when dinner was over. Johnny supported her as she limped to the door and opened it. They chatted for a few more minutes on the front steps. "I'm so glad you came over tonight, Johnny. Thank you for that wonderful meal. Give my best to Lance and tell him I look forward to seeing him again."

"Take care of that ankle, Maude," Johnny said. He kept one arm around her for support and kissed her on both cheeks. Her housekeeper appeared behind her for assistance, and Johnny closed the front door.

He strolled toward his car, hands in his pockets, grinning at the prospect of a partnership with Maude and her husband. He was so excited over the meeting with Maude, he became lost in the countless details running through his mind.

4

SCARLETT WAS DYING for a margarita. After she'd left Fleur at the Chateau Marmont and returned to the office to retrieve her car, she'd been tempted to deaden her misery. She'd been sober for two years now, a fact she was terribly proud of. Fleur wasn't worth breaking her record. Scarlett turned her car for home.

Her father had been an alcoholic, and he'd put her and her mother through emotional hell. Watching him die of liver failure in the prime of his life had left an indelible scar on her. Scarlett enjoyed a cocktail as much as anyone, but when she realized she was drinking alone more often than not after long days and her anger had quickened, she swore off the sauce. She knew of her high risk for continuing down the same dreadful path as her father, and she wanted a long, successful life instead.

As she threaded her way through residential streets to her

townhouse south of Santa Monica Boulevard in Beverly Hills, she thought about what Fleur had told her. Lucan had planted seeds of discord in Fleur's mind before their meeting with High Gloss, but why? How would it benefit him?

Lucan was a smart man; he hadn't become partner on his good looks alone. Was this about her spurning his advances, or did it go deeper than that? She couldn't imagine that Lucan would destroy a deal simply because she refused to play in the mile-high club.

There had to be more to this than she was seeing right now.

Scarlett stepped into the townhouse she'd rented after she'd been transferred to Los Angeles. Her heels echoed in the empty rooms. The only furniture she had was a bed and a desk. She kept meaning to call in a decorator, but she hadn't had time to look for one.

As she was kicking off her shoes by her bed, her phone buzzed and she answered it.

"Scarlett, it's Katherine. I received the most disturbing call from Olga a few minutes ago. Our deal was ready to go, but it seems Fleur really rattled Olga, and she's not one easily shaken. What happened to your client? Or is this a last minute tactic for more money? If it is, I have to tell you I'm appalled. I would never have expected this from you."

Scarlett had been expecting this call from Olga's attorney. "Katherine, I assure you that's not the case. This is our third transaction together for High Gloss, and I'd like to continue this relationship. Fleur never mentioned any of that to me before."

"It wasn't just Fleur's play for more money. It was also her attitude and her ideas. She was disrespectful toward Olga. And what's with the black-and-white cosmetics bit? That's far too avant-garde for a top prestige line. You can't believe that would actually sell."

Scarlett sat on her wrinkled, unmade bed and sank her forehead into her hand. She didn't blame Olga. "Tell Olga I'll get to the bottom of this as soon as I can."

"Honestly, I don't think it matters. Olga is livid. I've never seen her this upset. She said she wouldn't work with Fleur for half the price."

"Katherine, surely we can work this out. Fleur has been under a lot of pressure lately." Scarlett had pulled many deals back from the brink of disaster. "Let's arrange another meeting." In the meantime, she could coach Fleur and choke Lucan.

"I'm sorry, Scarlett, but Olga refuses to move forward with this. The deal is dead, and not even you can resuscitate it."

Scarlett felt like she'd been kicked in the stomach. "The last thing we want to do is inconvenience Olga and High Gloss. I'd feel terrible about leaving them without a partner and spokesperson for their line." She was pleading now, something she seldom had to do. But then, she rarely had clients go berserk on her. "Does Olga have other options?"

"Not at this time. She was all in with Fleur. I don't have to tell you I'll be working all weekend on this."

"Give me until end of business tomorrow, Katherine. I promise I'll come up with something." Olga might not be her client, but High Gloss was an important ally. Scarlett had made deals for other clients, and she had to continue working with Olga on their behalf.

Scarlett and Olga often spoke on panels together at *Fashion News Daily's* annual retreat for CEOs of cosmetic companies. At her level, it was a small world, especially for women at the top in the beauty industry. Word traveled fast. One wrong move and she'd stand to lose clients.

Katherine heaved a sigh on the other end of the line. "I don't know what kind of magic you can come up with, but I can tell you straight up, it better not include Fleur. Olga never wants to see her again. She can't imagine Fleur going out on personal appearances on behalf of High Gloss. Frankly, neither can I. No telling what would come out of her mouth." Katherine paused. "You've got until five tomorrow, Friday afternoon."

Scarlett punched her fist in the air, vastly relieved. "I'll call you then."

Scarlett woke the next morning at sunrise still dressed in her suit trousers and shirt from the day before. She'd fallen asleep working up a plan she hoped would be amenable to Fleur and Olga.

Her phone vibrated with a text message. Scarlett found her phone under a pillow and looked at the note. Her heart fell. Fleur texted to say she'd changed her mind and had just boarded a commercial flight to London. Scarlett immediately tried to call Fleur, but her message went straight to voicemail. "Damn it." She wouldn't be able to reach her other than by email for twelve hours. *Now what?*

Her next call was to Lucan.

"I need to talk to you about Fleur," she said.

"I'm running." Lucan's voice sounded labored. "Can it wait?"

The clock was ticking on Katherine's deadline. "The meeting with Fleur and Olga yesterday was a disaster. Fleur said you told her she was worth more, and she relayed that to Olga. Now High Gloss has pulled out of the deal. Olga won't work with Fleur."

"High Gloss was committed. What happened?"

"It was contingent on the meeting with Fleur, and she blew it."

"Didn't you try to salvage it?"

Scarlett wanted to scream. "After what you said to Fleur? How could I?"

"That's what partners do, Scarlett. We're a team."

"Okay, then. I need your help, Lucan." She'd never asked him for help before. Is that what he wanted to hear?

"Can't do it. I'm wrapped up today. And it sounds like it's too late. Take the day off, Scarlett. I don't want to see you in the office."

What? She'd never heard that before. A chill spiraled through her. Before she could reply, he disconnected the call. The fine hairs at her nape bristled and she rubbed her neck.

Besides being a disaster, something wasn't right about that call.

Scarlett threw her phone on the bed, crumpled the plan she'd worked on, and flopped back onto the bed. The deal was dead. She'd call Katherine later.

She stared at the ceiling. She'd been working nonstop for so long. *What did one actually do on a day off?*

She rolled off the bed, showered, and pulled on jeans and a bright coral shirt. Maybe it was time to take a break.

"Scarlett, what a surprise," Verena said. She waved her to the film set, which was a modern setting accented with orchids and large posters of Verena's new line, Skinsense.

"Hi, everyone," Scarlett said.

On high stools next to Verena sat Penelope, Fianna, and Dahlia. The skincare products were displayed on a table between them. Scarlett liked the new azure blue and white packaging. "I can't join you on set because of client conflicts, but I thought I'd come and watch. Is that okay?" Not being at the office today, she felt out of sorts. She couldn't get Olga, Fleur, and Lucan off her mind.

"Of course. And there's coffee and biscotti if you haven't had breakfast." Verena turned back to a hair stylist who was arranging her hair.

Scarlett glanced around. The film crew was checking lighting and sound levels, a wardrobe stylist was steaming garments, and a makeup artist was organizing her brushes and tools. A guy in jeans with a laptop leaned over the teleprompter to make adjustments.

Scarlett was impressed with the professionalism on the set, but she would've expected nothing less. Verena's partnership with Wilhelmina Jones looked like it was going to be successful. She poured a cup of coffee and sat in a director's chair near the set.

"Good morning. I'm surprised to see you here."

"Mia, it's good to see you." Scarlett embraced Verena's grandmother, who had founded Valent Skincare in Beverly Hills in the 1940s. "You're looking well."

"The doctors say I'm fit as a fiddle, too." Mia patted her silvery blond hair and eased onto a chair beside Scarlett. Her skin was still flawless, a testament to her treatments and products. "I like to think I got a tune-up for the third act. Plus, I'm on camera later."

"Are the twins with you?"

"Anika and Bella are attacking the biscotti. I swear those teenagers are bottomless pits."

Verena's fair, blond sisters sat beside them, giggling at the cute guys in the film crew.

"We'll need quiet on the set," the director told them with a wink. The girls pressed their lips together and turned their attention to the stage.

The filming began, and Verena spoke to the camera, welcoming viewers and sharing the back story of how her grandmother had created the special serum that was the basis for the line. Verena stumbled over a few words, and the director asked her to start over. The teleprompter was reversed. Three takes later, the director was satisfied and signaled for the next scene.

Verena cleared her throat, the director gave the cue, and the cameras rolled. "I'd like to introduce my friends Penelope Plessen, a model; Dahlia Dubois, a perfumer; and Fianna Fitzgerald, a fashion designer. All these women are in the business of beauty, and must look their best every day."

This take was more casual, with the friends chatting about the products, how they used them, and what they liked about them. They were genuinely enthusiastic.

Unlike some infomercials, Scarlett knew it was all true, because they'd helped Verena and Mia test the new line. They'd all given feedback, and it was overwhelmingly positive. Especially from Penelope. As a model, she'd tried most of the skincare lines, and was always looking for the most effective products on the market. Her career depended on looking the best she could every day.

Scarlett was so engrossed in the filming process that the morning flew by. She was surprised when the lunch trolley was rolled onto the set.

Before they broke for lunch, everyone was given strict orders to preserve their makeup and clothing. There would be touch-ups, but there wouldn't be time for more if they wanted to stay on schedule. They were trying to complete the shoot in one day.

Penelope stepped off the set. "Scarlett, it's been too long. Let's catch up."

"I'd give you a hug, but I don't want to mess up your

makeup."

"Don't be silly." Penelope flung an arm around Scarlett. At six feet tall, Penelope towered above her. For a high fashion runway model who lived on jets, wore the latest fashions from the best designers, and mingled with rock stars and celebrities, Penelope was surprisingly modest. She was from Denmark and had been modeling since she was a teenager.

A caterer had brought in a buffet lunch, so they lined up and took their plates.

"Love the new hair." Penelope had spiky, short hair in a dark blond shade close to Scarlett's natural color.

"It's this week's style." Penelope laughed. "Next week it will be henna red." Every fashion house wanted a different runway look, so her appearance was constantly in flux. She was a beautiful chameleon.

They'd met through Verena at the Valent skincare salon. Penelope had been a regular client for years. On Scarlett's visits from New York, she had often run into her while they relaxed in the sauna after their massages. Scarlett sighed. That was when she'd had the time to fit in a few personal activities, which she hadn't been able to do since she's returned to Los Angeles.

"So I hear you're working hard," Penelope said, as she heaped salad and roasted organic vegetables onto her plate. "You'll be a partner soon, won't you?"

"The meeting is next week." Scarlett drew her brows together. She'd thought she would be celebrating, but now she wasn't so sure. The timing for the High Gloss blow-up could not have been worse. "But there could be a delay." She followed Penelope's lead with salad and vegetables.

"What happened?"

"I had a major transaction for a client with High Gloss Cosmetics. They were looking for a spokesperson and partner for a new line. Yesterday morning, we had a deal, but by the afternoon, the spokesperson went crazy. This morning she jumped on a plane back to London." Scarlett felt like strangling Lucan and Fleur.

"Sounds like extraordinarily bad luck."

"Or something." Was there more to the story?

Penelope chewed thoughtfully. "You've done other deals with High Gloss, haven't you?"

"A couple of others. The CEO, Olga, is really good to work with. And that deal was worth a fortune."

"I know you can't tell me what happened," Penelope began, when they were interrupted by Fianna and Dahlia. The conversation shifted to the filming. Scarlett glanced at her watch. She had to make the dreaded phone call to Katherine.

She stepped away, taking care not to trip over wires, and called Katherine's phone. There was no answer, and Scarlett didn't want to leave a message. She'd try again later.

Scarlett was making her way back to the group when she spied a copy of *Hollywood Today* sitting in a chair next to the hair stylist and makeup artist. A photo on the front of the tabloid paper caught her eye. She stopped and peered at it.

"You can take it if you want. I'm through with it," the makeup artist said.

"Maude Magillicutty's new boy toy is pretty hot," the hair stylist added. Both women laughed. "Wonder who he is?"

"I don't know, but with a body like that, bet it won't be a secret for long."

Scarlett picked up the paper. Sure enough, there was a series of photos of the actress in the arms of a handsome young Latin man. The photos were a little grainy, but there was no mistaking her companion. Especially in the shot of him grinning in his Mustang convertible.

"But a bow-tie? Seriously?" The women laughed again. "Maybe he wears it for Maude."

"That's all he needs to wear."

Scarlett didn't know whether to be angry with Johnny, or pity him. The absurdity of it was incredible. She began to chuckle with the stylists, and the stress of the past week unleashed her emotions. Soon she had a torrent of tears pouring down her facing, though she was still laughing.

The two women shot her a look. Scarlett caught hold of herself. It wasn't *that* funny.

She snatched the paper and hurried away. She folded it with the photo inside, and stuffed it into her purse. On Saturday, she was supposed to meet Johnny at the Farmer's Market.

Just when she thought things couldn't get any worse.

The director was calling for people to return to the set.

Scarlett took her seat.

"Hey Scarlett, I've been trying to reach you," Fianna said. "Want to come by the shop this weekend? I can keep the shop open for you like we talked about. Chinese food, too?"

"I'd really like that, Fianna, but work is tough right now. Maybe after next week."

"Okay." Fianna paused. "Verena looked at my licensing plan. Do you have time to read it? I could really use your help. I want to be your next big client."

Scarlett smiled. "Someday you will be. After next week, I promise." Although she doubted she could help Fianna now. The firm was demanding so much of her time, and Fianna's account wouldn't be large enough for them. "Maybe I can refer you to someone else."

Fianna frowned, looking hurt. "I understand. I'm not important enough for you." She turned away to return to the set.

"No wait, Fianna, I didn't mean it that way." Scarlett followed her onto the set.

"Quiet on the set, please." The director motioned to Scarlett to return to her seat.

"Yes, sir." She slouched down in the chair, feeling awful. Her world was spiraling out of control.

But she'd worked hard to get where she was, and she wasn't going to let people like Lucan and Fleur dictate her life. Or ruin her friendships. She'd make time for Fianna.

On the next break, Scarlett told Fianna she'd call her

next week, but she could tell Fianna was still upset.

Scarlett told her friends good-bye and left the studio.

She drove for a while, thinking about how she could salvage the deal with High Gloss, but she couldn't come up with any new ideas. She pointed her car in the direction of Malibu, savoring the rare time she had to herself.

When she arrived in the colony, she parked and kicked off her shoes when she got to the beach. This was one of her favorite stretches of sand. It was quieter than the beaches of Venice and Santa Monica. She strolled along, watching the waves crest and break, relentless in their motion.

Her life was like that. Unending motion. It was so easy to wake up and go through the same tasks, day in and day out. All around her, her friends were dating, getting married, and producing children.

She watched couples strolling on the beach, hand in hand. Some had toddlers with them. What her mother wouldn't give for a grandchild.

Even if she never had children, there had to be more to life. Her friends were building businesses, taking vacations, and having fun. Why wasn't she doing this, too?

She knew the answer. She had been so focused on making partner she'd put her life on hold until then. Now, the partnership decision was close. But could she start living a different life once that goal was achieved?

If it were achieved. She flinched as she thought of Fleur and Lucan.

Or would she continue to be a legal slave to the practice?

She toiled far more hours than anyone else at the firm. Would that change? Or would she have to continue to work harder than anyone else to maintain her position?

Scarlett sighed as she watched shorebirds flitting around the sand, racing back and forth while the water lapped their pencil-thin ankles. She had started life from such a disadvantage that she'd always felt she had to work harder than anyone else. She'd had no family ties, no trust fund earmarked for college tuition, no country club connections. She'd kept a grueling academic schedule, earned excellent grades and had gone to school on a scholarship and loans.

But was it worth it now? Like the sand beneath her feet, she felt her world shifting.

She stopped and stared out to sea. It was time to call Katherine and give her an update. Dreading Monday, she wondered what awaited her next week at the office.

5

"HOLA, ¿QUÉ TAL?" An older man at a taco stand called out to Scarlett.

"Pedro, ¿cómo estás?" Scarlett stopped and spoke for a few minutes. Pedro had been a friend of her father and a fellow food vendor.

Scarlett had grown up going to the Farmer's Market on Fairfax Boulevard. She loved the historic market, although it had grown and changed into a much more metropolitan shopping area under new ownership.

The newer section next to it, called The Grove, had a movie theater, upscale shops, and fine restaurants. A train for children wound through the open air shopping addition, which often featured special effects like man-made snow in the winter. She shook her head thinking about it. Only in Hollywood do they manufacture snow amid sunny skies and palm trees. Still, some of the original vendors remained in the old section, and she loved putting on her jeans and visiting old family friends, though it had been a long time.

Scarlett looked at her watch. *Johnny should be here.* Maybe something happened to him, she thought, before remembering that in Los Angeles, the concept of *mañana*— meaning tomorrow, or a casual approach to time—was entirely acceptable. Life was different in New York, and she'd grown accustomed to its big city pace.

Yet after Scarlett returned to Los Angeles, she realized how much she missed it. Missed the warmth of the sun on her shoulders, the sight of palm trees silhouetted against a Pacific Ocean sunset, the flavors of the spicy Mexican food she'd known since childhood.

Her first few paychecks as a new attorney had gone to help her mother move from the barrio after her father passed away and her brother had gone to Afghanistan to serve in the U.S. Army. Every month, Scarlett sent checks to cover her condominium near Fairfax, where she could walk to the Farmer's Market, visit with old friends, and feel at home.

"Latte, *por favor, grande*," she said, ordering a cup of coffee from another vendor's stall.

Of all Scarlett's friends, only Johnny really understood where she had come from. The others knew, of course, and respected her for her intelligence and determination, but only Johnny understood what it had taken for her to leave the barrio, and move into a new circle of friends and business colleagues and earn their admiration. *Not that I need it,* she reminded herself, but still, she was proud of her accomplishments.

"*Gracias,*" she said to the server, taking the steaming cup. She was sitting down at a communal table when she heard Johnny call her.

"*Chica,* darling, sorry I'm late," he said, giving her a warm hug. "The parking was terrible."

Scarlett kissed him on the cheek. He was like a brother to her, always had been. "Where's your famous bow-tie?"

He grinned and shrugged. "I don't have one to go with this T-shirt. You're staying at your mom's place?"

"Not anymore. I've leased one of the old townhouses south of Wilshire."

"That's a convenient area." He hesitated, and his voice dropped a notch. "It's awfully nice to have you back in town."

Johnny sounded genuine, and Scarlett thought she heard something more in his voice, but she told herself she was mistaken. He probably spoke to all the women that way. She thought of Maude and the photo she'd seen. Johnny was her buddy, nothing more. "Need coffee?"

He shook his head, ran his hands through his thick, jet-black hair. "No, I've been up for hours already."

Scarlett grinned. "Did hell freeze over?"

"Hey school girl, you're not the only one with dreams, you know. I'm working on a business plan."

"Oh, really?" Scarlett looked at him with interest. "For what? A franchise for the Playboy mansion?"

Johnny winked at her. "So I like women. That's not a

crime, lawyer lady."

"Not until one of their husbands shoots you."

Johnny shook a finger at her. "I don't date married women. Nothing but trouble there."

"Right. That's not what I heard."

Johnny heaved a sigh. "Gossip, that's all it is, blondie."

"No, *mi amor*, gossip happens in a coffee shop or a locker room. You were splashed on the cover of *Hollywood Today*." Thinking about it, she tried to suppress a laugh, but couldn't. "The Latino boy toy of fading star Maude Magillicutty, silver screen siren of yesteryear. Wasn't that the gist of it?"

"Stop it, Scarlett, you know better than that. We had a business meeting. She sprained her ankle and I brought dinner to her."

"That's some service." She couldn't stop laughing.

Anger flashed in his eyes. "Of all people, I thought you'd understand."

"Actually, I do understand. The story said you were seen leaving her house at two in the morning, so I'm sure you delivered a great performance." She wiped tears of laughter from her eyes. "Maude Magillicutty, of all women, the blond bombshell, circa what, 1960?"

Scarlett noticed that people around them were taking in interest in their conversation, but she couldn't help herself.

Johnny took her arm and steered her through the crowd. "Wait, my latte," she said, hardly able to catch her breath.

"Let's get out of here. I'll get you another one." He

pushed his way past a couple of women with phones and a man with a camera. "What's the matter with you," he hissed in her ear. "You don't go blasting stories like that around in L.A. Every wannabe screenwriter and publicist is here on a Saturday morning. It's chock full of people dying to sell juicy stories to the tabloids. Believe me, they know how to embellish it. If there's a big star within a mile of here, the paparazzi are out in force."

"I'm sorry," she said, still laughing. "Just the thought of you and Maude—"

Johnny pulled her in back of a piñata stall. His rich olive skin was reddening and the veins in his neck were bulging purple. "Maude's a beautiful, smart woman who has made more money investing than you'll ever see in a lifetime at your posh legal eagle club," he said, clipping his words. "And for your information, miss know-it-all, I left at two in the morning because Maude and I were on a conference call with her husband in Shanghai. But that's something I can't talk about."

"Oh no, three-way phone sex? This keeps getting better and better."

Johnny started to punch a piñata before he caught himself and slammed his fist into his other hand. "Damn it, what's the matter with you? I thought you were my *friend*."

Scarlett blinked and stopped laughing. "I didn't mean... Oh, no, I honestly thought it was true."

An incredulous look crossed Johnny's face. "You, of all people? What's happened to you in that big fancy law firm?"

He turned away from her. "I can't even *look* at you."

Scarlett grew quiet. "Then, it's not true?"

"You're smart enough to know you can't believe everything you read in the tabloids, *chica*. Why didn't you just ask me?"

Scarlett passed a hand over her face, feeling embarrassed. *I shouldn't have assumed.* At that moment, she spied a long lens camera poking through colorful piñata streamers. She grabbed Johnny's hand. "You've been discovered, let's get out of here."

"Aw, hell." They darted out the side entrance past shoppers and began running through the parking lot. "Come on, my car, last row."

Johnny was fit, and Scarlett could barely keep up with him. Her heart was pounding by the time they reached his classic Mustang convertible. He jumped in, unlocked her door, and was wheeling out of the parking space as she was closing her door. In her review mirror, she saw a skinny young guy with a camera standing in the middle of the parking row, snapping away at Johnny's red car.

Johnny adjusted his mirror. "At least he's on foot." He banged the steering wheel. "I had shopping to do back there, too. Damned paparazzi."

"I didn't know," Scarlett said.

"No, you didn't, because you didn't ask." He turned onto Fairfax. "Where do you want to go?"

She shrugged. "Just drop me at my mother's complex."

Johnny looked across at her and sighed. "I'm under an

NDA with Maude and Mitchell. You do know what an NDA is?"

"Of course I know what a nondisclosure agreement is." She folded her arms. "So, what are you doing with them?"

"No, no, no, *mi chica linda*," he said, a smile curving his full lips. "Are you testing me? You know I can't discuss it."

Scarlett's natural curiosity was raised. "Say I'm your counsel."

"But you're not."

"You have counsel already?"

He grinned. "Maybe I do." He pulled into the driveway of her mother's building. "Here you are."

"But we didn't have a chance to catch up."

"Scarlett, I don't know what you want from me sometimes." He shook his head.

"Johnny, we're friends."

"Yeah, yeah." He reached across her and opened her door. "Then maybe I'll see you around," he said, staring straight ahead.

So cold, Scarlett thought. *Well, two can play at this game.* "Maybe, maybe not. *Adiós*, Johnny." She got out and slammed the door to his car.

She watched as he pulled away, not even glancing back at her in his mirror.

When Scarlett entered her mother's cozy apartment, her mother was in the living room, knitting. Her mother was traditional, and she hadn't worked since Scarlett and her brother Franco were born. She'd spent her life as a wife and mother, and she expected to continue as a busy grandmother. Unfortunately, Scarlett's older brother had enlisted in the army, gone to Afghanistan, and returned in a casket. And Scarlett wasn't married.

Scarlett missed Franco. He was always in her dreams. Johnny had been his best friend, too. Maybe that's why she remained so close to Johnny. It was a way of keeping Franco's memory alive.

From the scent of saffron and garlic, Scarlett could tell paella was simmering on the stove. Her mother was a fastidious housekeeper and an excellent cook. She had all the domestic skills that Scarlett hadn't acquired.

Everyone adored Isabel Sandoval, too. She donated her time to the church, looking after babies in the nursery during Sunday services. Scarlett wished her father had been more responsible. A woman as kind as her mother really deserved someone better. Now it was up to Scarlett to look after her mother and make sure she had a comfortable retirement.

Isabel looked up. "I didn't expect you so soon. Did you see Johnny?"

"I saw him."

Isabel put her knitting down. "And?"

Scarlett swirled around, ready to argue. She stopped herself, remembering her respect for her mother. "He didn't have long to talk."

"So he didn't tell you about Carla?"

"Carla Ramirez?" She and Carla had been friends in high

school, but Carla had always been competitive. In sports, fashion, and boyfriends. Carla proved to be an exhausting friend, and after Scarlett moved to New York, they hadn't spoken again. Carla had married a wealthy film director and recently divorced, but that's all Scarlett knew.

Her mother lifted her shoulders and let them drop. "I hear things, I don't know if they're true. Maybe you should call Carla sometime."

"I don't have time for this," Scarlett said. *Maude, Carla...*she couldn't keep up with Johnny's women. He had plenty of female admirers at the Polo Lounge.

"No, Escarlata, you never do." Isabel resumed her knitting.

Scarlett held her tongue. Whenever her mother used her Spanish name instead of her American nickname, she knew she was in trouble. "What are you making?"

Isabel patted the soft yarn. "Baby blanket."

"Who's having a baby now?"

"No one in particular, but I like to keep ahead. Seems like everyone is having children." She scrutinized Scarlett over her reading glasses. "Well, nearly everyone."

Scarlett ignored her remark. "I'm making coffee, would you like some?" Without waiting for an answer, she went into the kitchen.

She poured ground coffee into the coffee maker and filled the carafe with water. *What's Johnny doing with Carla? Are they dating?* He'd always been the popular one in school, while she'd been the brainy, bookish one. Other children had made fun of her, had teased her about her blond hair, her parents' European mannerisms, and their different Spanish pronunciations. She was called stuck up and worse, which only made her more withdrawn.

It was Johnny who had come to her rescue. He was the popular school heartthrob, the boy every girl wanted. Even then, he saw something different in her. He was awed at her intelligence, and her ability to read several levels above their grade. She read lessons to him, and helped him with his reading and writing, while he taught her local Spanish slang.

She sighed as she recalled their childhood past. Johnny wasn't diagnosed with dyslexia until high school. Until then, he had called himself stupid, but Scarlett had always known he wasn't. In fact, he was one of the most astute people she knew, even though he didn't have a college education.

Scarlett punched a button to turn on the coffeemaker. She leaned against the tile counter, waiting for the coffee to brew.

Johnny could play any instrument he picked up. His specialty was the guitar, and when he heard that she loved Spanish guitar, he studied with a master, exchanging lengthy English language conversation—American slang included—for his lessons. He'd taught Franco, too, and together they played at *quinceañera* parties in high school.

She loved listening to Johnny strum old Mexican love ballads, but she hadn't heard him play in a long time. In fact, the last time was a decade ago, the night before she'd moved to the east coast for school after earning a scholarship based on her superior academic performance.

They had always been a mismatch, but that's why they were such good friends. They could be honest with each other, since there was no sexual tension. *Well, not much*, she admitted to herself. *Not on his part, anyway*. She wasn't his type, and she knew it.

The coffee gurgled to completion. She poured two cups and went to join her mother.

Isabel patted a spot beside her on the sofa. "Sit here by me."

Scarlett placed the coffee onto two fine needlepoint coasters she was sure her mother had made. Each had a miniature bouquet of roses, her mother's favorite flower.

Scarlett sat down, took a sip of coffee, and looked at her mother. "So, tell me about Carla," she said, trying to sound nonchalant.

Isabel smiled and picked up her knitting. "I thought you'd never ask. Now that she's received a good divorce settlement, it seems she's decided on Johnny as her next husband. And you know how she traps them."

"How?"

"The old-fashioned way." Isabel held up the baby blanket she was working on.

Scarlett didn't understand. "But she didn't have a baby."

Isabel sighed patiently. "She had a miscarriage. Her husband was relieved and filed for divorce."

"Then how did she get such a large divorce settlement?"

"Some people say she had something on him." Isabel put

her knitting down. "Carla plays to win. Johnny better watch out."

Scarlett scoffed at the idea, but inside she was appalled. *The nerve of that woman.* Johnny would never fall for her, would he?

6

SCARLETT BEGAN HER day at the office much like any other Monday at Marsh & Gold, but the atmosphere seemed electrically charged. Something was different, but she couldn't put her finger on it.

Lucan was too busy to talk about the deal with Fleur and High Gloss. In fact, Scarlett couldn't get past his executive assistant, who made it clear he would not be available today.

David appeared at her office. "Hi, Scarlett, do you have time to start on that new licensing agreement for Grier Pharmaceuticals?" He gave her a sheepish grin.

This had been her assignment, and their roles should have been reversed. But Lucan changed that at the last meeting, the day after their return from London.

"Sure, I'll get right on it." She kept her voice level. David hadn't had anything to do with Lucan's decision.

"Sorry to hear about the deal with Fleur. She was always

out of control."

"She sure hit the wall this time."

David agreed and hurried away. His discomfort was almost palpable.

Instead of having lunch brought in, as Scarlett usually did, she decided to walk to a restaurant in Century City for a change of scenery.

She swung onto a stool in the restaurant and ordered a sparkling water with lime and a Cobb salad. While she was waiting, the television above the bar caught her attention.

It was tuned to CNBC, a popular business channel that reported on the stock market.

"Hello, I'm Caroline Wilson, and with us today is Los Angeles-based Greta Hicks of *Fashion News Daily*. Greta, the talk on the west coast today is about the demise of the deal between Fleur of London and High Gloss Cosmetics. What are your thoughts on the dramatic drop of High Gloss stock?"

Scarlett jerked her head up and spilled water from her glass. "What the—"

"Well, Caroline, it's the largest one-day stock price drop in a cosmetic stock. Funds are clearly flowing from High Gloss to other stocks in that sector. For example, we've seen an enormous jump in the stock price of newcomer Color Color, Inc., a competing color cosmetics firm, also based on the west coast."

"And why is that, Greta?"

Scarlett signaled the bartender. "Please turn that up, I

need to hear this." She fumbled for her phone and tapped the video record button.

"Fleur of London backed out of a deal with High Gloss last Thursday and subsequently created a new company, which inked a deal with Color Color over the weekend."

"I imagine the people who shorted High Gloss must be in high cotton today."

Greta laughed. "That's right, Caroline."

"Now, a short time ago we reached out to Olga Kaminsky, CEO of High Gloss, but she declined comment. However, we have a brief clip from Fleur of London we received this weekend, and we'll play that for you now."

Scarlett was aghast. *The temerity of that woman.*

Fleur's perfect face flanked with her purple hair snapped onto the screen. "On Thursday, High Gloss refused to consider my artistic vision as previously agreed, and for that reason, I felt it was impossible to move forward with our agreement. I think my fans will be happier with my true unfiltered creations from Color Color." Fleur ended the video with a smile so wide Scarlett wanted to slap it off her face.

Slap it off her face.

Scarlett blinked.

The program cut to a commercial and Scarlett shut off the video on her phone. She rewound it and played it again, squinting to make out details.

Scarlett threw some money on the counter for the salad, even though she didn't get it. "Can't wait, I've got to go," she said, racing out the door. She started back to her office, dodging through the lunch crowd.

"Scarlett, wait up."

She whirled around. It was Lucan and two of the other law firm partners. "We'd like to see you tomorrow morning."

"Hello, gentleman." Gaining her composure, she stopped and nodded to the other partners. "I just heard about High Gloss on the news."

Lucan raised a dark eyebrow. "We knew about that last week, didn't we?"

"No, I mean, yes, but High Gloss stock experienced a sharp decline today."

"Based on that unfortunate news, it would." Lucan spoke calmly.

Scarlett pressed on. "Do you know who Color Color is?"

"Just what we've heard on the news."

One of the partners glared at her. "We don't approve of clients going rogue. It's embarrassing for the firm."

"And costly," the other partner added with a frown. His expression conveyed extreme displeasure.

Scarlett was shocked. "I assure you, I did everything in my power to represent Fleur."

"Lucan filled us in." The partner paused. "We'll see you tomorrow."

The new partnership announcement. Scarlett caught her breath.

Lucan and the partner walked on, leaving Scarlett standing on the sidewalk in utter amazement. Something was very, very wrong. Too much was happening at once. She pulled out her phone and made a call to an investigator she knew and arranged to meet him later.

She returned to the office and asked her assistant to bring up a sandwich. After eating, she closed her door and focused on completing a draft of the licensing agreement for David to review.

The hours flew by, and by the time she left the office, it was dark outside. She hurried downstairs to the parking garage.

Scarlett was parked at the far edge of the concrete structure on the lower floor. The sound of her heels echoed off the walls. She had her key ready and pressed the sensor to unlock her doors.

In a flash, an arm swung around her head and a gloved hand clamped over her mouth, stifling her scream.

Adrenaline surging, she instinctively ground a heel into the top of the man's shoe, arched enough to drive her palm into the base of his nose and her elbow into his windpipe, and then kneed him in the groin as he was going down. He let out a yelp and spewed something in Russian.

Her heart pounding, she leapt into her car and squealed out in reverse. As she drove past, she saw a gun clatter onto the ground. "*Dios mio*," she cried, pressing the accelerator.

She wheeled out of the garage where she could get phone reception and dialed 911 for the police. Knowing her assailant had a gun, she thought against going home. What if he knew where she lived?

She pressed a number on her favorites. "Hello, Johnny? I need help."

"Hey *chica*, time for you to get up."

Scarlett stretched. For a moment she didn't remember where she was.

Johnny jiggled her arm, and the memory of the previous evening rushed back. He'd let her sleep in his bed last night, while he slept on the couch. "Wake up, I've got coffee for you."

She opened her eyes. There was Johnny, standing over her with a cup of coffee. He'd already showered, and a towel hung around his lean hips. His bare, bronzed chest was well-defined.

"Hmm, just a minute." The view was too nice to rush. She blinked lazily.

"You told me to wake you by 5:30. Come on, I'll take you to your place so you can shower. I'll guard the place while you get ready for work."

"Not like *that* you won't." She grinned and took the coffee. He'd made it exactly the way she liked it. Light, no sugar.

"Why not? Ancient Olympians didn't even wear this much." Johnny winked and disappeared into the bathroom.

When he emerged, he had on black jeans and a black T-shirt that hugged his muscular shoulders. His thick hair was still damp. He tossed his robe onto the bed. "I hung up your clothes last night. They're in the closet." He shut the bedroom door behind him.

Johnny lived in a classic 1930s residential apartment built over a quadruple garage on a large estate north of Sunset Boulevard, just minutes from the hotel.

Scarlett stayed in bed for a little longer, enjoying the masculine scent that clung to his bed linens. Finally, she swung out of bed and looked around.

His apartment was surprisingly tidy. In the closet, his clothes were arranged by color and style. Framed photos of Johnny with famous clients sat on his bureau. "*To Johnny,*" they read, with glowing inscriptions. One drawer was partly ajar. Looking inside before she closed it, she spied his collection of bow-ties in a rainbow of colors.

Her eyes fell on the bookcase in the corner. She looked closer. The titles surprised her. Business, restaurant management, accounting, and business law books were neatly organized. She flipped one open. Johnny had highlighted passages and made notes on some pages. She put the book back.

After she splashed water on her face, she dressed in the clothes she'd worn the day before and opened the bedroom door.

"Ready," she said.

"Here, I'll take your cup." He rinsed it out and put their mugs into the dishwasher.

Scarlett leaned on the kitchen counter. "I'm sorry I insulted you at the Farmer's Market. I'm afraid my teasing got out of hand."

He raised an eyebrow. "Surely you didn't believe that story in the tabloids."

"No, of course not. I know you and Maude Magillicutty aren't having an affair." Scarlett fell quiet, biting her lip while she recalled the events with the paparazzi.

Johnny pulled her close to him and tapped her on the nose. "You're never dull. But I like your passion, *chica*."

Scarlett wrapped her arms around him. "Thanks for letting me stay here last night." Feeling slightly embarrassed at his closeness, but not understanding why, she pulled away. Something had changed between them. Or maybe it was just her.

Johnny cocked his head. "You're welcome anytime."

They clomped down an exterior wooden staircase to his car. "How'd you find this place?" she asked. The enormous French Normandy house on the grounds was vacant and undergoing an extensive remodel, but the bougainvillea and lilies were still in bloom, and the fruit trees still bore lemons, oranges, and grapefruit.

"One of my customers offered it to me about a year ago, rent free. It used to be the chauffeur's quarters. They're remodeling the house, and they like to have someone living on the grounds to keep an eye on things, open the gate in the morning, that sort of thing. Sure saves on rent."

"And you have fresh fruit. How long is the remodeling going to take?"

"Probably another year, at least. It's a sizeable job." He opened the car door for her and she slid in.

Johnny started the car. As they drove through the gates, he glanced at her. "Tell me again what happened last night. Slowly, this time."

Scarlett sighed. She'd told the police everything she recalled. "He came out of nowhere. I think he must have been hiding by the front of the car. I didn't notice until he attacked me. That's it."

"But you got away pretty quickly. That was impressive."

"I took a self-defense class when I moved to New York. Never needed it there, though."

"You're quite a woman," Johnny said, admiration in his voice. He pulled the car in front of her classic townhouse. The sun was rising, and birds were chirping in the purple blossomed jacaranda trees.

Scarlett stepped out of the car with trepidation. Johnny put his arm around her and escorted her to the front door. Even though she'd vanquished her attacker, she felt safer having him so close to her. She turned her key in the lock and Johnny went in first, checking each room.

"This is the cleanest place I've ever seen," he said, taking in her near-empty rooms. "But that's only because you don't have anything but a bed in here."

"That's not true. I have a desk and a chair, too."

"What do you do with this emptiness, throw sock hops on Saturday nights?"

Scarlett started laughing. "Sock hops? Have you been watching *Happy Days* reruns again?"

Johnny crossed his arms and grinned. "It's good to see

you laugh. Now go get ready. I'll make myself comfortable… on the floor."

She hurried into the bathroom and showered, feeling much safer that he was here. As the warm water streamed over her hair, she thought about the incident. Was it a random attack? Her car was the only one left there. Didn't the guy have earlier opportunities? Or was she the target. If so, the man had to wait a long time for her.

She dressed and just before she left, she sent the video she'd taken on her phone of Fleur to the investigator. She'd planned to meet him last night. But she'd never made it.

"I can take it from here, Johnny." They had left her car here last night.

"Are you sure? I don't want you parking in that garage again."

"The police seemed to think it was a random occurrence."

"The police." Johnny stared at her. "Is that what *you* think, counselor?

Sometimes she thought he knew her too well. "I don't know for certain, but I have to go to work. I'm meeting with the partners this morning." Eight years she'd been waiting for this day. She wasn't going to let the events of last night stop her from getting the partnership she'd earned.

"Promise to call me after you meet with them?" Johnny faced her and took her hands in his.

She glanced down. His hands felt firm and seemed to transmit strength through her hands, warming her to her core. "I promise," she said, her voice sounding a little thick to her ears.

He kissed her on the cheek. "Good luck, *chica*. I'll be thinking of you."

7

JOHNNY PULLED INTO a parking place in front of the restaurant and waved to Lance and Maude, who were already standing in front of the little stone cottage. Maude had called him yesterday saying that she and her husband had spoken, and she wanted to see the restaurant right away.

"Good morning," Johnny said, kissing her on the cheek. Maude looked lovely in a white silk pantsuit and a broad-brimmed hat. He turned to Lance and said, "Thanks for bringing Maude this morning. I had an emergency with Scarlett."

"And a good morning to you, my—what was it?—my Latin lover boy toy. Yes, I think that was it." Maude patted Johnny's muscular arm.

Lance chuckled. "Look, Maude, I think I see paparazzi." Joking, he pointed across the street.

"Why do think I wore this giant hat?"

"To hide?"

"No, for a better shot. It frames my face, don't you think?" Maude struck a pose. "There, I hope they got that. It was my best side."

"The owner's not here yet?" Johnny was anxious to get inside.

"He called and said he's running late," Lance replied.

An attractive woman with a groomed standard poodle on a leash approached them. "Why, I don't believe it," she said, pushing oversized sunglasses over a mane of dark curly hair.

"Carla?" What are you doing here?" Johnny gave her a quick hug, trying not to touch too much skin, which was easier said than done. She wore a tight spandex sports bra and tiny shorts.

"It's my regular morning walking route. What are *you* doing here?" She gazed behind him.

Johnny introduced her to Maude and Lance. He and Carla had gone to school together. Carla had married—and divorced—a well-known film director. Now she was a wealthy woman who spent her days doing zumba, having lunch, and going power shopping.

Lance spoke up. "We're thinking about opening a restaurant here. Do you live nearby?"

"Johnny knows I do. I could bring in all the neighbors." She smiled up at Johnny. "And then I wouldn't have to drive so far to see you."

"Ah, Carla, Carla. Always teasing me." Johnny feigned surprise, but he knew all he had to do was call her, and she'd come running. Not that he had, but Carla definitely had an eye for him. She'd been showing up at the Polo Lounge right before closing and dropping hints for him to invite her out.

Or take her home.

But that wasn't his style. He liked to choose, and he was very selective. Of course, Carla was attractive, and normally he'd call on her. But someone else had just landed in his life again.

"Johnny, I asked you a question." Carla touched his chin and turned his face toward her. "Are you free on Saturday night?"

"Saturday? Our busiest night, you know. Private party, I'm afraid."

Lance and Maude traded looks.

"Well, keep it in mind all the same. And if you need a decorator for this place, give me call."

"Look, here's the owner," Lance said.

Carla brightened. "Great, I'm dying to see the inside. I can give you some ideas right now."

Johnny sighed, and Maude winked at him from under her broad-brimmed hat.

Scarlett sat down at the conference table and folded her hands on the table. From all outward appearances, she was cool, competent, and confident. But inside, her nerves were doing a cha-cha in her stomach.

She gazed around the table at the partners. Every seat was taken by a man in a dark conservative suit. The mood was as somber as a funeral parlor. The scent of men's cologne was overpowering, which wasn't helping her queasiness.

Lucan cleared his throat. "We called you here today for

the obvious reason. Scarlett, let me begin by saying how much we appreciate your dedication to Marsh & Gold. We are a better firm for having you in our midst."

Scarlett inclined her head in a slight acknowledgement of his compliment. Why then, did she feel like she was waiting for the guillotine?

"You have certainly put in the hours necessary to become a partner here. However, our decision is predicated upon a number of points."

Scarlett sensed a swirling undercurrent and felt the need to reinforce her value. "Among the associates, I'm the best candidate for partnership at the firm. I've brought a substantial amount of business into the firm and will continue to do so, in addition to pro bono work."

"Of course. We appreciate that. Your future compensation will reflect such contributions."

A small silence ensued.

The conversation was not going as she'd expected. Equity partners had ownership stakes in the firm. Were they going down the path of a non-equity partnership?

"As you know, we have many talented associates and only a limited number of partnership openings. Our decision is no reflection upon your skills, which are quite fine, as we all agree."

Heads bobbed around the table, and she couldn't shake the thought of bobble-headed attorneys going through the mechanics.

Scarlett braced herself. Every nerve in her body was

tingling with apprehension.

Lucan lowered his gaze. "We will make an announcement this afternoon that David Baylor is the newest partner in the firm."

Stunned, all Scarlett could do was blink. *Eight years of her life.* Her mouth felt dry, and she had to remember to breathe. *This can't be happening.* She struggled to compose herself and find her voice.

"Of course, we'd like—"

Scarlett jerked to her feet, cutting off Lucan. She'd heard enough. She faced the partners. "Gentleman. Thank you for your consideration."

She threw a glare at Lucan, whipped around, and strode to the door. She hurried through the hallway on legs weak as putty. The dark green walls were closing in on her, robbing her of her breath. Everything felt surreal, as if this nightmare were happening to someone else.

Not her.

Not the woman who had given her life to the firm, who had endured snide comments, unreasonable clients, and biased partners; who had passed up weekends, trips with friends, even sleep and love. And who had endured Lucan Blackstone's harassment.

How dare they?

Sure, David was a fine attorney, but even he didn't think he'd performed well enough to make partner this year. He'd told her so just last week. She was the best partner candidate that firm had, and she knew it. Everyone knew it.

So what had just happened?

Her heart pounding, she stopped by her office, snatched her purse, rode the elevator down, and burst into the bright sunshine. She gulped the fresh air. But it did nothing to assuage the hurt and anger surging through her.

She could've asked them why, but she'd known the answer would be vague and inconclusive.

In short, a lie.

She circled a flowing fountain a couple of times in an effort to reign in her flailing nerves, and she then tapped an email to her assistant saying she was taking the remainder of the day off.

As she headed to her car, she couldn't help but think there was more to this denial than she'd been told. The back of her neck was crawling with alarm.

In her experience in the legal field, she'd learned there were few true coincidences. And in the past week, there had been far too many. Fleur, High Gloss, Lucan, her attacker.

Someone was pulling the strings of her life, and it had cost her the partnership she'd worked her entire adult life for. She brushed an angry tear from her eye.

She was determined to find out who it was, and why they were doing it.

Scarlett gritted her teeth. This was not over. *Far from it.*

She punched a number on her phone.

Zelda Robinson stood and splayed her fingers on her antique desk. "Scarlett, what seems to be the problem?"

Behind her mentor, palm trees swayed over the village streets of Beverly Hills. With tapestry cushions and potted orchids, Zelda's comfortable office was a far cry from Scarlett's cold corporate offices in Century City. "I was passed over for partner."

On the way to Zelda's, she'd called Johnny as promised. When Johnny asked her if congratulations were in order, she'd lost her temper, spewing a string of Spanish expletives over the phone. Then, when she heard Carla Ramirez talking in the background, she hung up. Why give him the chance to lie to her, too?

Scarlett shook off her anger. She had immense respect for her former law school professor. Zelda was a high profile attorney whose specialty was women's issues, including sexual harassment, equal pay, healthcare, education, and child care. More than that, Zelda was a friend, and she valued her advice. Pent up words tumbled out. "I thought I had it. I was the best choice at the firm. A partner told me last week I had it." She bit her lip in consternation. "Something rotten is going on."

"That's a natural reaction." Zelda nodded her short, stylish grey hair and sat down. She'd been one of Scarlett's law professors, and she had a private practice. "Is there anything specific you might attribute this to?"

Scarlett outlined the events of the past week, disclosing only what she could without breaching her attorney client privilege with High Gloss. However, she told her about the CNBC news report and other public details.

Zelda listened thoughtfully. "And how are your relationships at the firm?"

"They were excellent. Before the return trip from London," she added. She went on to tell Zelda about Lucan's behavior on the flight.

"Sexual harassment. Not surprising." Zelda steepled her hands. "Plan to do anything about it?"

"I thought about filing a complaint with Human Resources, but with the partnership decision so close, I didn't. I know whistleblowers are often crucified, so I didn't say anything. Once I made partner, I thought I'd have more leverage to make positive changes at the firm."

"That's logical. But it didn't work out that way, did it?"

"No." Scarlett considered Zelda's comments. "At least I still have a job, and they indicated my compensation would be raised."

"Did they give you a new employment agreement?"

"I left in a hurry."

"You have two choices. Stick it out or leave. It's really that simple."

After Scarlett left Zelda's office, she called the investigator she'd sent the video of the CNBC segment to. One of her law school classmates who practiced personal injury had referred him to her. He was a whiz at technology.

"Rob, have you had a chance to take a look at that video?"

"Not yet, Scarlett. Give me a few days. I'm pretty swamped right now."

Scarlett had watched the video several times, but the quality on her phone was poor. Rob had the tools to sharpen the image and look closer.

"Great, and let me know as soon as you have something." Scarlett hung up. She had to solve this puzzle before things really got out of hand.

8

THUNDERSTORMS HAD plagued the Van Nuys airport throughout the night. This morning it was still raining, but the tower had given pilots clearance to fly. Scarlett shook out her umbrella.

"Good morning, David. Scarlett." Lucan barely acknowledged her as he stepped onto the firm's private aircraft at the Van Nuys airport. His eyes were sunken and smudged with dark circles as if he'd been up all night.

Scarlett wondered why.

After Lucan boarded, Scarlett hesitated before stepping aboard. "I didn't know he was coming with us, David."

"Neither did I. Not until four o'clock this morning." David yawned. "Sleep is clearly optional at Marsh & Gold."

"You're just noticing that, partner?" Scarlett grinned. As much as she thought their roles should be reversed, David was such a likeable guy she couldn't fault him. He was an excellent colleague and had always shown her respect.

Lucan's presence troubled her. Scarlett eased into a white leather club chair next to David. "We should catch up on the client's needs while we travel." She plugged in her laptop.

"Bring on the coffee," David said, flipping open his briefcase.

Lucan shrugged out of his wet raincoat and threw it over a seat. Lavender, the flight attendant, hurried to retrieve it and hang it up for him. Lucan jerked around. "I don't want any disruptions on this flight from either one of you. No matter what, understand?"

"Yes, sir," David said.

Scarlett nodded. Lucan's dark mood reflected the morning's dismal skies, creating an oppressive mood on board. Something seemed seriously wrong. Could it have anything to do with the High Gloss deal? Scarlett picked up an unsettling vibe emanating from Lucan.

With a gruff word to the flight attendant, Lucan disappeared into the stateroom.

Whatever was bothering Lucan was grave. Feeling nervous, Scarlett tapped a text to Rob. She hoped he'd had a chance to start looking at the video she'd sent. She needed confirmation. *Don't email,* she added as an afterthought. She didn't want his message going through the firm's email system. *Text or call only.*

As the plane's engines rumbled to life, Lavender brought sparking water for Scarlett and fresh coffee for David.

David sipped from the steaming cup. "No coffee?"

"I've had my quota for the morning." Johnny had made her coffee, taken her by her apartment to change and pack, and ferried her to the airport. "Besides, hydration is important when you fly."

"Did you learn that from one of your clients?"

She sipped her cool water. "Verena Valent."

"I read in the *Wall Street Journal* that she's in partnership with infomercial guru Wilhelmina Jones. Verena has a new skincare line coming out, right?"

Scarlett nodded. "The new line is called Skinsense, and it's fantastic. After that debacle with Herringbone Capital, I predict she's going to climb right back on top." Verena deserved it. The infomercial was in editing now, but what she'd witnessed on the film set had looked very professional and effective. The products certainly were. Scarlett had been using them for months.

David cupped his hands around his coffee. "Good for her. They gave her such a rotten deal."

Scarlett squeezed lime into her water and took another sip, thinking of her friends. Among them all, she was growing closer to Johnny. He'd insisted she stay with him again last night, and slept on the couch for a second night.

Before he'd sent her off at the airport, he'd warmed her with a giant bear hug, helped her with her bag, and held her umbrella to keep her dry. She remembered now that it was the little things he did that had always endeared him to her. When they were young, she'd taken those kindnesses for granted. She'd even called him chauvinistic. But now that she was older, she saw him in a different light. He was a kind soul, he and truly cared for her well-being.

Scarlett glanced outside, watching rivulets of rain streaming down the cabin windows.

She had to admit she had a way of complicating issues. Sometimes, in her quest for the truth, she examined every infinitesimal detail. With Johnny, there wasn't an ulterior reason behind his kindness.

She sighed, trying to quiet her mind for a few moments before she and David tackled their preparatory work.

Johnny planned to meet her in Spain after she'd completed her work. David had quickly agreed to her request for vacation days. Lucan would not have been as amenable, but she was on David's team now.

Lavender stopped by their seats. "Hi, folks. It's going to be a bumpy take-off with this weather. Be sure to buckle up."

"Thanks."

Lavender raised her brow. "Everything okay with you, Scarlett?"

Scarlett knew what she was referring to. "Just fine, thanks, Lavender." She gave her a warm smile. She owed a lot to this woman. If not for her, no telling what Lucan might have done.

Soon the plane hurtled down the runway and lifted off. The turbulence rocked the aircraft as it climbed above the clouds and burst into blue skies above.

Once the turbulence dissipated, Scarlett and David began to work, laboring through most of the twelve hour flight to Madrid. During this time, not once did Lucan emerge from the stateroom. Occasionally they heard murmurs wafting from behind the closed stateroom door, as if he were on a Skype call through the plane's internet system.

Yet even when Lucan was in a sour mood, he had always been sociable, making wry comments until everyone around him began laughing. It was part of his charm. Today's behavior was highly irregular for him.

As the pilot touched down on Spanish soil at sunrise, Lucan emerged from the stateroom. He still looked like hell. Scarlett's senses snapped to high alert. What had Lucan so worried?

After arriving at the hotel from the airport, Scarlett and David agreed to catch three or four hours of rest and meet at noon. Scarlett was so excited to be in Spain, she couldn't sleep. She ordered coffee from room service and took a leisurely bath surrounded by white marble. Wrapped in a plush robe, she swung open the double doors to the small balcony of her French antique-furnished suite at the Ritz Hotel, which was situated in the central part of Madrid between Retiro Park and Teatro de la Zarzuela.

Breathing in, she looked out over a private garden filled with calla lilies and potted topiaries. Directly across rose the majestic Museo Del Prado with its Grecian columns and vast collection of Francisco de Goya paintings. The romance language of her youth rose and fell in a mild spring breeze that lifted gauzy curtains flanked with heavy silk damask.

España. This was the country of her birth, and yet she knew so little of it.

Scarlett changed her heels for flat shoes and went for a walk to soak in the sights of the beautiful city she'd often heard her mother speak about. She strolled along the dining terrace, where royal blue canopies and umbrellas provided shade against the warm Spanish sun. She trailed her fingers along carved stone balustrades.

She continued on into the city streets. The scent of garlic, saffron, and spices filled the air, making her hungry. She stopped at a sidewalk café and ordered a calamari sandwich with lemon and mayonnaise and *patatas bravas,* crunchy cubes of double-fried potatoes topped with spicy red sauce. As she ate, she thought of her mother. She vowed she would bring her for a visit.

Afterward, Scarlett explored, passing rippling fountains and throngs of school children lining up for the museum. Hearing their laughter, Scarlett smiled, recalling visits to the museums with her brother and Johnny. Her mother had always been determined to bring culture into their lives, even if they barely had money for bus fare. Now she understood her mother's frame of reference.

Scarlett paused at a fountain. Thinking of Johnny, she flipped a Euro into the water. But what, exactly, was she wishing for?

Before she could answer that question, church bells tolled the noon hour. She hurried back to the hotel to meet David and Lucan. A long week of work loomed ahead.

After spending the week advising their client, a multinational company, on its intellectual property holdings, Scarlett was more than ready for her holiday. Her head was spinning with beauty trademarks and figures, and she couldn't wait for a morning sleep-in. She and David had worked late last night to wrap up all the details.

She rolled over to check her phone and saw a text from Rob. *No discernible injury,* it read. A chill coursed through her. She let her head sink back into the Egyptian cotton covered pillows. It was what she'd expected. Her mind whirred.

She wished she had an off-switch on her brain. This was the first day of her holiday, and Johnny would soon be arriving. Fleur could wait until next week. She turned off her phone ringer and stretched.

Deciding she was officially off duty, she languished in the bath and dressed leisurely. She wiggled into svelte new jeans she'd found at Adolfo Domínguez and buttoned a casual white blouse from Zara she'd bought one day during lunch. She slipped her feet into a new pair of leopard print Manolo Blahnik heels she hadn't been able to resist. She adored gorgeous shoes. It was one of the perks she allowed herself for working as hard as she did.

She glanced at her phone and saw that David had tried to call. She rang him back.

"I'm checking out," he said. "Meet me in the lobby?"

"Sure," she said. "I'll be right down.

When the doors slid open, David was pacing by the elevator, his hands thrust into his pockets. She stepped out. "It's been a good week, David. I hope you and Lucan have a good trip back."

David's eyes darted around. Perspiration dampened his upper lip. "Listen, I've been thinking about what you told me about Fleur." He sounded nervous. "This morning I got a call—" He stopped.

Another elevator opened and Lucan emerged. He stuffed his phone into his pocket. "Good morning. Good job on this transaction, David. Looks like this is going to be a long, profitable relationship with the client." Lucan rested his eyes on Scarlett, but didn't say a word.

Lucan's blank expression was unnerving. He'd been like that all week. It was almost as if his soul had been hollowed out of his body, and he was merely going through familiar paces.

"Scarlett really won them over, didn't she?" David nodded toward Scarlett. He put on a smile, but Scarlett wondered what was worrying him.

"I think they were impressed with the whole team, especially you, my good man." Lucan shook his hand. "Now Scarlett, I know you're taking holiday time. I insist you stay here at the Ritz."

"Actually, I'm transferring to another hotel for the weekend, and then driving south." Did he honestly think this was a magnanimous gesture? He often spent more on a bottle of wine.

"No need to move, your room is paid for." Lucan spoke like a benevolent dictator.

"That's really not necessary. I have a friend joining me. The Ritz is not in the budget." Johnny had told her he was saving his money for the restaurant and asked if they might stay at a charming pensione nearby that Lance had recommended.

Lucan blinked, his eyes deadened in their sockets. "Put their room on your bill, too. Think of it as a bonus." His mouth was a tight, thin line that revealed neither regret nor sorrow. "We'll write it off to marketing."

"That's generous, but I can't accept it. It's inappropriate." Scarlett shot a look at David, who seemed nonplussed over Lucan's behavior. A hotel room for a weekend would hardly repair the damage Lucan had inflicted on her. What about his lecherous attack on the plane? What about the partnership that was rightfully hers?

Lucan's professionally groomed eyebrows drew together. "Scarlett, that's a direct order. The firm wants you to be comfortable. Think of it as a consolation award, if you wish. Charge whatever you want to the rooms, but you're staying here." He nodded to David.

"Scarlett, I'll take your laptop back to the office for you," David said. "You don't want to lug it around with you on vacation."

"Thanks, David, but it's no problem." Scarlett thought his face looked flushed and wondered if he was ill.

David mopped sweat from his hairline. "I've already got

it, Scarlett. You left it with me last night."

"I did?" Scarlett didn't remember doing that, but they'd worked late, and she'd been tired. "Well, okay, thanks."

Lucan dipped his chin. "Now David, come along, it's time we're off."

Scarlett wished them a safe flight, but in truth, she'd like nothing more than to see Lucan expire in a flaming inferno. He was a vicious, despicable man. Something didn't seem quite right this morning. She rubbed her neck.

Lucan stopped at the front desk and spoke to the manager on his way out. Scarlett leaned against a pillar and watched them go, thinking she'd never seen a man so calloused, or so tormented, as Lucan Blackstone.

And then there was David. He looked back over his shoulder, his brow furrowed with anxiety.

Scarlett exhaled, relieved they were gone. Already the tension was lifting from her shoulders.

The manager motioned to her from the front desk. "Senorita Sandoval, we'll have your second suite ready soon."

"Johnny!" Scarlett called out to him as he exited customs. Her heart thumped with excitement. She'd been yearning to see him all week.

"Look at us," he cried. "We did it, we broke free, *chica*." He flung his arms around her, lifted her from the ground, and swung her around.

She laughed and ran her hand across his muscular shoulders. He wore black jeans and a silky black T-shirt that hugged his well-defined chest. With his thick black hair and dark sunglasses, he looked so much like a Hollywood star that she had to laugh. "What happened to the ubiquitous bow-tie?"

"I'm on holiday. I've got a couple packed, but I want to buy some new ones here. Hey, you look pretty hot, love the high heels with jeans. Nice new style for you." He held her hands away from him to check out her new casual look. His eyes crinkled at the corners, and a smile played on his lips.

Scarlett glanced down. "And it's all from Spanish designers, too. I had to contribute to the local economy."

"Much better that your corporate grey and black suits. Not that you don't look great in those, too. But this is so much more you."

Scarlett's cheeks grew warm. "Guess I've been overdue for a holiday."

"You've been overdue for life. And we're going to change that." He stopped at the luggage carousel and grabbed his suitcase. "So where are you taking me first?"

She tossed her hair over one shoulder. "How about the Ritz, handsome?"

Johnny made a face. "That's really out of my budget. Someday, after the restaurant is a huge success—"

"Relax, it's a gift from the firm."

"You're kidding." He took her hand, twirled her around, and executed a perfect dip. "Then let's go, *chica*."

Johnny and Scarlett started at a restaurant that served Basque food from the northern part of Spain and then went to a tapas bar in the La Latina district. Johnny insisted they finish off with churros and chocolate at San Ginés Chocolateria, a restaurant he'd read about which had been operating for more than a century. With its dark green paneling, mirrored walls, and marble counters, the jewel box of a shop was tucked away on a small side street and was open around the clock. The air was permeated with the rich patina of chocolate and fried dough.

They entered the shop, and no sooner had they sat down than a waiter whisked by. Without inquiring about an order, he simply served two sturdy porcelain cups of warm, thick sweet chocolate, along with plates of hot-from-the-fryer churros.

"Smells incredible." Johnny sprinkled powdered sugar on his churro, dipped it into a cup of chocolate, and then took a bite. "Is this even legal?" he asked, exclaiming over the chocolate treat.

"If it isn't, I'll defend you," Scarlett said, following suit. "Oh, this is delicious! You should put something like this on your menu."

A smile spread across Johnny's face. "Who knows? We might." He snapped a photo of the churros and chocolate with his phone.

"That's why you're here, isn't it?"

Johnny met her eyes over the rim of her cup. "Among other reasons."

As heat gathered in her chest, Scarlett averted her gaze. "Let's work out a plan," she said, her words tumbling out.

"We'll take notes and photos of everything you like, and when we return, we'll see if Lance can make it."

Johnny touched her hand. "Lance can make just about anything. Relax, Scarlett."

She inhaled deeply, and released a breath. He was right, it felt good.

Afterward, they strolled through the central shopping district. Scarlett stopped by Loewe and splurged on a bright yellow Amazona purse for her mother.

"Isabel will love that," Johnny said.

"She's always wanted one. Someday I'll bring her here, too."

"You're a good daughter, Scarlett. I know your mother appreciates you. No one knows better than I do how rough it was when Franco died. And your papa, of course." He dodged a crack in the sidewalk and offered her his arm for support.

She hooked her hand in the crook of his elbow. "We'll always miss Franco, won't we?"

"Hardly a day goes by that I don't think about him," Johnny said. "Whenever I hear a Spanish guitar, I always think of Franco."

"Me, too. He played so beautifully. In fact, I couldn't bring myself to listen to acoustical guitar music for a long time after he died. Even now, I often tear up." She turned her face up to his, and saw him blink back emotion.

"I haven't played much since then either." Johnny pulled her closer and draped his arm across her shoulder. "He really loved you, Scarlett." As they walked, they reminisced about their families and childhoods. There wasn't anyone else who understood what she had been through, or where she had come from.

"Dinner is served late in Spain," Johnny said. "Feel like a massage or a work-out?"

Scarlett laughed. "If we're going to continue eating like this, I need to visit the fitness center."

"I'll join you." Johnny patted his taut stomach, but Scarlett thought he looked just fine.

They returned to the Ritz, and Johnny checked into his suite, which was one floor above hers. "I'll meet you at the gym when I'm ready," he said.

Scarlett changed into her fitness gear and made her way to the exercise area. Johnny was already there. She paused by the door to watch him. He was incredibly fit and perfectly muscled. If she didn't know him already, he was definitely a man she'd want to meet.

"Hey, look at you." He squeezed the toned muscles in her arm. "No wonder you flattened that guy in the garage."

She flexed an arm. "That was the result of good training. Any woman can learn that."

Johnny let his hand glide from her shoulder to her hand, and his eyes followed, lingering on her skin. "I think you're in pretty good shape, counselor."

Flushing, she climbed onto a stationary bike and began pedaling. "I'm not as buff as you are though. I get most of my workouts from a laptop, rather than a lap pool."

"You're perfect as you are. I like feminine women. A few soft curves are sexy," he added with a wink. He joined her on an adjacent bike, and they continued talking while they warmed up. Half an hour later, he moved on to weights. Scarlett followed him and looked on while he showed her some new exercises.

"Are you watching?" he asked, as he executed a perfect curl.

Am I ever. Scarlett grinned. "What Maude wouldn't give to be here right now."

Johnny shot her a dirty look.

"I couldn't help it," she said, giggling to break the tension between them. Besides, she loved to tease him.

Feigning anger, Johnny returned the weight to its stand and pulled her close to him. "What am I going to do with you?"

His body was warm with exertion. Scarlett gazed at his firm chest, and then let her eyes travel up. She saw emotion in his eyes, and his intense expression surprised her. She laughed with nervousness and pulled away. "I think I need a bath. Call me when you're through."

Her heart pounding, she strode from the fitness center. Her attraction for Johnny was getting out of control. He was a childhood friend, the best friend of her brother. The last thing she wanted to do was to endanger their friendship. One more step and she might ruin everything between them.

But why did he have to be so damned appealing?

Scarlett opened the door to her suite and ripped off her

clothes. She slipped into her robe, and then flung open the balcony double doors to let the early evening breeze clear her mind. The sound of flamenco music filtered from the street below, and faint stars twinkled in the twilit sky.

She gazed over the city she'd grown to love in the past week. This was a journey of discovery for her. Perhaps in more ways than she'd imagined. She eased into a bath and let her muscles relax. When she was through, she stepped from the bath, wound a fluffy white towel around her hair, turban-style, and tied the white terry cloth robe around her waist.

Her neck still felt strangely tight, and she rotated it a few times.

A soft breeze wafted through the open doors, fluttering the sheer white panels that billowed like sails into the room. By now night had fallen, and Scarlett stepped through the door to look out. As she did, she stubbed a toe, and leaned over, hopping to keep her balance.

Suddenly, the air above her cracked and her toweled turban sustained a sharp thud, the force of which knocked her on her back. She cried out. "What the—"

Another sound cracked the night air and splintered the moulding on the wall across the room. Instant panic seized her.

Adrenaline surging through her, she flattened her body against the carpet and belly crawled behind the open door. A third shot blew apart the leg of a cherry wood antique desk. It teetered precariously over her.

Her heart pounding, she rolled over on her back and

tried to catch her breath. *Now what?*

Who was shooting at her? A terrorist? Television news reports flashed through her mind. Was she about to be tomorrow's headlines? She was breathing so rapidly she was growing lightheaded, but she had to keep her wits about her.

Is this how it ends?

She spied her phone on the bed and inched her way to it. Her fingers shaking, she pressed Johnny's number. It rang once, twice, three times.

Answer your phone, Johnny!

Four times. Five.

"Hi *chica*, almost ready, just getting dressed."

"Johnny, I'm in my room," she cried, shivering with terror. "Call security! Someone is shooting through the open door from the street! Oh God, please hurry, come quickly." She squeezed her eyes shut, thinking about her brother, who'd been killed in an ambush in Afghanistan. *Possibly like this*, she thought, praying. *Franco, if you can hear me...*

"Stay on the line, Scarlett, stay with me!"

9

THE NEXT DAY, Scarlett strode into the office with confidence, wearing her best black Armani suit with a white silk blouse and pearls. But she'd barely had a chance to open her briefcase when her assistant buzzed her.

"Lucan wants to see you in his office."

And she wanted to see him. Straightening her shoulders, she walked into his office. Unfortunately, David was there, along with Lucan's assistant.

"What's up?" Scarlett acted calm, as if her world had not exploded yesterday.

Lucan looked up. "David brought in a Spanish cosmetics company who needs to have their intellectual property agreements reviewed before they go public. They're moving their operation to New York."

David's face turned red. "Well, I didn't exactly bring it in. Scarlett, you made the contact and the pitch. I just took the call this morning."

Scarlett tapped her foot. "So where do we begin?"

"The two of you are going to Spain. Scarlett, you can interpret for David."

Now she was being demoted to interpreter. "They speak English just fine."

"We'd still like for you to go," Lucan said smoothly. "David, why don't you brief Scarlett? Take the small conference room. I'll join you shortly." He swiveled in his chair and addressed his assistant, signaling the end of the meeting.

As they walked to the conference room, David turned to Scarlett. "What can I say? It should've been you. Maybe next time."

"Sure, maybe so." Scarlett couldn't be angry at David. They'd been colleagues for years and law school students before that. She quirked up a corner of her mouth in an attempt at a smile. "Your fiancée must be happy for you."

"She was planning a celebration dinner this weekend, but now it will have to wait. Reality is quickly setting in, I suppose." He held the conference room door for her, and they sat down at the table and spread out their notes.

"For the record, I think you did one heck of a job with Fleur." David made a face. "She was one tough client. A real nut case."

"I appreciate the sentiments." She took a breath to say something and then hesitated.

"What were you going to say?"

Scarlett rested her chin on her hand, thinking. "I saw Fleur on CNBC. She'd sent them a video to air about her decision to go with Color Color instead of High Gloss."

"What a prima donna."

"There was something strange about the video."

"What's that?"

"When I picked her up the Chateau Marmont the morning after we returned from London, Fleur had a fat lip. She said she'd slipped in the shower." Scarlett narrowed her eyes.

"And did you believe her?"

"Not really, but that's not the point."

David leaned closer. "So what is your point, counselor?"

"Supposedly she made her decision to go with Color Color based on High Gloss's reluctance to share her artistic vision. And she made that decision after the meeting with Olga."

"I'm not following you."

Scarlett ticked off points on her fingers. "High Gloss stock soared on the announcement of the deal with Fleur of London. The market anticipated their increased profits. Then, when Fleur backed out, their stock tumbled. When she signed with Color Color, their stock skyrocketed."

"That's normal, isn't it?"

"True, but on tape Fleur said she made the decision after her meeting with High Gloss and signed with Color Color after she returned to London. I don't think that's true."

David leaned back and laced his fingers behind his head.

"Why not? And why would it matter?"

"In the video, Fleur's fat lip had miraculously healed. It was a real bruiser, and swollen, too. There's no makeup in the world that good. Not even High Gloss can make a foundation to cover a lump the size of a golf ball."

David's eyes widened. "So you think the video was shot beforehand?"

"Probably before we left London. She was in her office."

"Someone could've made some serious money on the news."

Scarlett pitched forward. "That's exactly what I'm thinking." She still had to verify what she'd seen, but she was ninety percent certain.

Later that evening, Scarlett stopped by her mother's apartment for a late dinner. Isabel had made a salad and cold gazpacho, along with sweet empanadas for dessert. Scarlett loved the little half-moon pastries from her childhood.

The hardest part of the evening was telling her mother that she had not achieved her partnership goal.

Isabel hugged her. "When you were born, I didn't look into my baby's beautiful eyes and say, 'I hope you make partner one day.' No, I said, 'I hope you have a beautiful life.'" She smiled at her. "Is there beauty on your path, *mi niña?*"

Scarlett clung to her mother and wiped tears from her eyes. Her mother always had a way of putting things into perspective for her. Perhaps it was the deaths of her husband

and her son that made Isabel appreciate a simple life. To Scarlett, these were deep scars, and a large part of what drove her.

But was there beauty on her path? Once Scarlett had thought so. What had happened to it?

As Scarlett was washing dishes with Isabel, she told her about her business trip to Spain.

"Why, that's wonderful." Isabel paused, a faraway look in her eyes. "You'll love España, there's magic in the air."

"I wish it were a vacation and you could come, too."

"Someday we'll do that." Isabel dried her hands on a dish towel. "Do you think you'll have time to visit family?"

"I'm not sure, though I'd like to. We're going to Madrid."

Her mother scurried to her desk and picked up an old address book. She slipped on her reading glasses and ran her finger down handwritten pages. "Here they are. I'll write down these addresses and phone numbers for you."

Scarlett smiled at her mother. After moving to America, Isabel had never returned to Spain, though she and Scarlett had often spoken of doing so. It was another one of the things in her life she'd put aside in her quest for success.

She thought about her friend Verena, who had lost both her parents in a tragic car accident when she was eighteen. Her grandmother Mia had made a point of taking her and her sisters to Switzerland to share their heritage with them.

Scarlett had always thought she would do that one day with her children and her mother. Now, as she looked at the fine lines on her mother's face, she thought that day should be sooner rather than later.

Isabel folded the piece of paper and gave it to her. "Please try to make time to see your family. They ask about you so often."

"Honestly, Mamá, I don't know how much time I'll have."

Isabel smoothed her hair. "At least call on my cousin Teresa in Cádiz. She's very special to me."

Her mother often talked about Teresa. Scarlett could hardly remember any of her mother's family, and they'd lost touch with her father's side. Her mother told her they had scattered around the world.

She kissed her mother on the cheek and tucked the addresses into her purse. "I'll try," she said. Just before she snapped her purse shut, her phone rang. She glanced at the caller information on the screen. "It's Johnny."

"Answer it." Isabel smiled and busied herself at her desk, although Scarlett knew she was listening.

Scarlett spoke to him and then clicked off. "Mamá, I need to see Johnny before I leave." Besides, she was anxious about going home alone after the attack in the garage. She hated feeling like that, but in truth, she'd enjoyed waking up in Johnny's bed. They were friends, but he made her feel safe.

Isabel said, "Go see him, *nena*."

Scarlett kissed her mother on the cheek. She loved that little term of endearment, *nena*, pronounced nay-nah. If she ever had a daughter, she'd call her that, too.

Scarlett pulled under the striped porte cochère in front of the Beverly Hills Hotel. The valet took her car, and she started up the red carpeted steps that led into the hotel. The landmark hotel had been built in 1912 and had long been a glamorous mainstay of the community.

Johnny had done well here as maître d' of the Polo Lounge. He had made many important connections, which would serve him well in a restaurant of his own.

She veered to the right toward the lounge. She stepped inside, thinking that the ambiance, though modern, was still like something out of a Hollywood movie. Behind the sleek wooden bar a vintage picture of polo players was suspended over bottles of coveted cognacs. Curved semi-circular booths were the perfect spots to see and be seen.

When Scarlett arrived, Johnny was seating a film producer and his wife. She watched him, proud of the impeccably mannered man he'd become. The couple chatted with him, clearly enjoying his company.

Tonight he wore a purple and silver polka-dot bow-tie, and Scarlett couldn't help but smile. To her, he was the most handsome man in the room, more so than some of the famous faces dotting the restaurant. But then, she knew him too well.

When he saw her, a grin lit his face.

"Where is everyone tonight?" The lounge was uncharacteristically quiet.

"It's a weekday and we're winding down early for the

evening. I've been training a new guy for the door, since I won't be here much longer. I'll sit with you. He's got this now."

Scarlett slid into the booth he indicated, and he sat beside her. Johnny had a charismatic presence, and she felt drawn to him. "You're really serious about this new restaurant, aren't you?"

"Absolutely. Here's my partner now." Lance, still in his white executive chef jacket, made his way toward them.

"Hello, Scarlett." Lance sat on the other side of her. "What brings you out tonight?"

He smelled delicious, of herbs and garlic. No wonder Verena adored him. "I'm leaving for Europe tomorrow, and I wanted to see Johnny before I left."

Johnny took her hand. "Any word from the police on your attacker?"

"Not a word." His hand was warm on hers. It was a friendly, protective gesture.

"I'd feel better if you stayed with me tonight," Johnny said.

Scarlett started to protest. It wasn't as if she were afraid to stay alone, even though she'd enjoyed his bed. "I'll be fine, Johnny."

"Probably. But it's just one night. Maybe they'll find the guy while you're gone."

"Where in Europe are you going?" Lance stretched his long frame against the back of the booth.

"Spain. The firm has a client there." She didn't mention

the fact that she'd brought them in.

"I love Spain. The food is spectacular." Lance threw a glance at Johnny. "Actually, we should put tapas on the menu in our restaurant. It's hard to find those authentic little dishes in the states."

Johnny glanced at Scarlett. "If they're anything like your mother's cooking, how fast can I leave?"

"Wouldn't that be fun?" She laughed at the thought. "You and my brother sure kept her busy cooking when you were kids." Scarlett fell silent, thinking about how much fun it had been having them around. She'd never imagined those days would disappear so soon.

Johnny squeezed her hand. "I miss him, too, Scarlett," he said softly.

"Why don't you go, Johnny? You haven't had a vacation in forever, and now you've got a pretty good understudy here." Lance nodded toward the young man at the front.

Johnny's eyes lit with interest. "I'd love to. How long will you be there, Scarlett?"

"About a week. But we're going to be awfully busy working with our client."

"Can you stay over a few days?"

Could she? In the past, it would have been out of the question, however, she no longer needed to prove herself to make partner. "Why not?" The thought of having a short holiday was quite appealing.

"Good, then it's settled," Lance said. "I'll give you a list of things to order. When I worked in Paris, I used to go to

Spain every chance I got."

Scarlett laughed. "I can help him with that, too."

"Then it's a deal," Johnny said. "I'll book a flight tomorrow. Now, come home with me, Scarlett?"

"Sure, only this time, I'll sleep on the couch. It's only fair."

"No way. Guys like couches, haven't you heard?" Johnny helped her up, while Lance winked at him. "No better place to fall asleep."

Men are so funny, Scarlett thought, though she was excited he was going to join her in Spain.

10

AS SOON AS Johnny heard the distress in Scarlett's voice, he raced from his suite and pounded through the hallway at the Ritz in a T-shirt and yellow-striped boxer briefs, dodging shocked guests. He yelled over his shoulder. "Call security to Room 410, Scarlett Sandoval's room. There's a shooter outside!" He repeated his words in Spanish, pleading for help.

A couple of women screamed. A man turned and ran into his own room. "I'll call," he said.

"Hurry, my girlfriend is still in there."

Johnny thudded down the stairwell, taking three steps at a time, and burst onto her floor.

He still had her on his cell phone. "Scarlett, can you get to the door?"

"No, it's in the direct path of the balcony door, where the shots are coming from. Don't get too close, Johnny. Please don't." As her voice cracked, his heart splintered. He couldn't lose her. Not now, not when they were so close.

"I'll be careful. Where the hell is security?" He arrived at her door. "I'm here. Wait a minute, I think someone is coming."

"Please be careful, please. I need you, Johnny."

"Hang on. It's security, and he's a big guy." Scarlett was suppressing sobs on the phone, and it ripped his heart out.

The guard put a beefy hand on his two-way radio. "Do you have an ID, sir?" His eyes dropped to Johnny's bright boxer briefs.

Johnny put his fists on his hips. "Do I look like I do?" He quickly explained the situation.

The guard stepped to one side. "We'd better call the police." He spoke into his radio.

"How long will that take? Can't you open the door?"

When the guard shook his head, Johnny said, "Come on, my girlfriend is in danger. I'll take the responsibility." He spotted the man's wedding ring. "What if it were your wife?" The security guard sighed and relented. He swiped the passkey, and Johnny swung open the door. "Scarlett, can you hear me?"

"Yes, yes I can."

"Stay there. I'm coming in to get you." He wiped sweat from his brow and inched along the wall.

"I can see your shadow. Get down, Johnny."

"Think they're still there?"

"Don't take that chance."

Johnny looked around. "Hey, *amigo*, I need your hat."

He snatched it from the guard's head and tossed it into the room. A shot ripped through it.

Scarlett screamed.

"Holy *caca*, we need help," Johnny said grimly, passing a hand in front of his face. "And you need a new hat."

He spoke into the phone. "Scarlett, the police are on their way. Stay with me, *chica*. Stay calm." She sniffled on the other end of the line, and he could hear her murmuring a prayer in Spanish. Johnny fell to his knees. He felt so helpless. "Listen, I'm coming in."

"No, no, stay there, Johnny."

"I've got to help you." He heard her ragged breath through the phone.

Outside, a police siren bleated in the night, drawing closer. "Do you hear that?"

"Yes," she whispered.

Red flashing lights burst through the night, blazing through Scarlett's open doorway. Moments later, screeching patrol cars closed the street, and an armed team moved into the hotel, which had been placed on lockdown. An announcement blared though the hotel, asking people to stay away from exterior windows.

Doors in the corridor flung open, and guests in all manner of dress—from bathrobes to tuxedos and evening gowns—spilled into the hallway. "What's going on? Is it a terrorist attack?"

Johnny angled away from the crowd. "Still with me?"

"Yes," she replied softly.

The minutes ticked by like hours. Johnny wiped perspiration from his face. Clutching his phone, he slid down the wall by her open door. "Can you hear me?"

"Yeah," came the faint reply.

"Try to stay calm. We'll get you out of there." He didn't know how, but losing her was not an option. He had to keep her calm.

"Johnny, I'm so scared," Scarlett whispered.

Her distress was palpable. He pressed his hand to his forehead. "Think about how you whipped that guy in the parking garage. Be that strong woman now, *mi corazon.*"

She was silent for a long time. Her breathing became wispy.

"Johnny, if I don't make it—"

"Shh, you're going to be fine. Just wait." Filled with anguish, he leaned his head against the wall. "I'm here, Scarlett, I won't leave you."

The phone went silent again. After a while, Scarlett whispered. "Who's trying to kill me? What do they want?"

He gritted his teeth. He wished he knew. "Maybe it's a mistake." Who would want to do Scarlett harm?

"No such thing…" Her breath caught.

Johnny squeezed his eyes shut against his agony. "Relax, just breathe."

"Tell my mother—"

"You'll tell her yourself, *mi amor.*"

He *had* to reach her. Where the hell were the police? He leaned into the doorway. If he could crawl on the floor to her—

"Sir, please stand aside."

Johnny looked up at a group of armed officers in protective gear. "Am I glad to see you guys." He scrambled to his feet.

Working in unison, the men entered Scarlett's room with caution.

Johnny sank his head into his hands and prayed as he had never prayed before. *Please, please save her.* Every nerve in his body was on high alert.

He waited for the sound of more gunshots, but it was all clear. He peered in.

Two men were helping Scarlett out. When she saw Johnny, she fell into his arms, clinging to him with all her might.

"Hey, hey, you're safe now," he said, clutching her. He'd been so frightened of losing her, and their lives had flashed through his mind. Their time together had been too short. *You don't always have tomorrow,* he realized. Scarlett was shivering with shock in his arms.

The team cleared the room and secured it. One of the burly officers approached him with his hands on his hips. "Evidence from the sniper was found across the street."

"Was it a terrorist?" Johnny asked.

"No. It looks personal. We need to speak with both of you. Wait here."

As if they had a choice. Another officer stood guard beside them.

"Can I get some blankets?" Johnny asked, pressing Scarlett to his chest. Her hair was damp, and she was trembling in her robe.

The officer signaled a hotel employee, who reappeared with a stack of blankets. Johnny sat on the floor and draped blankets around Scarlett. He cradled her in his lap.

She managed a small laugh though chattering teeth. "You need one, too. Sitting here in your shorts and T-shirt."

Johnny grinned at her. At least she was speaking again. "How about a cup of tea? Or hot chocolate?"

A smile twitched her lips. "Tea. I'd like that."

Johnny requested hot tea, and within minutes another employee arrived with a tray. Scarlett gripped a steaming cup in her hands.

Johnny leaned his head against the wall and gazed around the lavishly decorated corridor. "Hell of a way to spend an evening at the Ritz, isn't it?"

After the commotion died down and guests returned to their rooms, the police escorted Johnny and Scarlett to Johnny's suite, where Scarlett sank onto a tufted loveseat. A fresh pot of Earl Grey tea sat on the French coffee table before her. The hotel manager couldn't do enough for them; he promised he would have Scarlett's personal effects moved to another suite after the police had finished their work in her rooms.

Scarlett still wore her bathrobe. Johnny grabbed a pair of worn jeans and slid into them. He figured enough people in the hotel had seen his underwear.

Johnny joined Scarlett on the beige settee and wrapped his arm around Scarlett, who was still shivering from shock and adrenaline. The color was returning to her face, and she seemed stronger. He never wanted to let her out of his sight again, though he knew that was an unreasonable expectation. He'd settle for tonight.

The police officer asked for their passports. "Scarlett Sandoval, Johnny Silva." He scribbled notes on a pad of paper.

"What happened?" Scarlett asked, sitting up straighter with a burst of energy. "Why was I targeted? Who did this?"

Johnny grinned at her. *Interrogating the police officers.* That's more like the Scarlett he knew.

"We found evidence in an empty office facing your room." The officer wagged his head. "Do you recognize this photo, Senorita?"

Scarlett peered at it. "It's my headshot from the law firm I work for."

"How would the sniper have gotten this?"

She adjusted her bathrobe, hugging it closer to her. "It's on the company website. Anyone could have printed it from the web."

"And who knew you were staying here?"

"Not many people. My office, travel agent, client, mother, and a few friends." Scarlett ticked off people on her fingers. "No one who'd want to kill me, though."

"Family or friends?"

"I have very good personal relationships. I can't imagine

any of them would have tried to kill me."

The officer shot a look at Johnny. "Husband?"

"Johnny? No, of course not. I mean, I'm not married. Yet. Or rather, no plans, immediate or otherwise." Scarlett seemed flustered. "Not that it's out of the question, you understand." She sighed and gulped tea from a gold-rimmed porcelain cup, her hands shaking.

The officer swung his eyes from Johnny to Scarlett. "And how would you define this relationship?"

"Friends," Scarlett said, answering too decisively for Johnny's taste. "Maybe it was a random person I met here in Madrid."

"It's possible. And in case we need to contact you, where will you be tonight?"

Scarlett shot a questioning look at Johnny.

"She's staying with me tonight."

"I suggest you change rooms, too, Mr. Silva. Put the room under a different name." The officer rose. "We will contact you when we have more information."

Johnny called the front desk, and minutes later, the manager showed them to another suite, which was recorded at the front desk under a false name. Johnny glanced around the suite, taking in the gleaming chandelier, the thick carpet, the twin marble bathrooms, and the living room filled with fresh roses and lilies. This larger suite had an inner sleeping chamber, and Scarlett looked relieved. "This will do," he said, and thanked the manager.

Her personal effects were delivered shortly afterward.

"Don't you feel like a real celebrity now?" he asked.

"I can't imagine having to live like that, traveling under assumed names and all." Scarlett shuddered. "No privacy at all. Stalkers, threats…"

"Yeah, and people shooting at them," he added wryly. In Beverly Hills, Johnny had observed both the perks and the limitations famous people had in their daily lives. He liked his life just fine, anonymity and all. "Be honest, Scarlett. Any idea who's trying to kill you? Or does Marsh & Gold knock off associates who don't make partner?"

"That's usually not the case." She drew her hands over her face. "David was trying to talk to me before he left this morning. He was disturbed. He said something about a call before Lucan arrived on the scene, and then he clammed up." She picked up her phone and checked the time. "They haven't landed yet. I'll send him an email."

"No, don't email." Johnny didn't know why he said that, but he didn't have a good feeling about the firm she worked for. When she told him the New York office called the Los Angeles office *the wild west*, he'd had an uneasy feeling, even then.

Scarlett stared at him, but after a moment, she nodded and put her phone down. The smooth skin over her high cheekbones flushed pink.

"Who at the office might have wanted to harm you?"

"I can't imagine. No one is perfect there," she said, arching a fine eyebrow. "But there aren't any wild, axe murderer attorneys roaming the halls." Scarlett fell silent.

JAN MORAN

"What, that's just your clients?"

A smile tugged at a corner of her mouth. "We're lawyers. We agree to disagree. We fight for our clients."

The telephone on the desk rang, and Johnny answered it. After he hung up, he said, "That was the manager. Unless you want to go out and try to find a crazed maniac tonight, let's stay in. They'd like to send up dinner, along with a massage therapist and a bottle of champagne." Johnny picked up the room service menu. Scarlett needed to eat something.

She rubbed her arms. "First dibs on the massage. You can have the bubbly."

"I'll take that deal. I can sure use a soothing tonic. Hmm, Dom Pérignon, or Perrier-Jouët Rosé?" He flipped open the room service menu and ran his finger down the page. "Let's see, we can order from the Goya restaurant. For starters, how about the tuna tartar with caviar and papaya vinaigrette? Then there's the oxtail ravioli—you might like that—or the sea hake loin with Iberian vinaigrette."

"Johnny?"

"Yes, Scarlett?"

She sipped her tea. "I heard you call me your girlfriend over the phone."

His heart quickened. "Did you? Well, you'll always be my girlfriend, *chica*." And to prove it, he dropped the menu on the table, pulled her to her feet, and wrapped his arms around her. She was still trembling. He tightened his arms to convey his protection. "I was so worried about you, Scarlett."

"I could never have imagined anything like that," she

said, her voice cracking as the adrenaline drained from her. "I thought I was going to die."

Johnny couldn't hold back anymore; his eyes welled with emotion. Scarlett arched her neck and gazed at him, her eyes glistening in the soft light of the chandelier above. "Oh, Scarlett, *mi corazon*," he murmured, brushing his lips against hers.

Scarlett hesitated at first, and then responded with sweet tentativeness. To him, it was a moment he'd waited a lifetime for, and he was swept away on the soft fullness of her lips. She relaxed in his arms for a moment, and then took a half-step back, a smile playing on her lips.

"I should take a bath," she said, her eyes never leaving his. She moistened her lips.

"And I'll order dinner. I think I know what you like."

"I think you do." She disappeared into one of the bathrooms and closed the door.

Johnny whirled around and clenched his fist. *Yes*, he thought to himself. *Snipers be damned.* He ran a finger across his lips and closed his eyes.

11

SCARLETT AWOKE WRAPPED in Johnny's arms, the same way she'd fallen asleep. With his warm, muscular body curving around hers, she felt cosseted in love and luxury, despite the frightening events of the evening before.

As she shifted in a bed that cushioned every inch of her body, silky cotton sheets slipped from her shoulder. Johnny nuzzled her bare skin, dragging his lips across her shoulder. Never before had she felt such a sense of belonging, and it was truly an awakening for her.

Could a brush with death do that to a person?

She ran a hand down the satin gown that covered her thigh. Her fingers brushed Johnny's leg, which was draped over her leg. She loved the feeling of being tangled in his limbs.

Gazing at the chandelier above, ensconced in a muted world of opulence, it almost seemed as if last night had never occurred, that shots had never rang out over her head. But it had happened, and Scarlett knew that it hadn't been an accident.

Lucan had been so keen to have her stay the weekend at the Ritz. And yet, that was such easy assumption to make. Lucan was a smart, shrewd man. If he were the culprit, would he have been so obvious? Especially with David as a witness?

And why?

She thought of Fleur and the video, and the dramatic stock gyrations her decision had caused. Seismic price swings meant profits for those who shorted stocks, traded options, or bought and sold at opportune times. Magnify stock prices by tens of thousands, and millions might be made overnight.

Might that be worth killing for?

Johnny slid his leg over her gown. "*Buenos días, mi corazon.*"

Corazon. Spanish had the loveliest terms of endearment. She loved the romance and feeling of the language of her childhood. "*Buenos días, mi corazon, mi cariño.*" My heart, my darling. From the moment bullets had ripped through the surface of their relationship, their feelings for one another had burst through, as if freed from chains around their hearts.

They hadn't made love last night, but they had expressed the depth of their feelings in ways she'd never known existed. From the touch of his hand, the heat of his breath, the scent of his skin…her senses had been fully aroused.

The harrowing events had emotionally drained her, and after her in-room massage she'd been physically and mentally spent. Johnny had been so protective of her, treating her as if she were made of porcelain. But she was a woman with desires. Fortunately, that night Johnny had invaded her dreams with infinite sweetness.

And God willing, she would live another day. She turned to him.

Johnny trailed a finger along her neck, pausing to circle the tender hollow where her collarbone began. "I could stay here all day with you, but I think we should leave." He kissed her forehead. "I don't want you to be target practice again for some crazy shooter."

"It's time we left." She stretched, and Johnny cast an appreciative glance over her body.

"Let's rent a car and drive to Cádiz as we'd planned." He frowned. "Does anyone at the firm know you're travelling there?"

"Only Mamá."

"Good." He kissed the tip of her nose. "I think we can trust Isabel."

While she dressed, she heard him call the concierge and order breakfast. Johnny was certainly at home in a hotel, she mused. But then, he worked at an exclusive hotel and was not easily impressed.

They ate and checked out of the Ritz, and Scarlett thought the staff was relieved to see them leave. Near the hotel, Johnny arranged a rental car.

"*Andalucía*, here we come." Johnny opened her door and helped her in.

Scarlett settled into the Citroën convertible. She was looking forward to their journey through the southern part of Spain. Her mother had told her she had family throughout the region, from Seville to Cádiz, Granada to Málaga. She didn't know how many areas in Andalusia they could visit, but she definitely planned to return with her mother as soon as she could. Johnny got in behind the wheel.

Scarlett said, "I have distant relatives scattered all over Spain, but Mamá asked that I visit her cousin Teresa in Cádiz."

"Any family of yours I'd love to meet, Scarlett. *Su familia es mi familia.*"

"Careful, I don't know if I'd take it that far," she said with a mock grimace. "You might not want my family as yours. I don't really know them. I haven't seen them since I was a preschooler."

Johnny turned the ignition while Scarlett unfolded a map she'd bought while he was renting the car. He steered through Madrid, glancing in his rear view mirror often to make sure they weren't being followed. Once they were out of Madrid and onto the open road, they both breathed easier.

Johnny, satisfied that they had not been followed, pulled over and put the top down, opening up the car to the outdoors. Fluffy clouds floated in azure skies overhead. He eased back onto the road.

As they drove on, Scarlett followed their progress on the map. Johnny watched her wrangling the large map with amusement.

"That's sure old-school," he said. "Thought you were the kind of girl who only navigated on a cell phone." He punched a button for the built-in navigation system, but the digital display froze. "Aw, geez. Look at this." He fiddled with the buttons. "It's not working. Let's use your phone."

Scarlett threw him a quick glance. "It's off."

"You? Without a phone? I don't know whether to be awed, impressed, or check you in for psychiatric evaluation. Come on, tell me what's wrong." He squinted at her. "Is it a client, or someone at the office?"

"First, you know I can't divulge privileged client interactions."

"I respect that. Unless they start taking shots at you." He grimaced. "Then you might want to reconsider that professional relationship."

"I don't think it was a client. And remember, I took an oath to practice law."

"Yeah, and I unloaded a few oaths last night, too."

"I'm serious."

"So am I. What's an oath if you're a dead lawyer? Scarlett, you have to tell me what's going on. You don't turn on your mobile phone, so that tells me that you're afraid of being tracked."

"Good deduction, Sherlock. Actually, the battery died last night."

"And you didn't recharge it this morning?" He shook his head. "Someone was intent on taking you out last night. I'm sitting beside you in the line of fire, so don't you think I have a right to know what's happening?"

He had a point. "I thought it could wait until after I returned." She bowed her head. Without breaching client privileges, she told him about seeing Fleur on CNBC, and the miraculous disappearance of her busted lip.

Johnny listened, taking it all in. "So you think she made the video before she met with High Gloss."

"That's right. I'm sure of it. I had the video analyzed. Her face showed absolutely no sign of injury or swelling of any kind."

"Then she sabotaged the deal. Why?"

Scarlett went on to tell him of her suspicions about possible stock manipulations and insider trading.

Johnny let out a whistle. "Who did you tell about this?"

"I mentioned the news clip of Fleur to David, though I didn't have confirmation then. And that's public knowledge. It was on the news." She drew her eyebrows together. "I also said someone could've made some serious money on that information."

"When did you tell him that?"

"Before we left. We were at the office, in the conference room—" Scarlett stopped and bit her lip. Could their conversation have been recorded?

"Is it possible someone overheard your conversation?"

"The main conference room is equipped with a recording device for board meetings. I didn't think it was used much anymore. We were in a small meeting room. I guess it's possible it might have been recorded, or someone listened in." She didn't think David would have repeated the conversation.

"Sounds like someone thinks you're onto them. Who do you think it might be?"

Scarlett narrowed her eyes. "Lucan is too smart to be that obvious."

"What about the other partners?"

This might be more involved than she'd realized. "I need to speak to someone when I return," she said quietly, thinking about Zelda. Inwardly, she was shaken. *What had she stumbled into?* "If they're technologically savvy, then my phone could be used to broadcast my location. I don't want that to happen."

"Scarlett, if that's your concern, I'm pretty sure the technology exists to find your phone without it being on."

Scarlett sucked in her breath. He was right. She shoved her hand into her purse, grabbed her phone, and tossed it from the car as they careened down the motorway. She watched it soar through the air and land in a field of cattle, which were lolling in clover and barely noticed a thing.

Johnny glanced at her from the corner of his eye. "I've always liked a decisive woman."

Scarlett looked at him and burst out laughing. "Let them track that."

"You can use mine, just don't call the office."

"Wouldn't dream of it."

He placed his hand on her knee. "Let's have some fun on this road trip."

They drove in silence for a while, and Scarlett stole glances at Johnny. Did she dare let their feelings progress? If she did, and their romance ended in disaster, as some of her relationships had, their friendship would be ruined. Johnny was an important thread in her life; he was a connection to her brother. Was this a risk she was willing to take?

They whizzed past a directional sign for *Sevilla*, and Johnny veered off the road. They stopped at a tapas bar, where Scarlett explained some of the traditional dishes she'd grown up with.

Johnny loved the food. "Maybe Isabel can share some of her secret recipes with Lance."

"She'd like that. You know she's always been an excellent cook. It would give her something to do."

"And lessen her fixation on your producing grandchildren, you mean?"

Scarlett widened her eyes. "How did you know?"

"Lucky guess," Johnny said with a wink.

Afterward, with shops closing for the afternoon siesta, they spied a magnificent stone fountain in the midst of a square, which, judging from the number of people there, was a favorite spot for lovers, both young and old.

The warm afternoon sun hung high in the sky. They sat on a bench covered with blue and yellow hand-painted tiles, listened to the fountain's gentle splashing, enjoyed the cool breeze that touched the water, and talked about Johnny's plans for the restaurant. It was a perfect afternoon.

Succumbing to the relaxed pace, they decided to stay in

Seville that evening. They found a quaint pensione covered in a riot of pink bougainvillea.

Later that evening they cuddled together in a large iron bed that squeaked whenever they moved. Wearing a short, though modest gown, Scarlett faced Johnny in bed on cool, crisp white bed linens. He wore multicolored polka-dot briefs, and his chest was bare. She suppressed a grin. Did he match his underwear to his bow-ties? He sure favored wild prints in both.

She ran her fingers through his thick curls as they whispered in the night. He caressed her skin and nuzzled her shoulders, but he didn't pressure her to go on. Was Johnny having similar reservations about her, too? Yet his speech was peppered with endearments.

"So, *querida*, how many boyfriends did you have in New York?" He smoothed wayward strands of hair from her forehead. "Did you leave any broken hearts behind?"

Scarlett laughed softly. "I'd like to say I left legions of love-starved men in my wake, but I'd be lying. As an associate, I didn't have much time for a personal life."

"You didn't *make* time, you mean."

"No, because I didn't meet anyone who meant that much to me."

"Yet you're making time now." Johnny kissed her forehead.

Her heart pounded so loudly, she was sure he could hear it. "I needed a break." She saw a flicker of disappointment in his eyes. Why couldn't she admit that she was incredibly drawn to him? "And you're different," she added. The light of happiness returned to his eyes.

They continued talking about their families, and their future goals. Johnny told her more about their plans for the restaurant, and Scarlett listened, enjoying the passion in his deep voice.

He truly cared about making people feel welcome and comfortable and special, whether they were an A-list star, or a tourist they might never see again.

"You never know who they'll tell," Johnny said. "With social media, any good—or bad—experiences can be blasted around the world in mere seconds."

Johnny ran a finger along her neck, and she shivered with pleasure. "Now that you're off the partner track, have you thought of doing something else? If you could do anything in the world, *mi amor*, what would you do?" he asked. "Anything, anywhere."

Scarlett considered his words. "There's still a chance I could make it next year." Much less of a chance, she knew. "I enjoy helping people, especially entrepreneurs in the creative arts who are just getting started. If I weren't at Marsh & Gold, I'd still want to practice law. It's intellectually fulfilling, and empowering."

Johnny's deep brown eyes crinkled at the edges in a warm smile. "Scarlett, you have the ability to do whatever your heart desires."

If she didn't make partner, what would she do? Would she want to stay there? Many firms had an up-or-out policy, though exceptions were made for stellar specialists. "Actually, I think I'd like to run my own firm someday."

"Then you want to be an entrepreneur, too."

"I guess so." She rolled onto her back and flung an arm over her head, while Johnny trailed his fingers along her other arm. She'd never felt so at ease with a man before. "But that's probably a long time away."

Johnny slid a hand under his head. "Whatever you decide, you have my support."

Scarlett sought his eyes out, checking for truth. "You mean that? You're not going to deride me if I make an error in judgment?"

"No, why would I?"

She blinked a few times, recalling childhood dramas. "I loved my father, but when he drank alcohol, he became verbally abusive toward my mother. He would ridicule her ideas, and belittle her efforts, and scorn her for simple mistakes. He never actually struck her, but his words damaged her self-esteem all the same. I saw it, and I always jumped to her defense."

"I remember that, too," Johnny said, smoothing her furrowed brow. "I always felt sorry for your mother. She's a class act. Just like her daughter."

"My father was frustrated. He came here for a better life for his family, but he was never able to hold the same positions he could have in Spain. His command of the language was never quite good enough. In many ways, it was hard for him to adjust. But once they arrived, my mother was determined to remain in America and become a citizen, though she loved her native country, too. She thought she was doing what was best for her children's future."

"Times have changed, Scarlett. Women don't have to live like that anymore."

"Thank goodness. I'm so wary, watching for signs like that in men I've dated."

"Nothing wrong with wanting to protect yourself, or insisting on a good relationship. You're worth it, Scarlett. A thousand times over, *mi amor*."

Scarlett's eyelids grew heavy. She heard Johnny's breathing deepen, and she rolled toward him, running her hands over his torso and cuddling close enough to feel his strong heartbeat. *Utter perfection*, she thought, before drifting off to sleep.

12

THEY ROSE WITH the pink sky of dawn the next morning. While Scarlett bathed and dressed, Johnny went out for an early morning run.

When he returned, Johnny tapped on the door. "Decent?"

"Come on in. You've seen most of what there is to see." She was just zipping up a tangerine-colored sundress. Still, she liked his manners. "Is that coffee I smell? If it is, I promise I'll love you forever."

"If I'd known you were that easy, I'd have started with the coffee angle long ago." He kissed her on the forehead. "*Café con leche*. Light, just the way you like it. We'll stop for a proper *desayuno* later."

"Mmm, I'd like that. I don't know why I'm starving." She glanced at the damp T-shirt clinging to his chest, and then dropped her gaze to his muscled legs. "Oh, sweaty man.

Into the shower with you."

"That was a great run. Such beautiful architecture."

"It's been a cultural melting pot. Lots of Moorish influence here."

"The lady who made our coffee gave me some places we need to see, like Las Setas." He swirled his hands in the air with excitement.

"Mushrooms?"

"That's what they call it. It's a giant wooden structure. Seems a lot of people love to hate it here."

Scarlett laughed and tossed him a towel. "Hurry up. In the shower. I won't get into the car with you like that."

After they checked out of the pensione, they had breakfast and took in the sights. They climbed the steps to see Las Setas, formally known as the Metropol Parasol, an enormous German-designed wood structure near La Encarnación Square, which Johnny found intriguing. "Who would imagine seeing this here?"

They strolled around the expansive Plaza de España, exclaiming over a sea of ornately painted tiles. They found the beauty of the Seville Cathedral and its towering gothic architecture awe-inspiring, as was the opulently layered Royal Alcázar Palace, called the Reales Alcázares de Sevilla, originally a Moorish fort dating from the thirteenth century.

Scarlett's imagination took flight in the dazzling Arabian palace. Mosaics twinkled with gold leaf, and carved ceilings were light and lacy. She was astounded by the Alcázar's intricate decorative designs and graceful arches. "Fianna and

Dahlia would love to see this, too," she said, twirling under a soaring dome as Johnny swung her around. "They're so artistic; I can just imagine how inspired they'd be by all of this."

In the gardens, they wandered through a clipped hedge maze, while scented orange groves perfumed the sunny grounds. Scarlett thought she'd never had a day filled with such beauty in her life.

Later, after lunch, they strolled through the Parque de María Luisa, where horse-drawn carriages ferried lovers around the grounds. Scarlett felt as though she'd been whisked back in time.

They walked on, admiring the botanical gardens and enchanting tile work. Soon Johnny swept her into a round, domed pergola with an ancient stone foundation. Scarlett leaned against a wooden railing and gazed out over a sun-dappled pond, where ducks plied the placid water.

Johnny stood behind her and ran a hand over her hair. "I've always loved your hair," he said, letting strands fall through his fingers. "I wish you could see how the sun lights your bronze curls, Scarlett."

She shook her hair out in the gentle breeze that wafted through the open pergola. He lifted her hair and touched his lips to her neck, sending waves of desire through her. But they were life-long friends, and she had to know what his thoughts were before they made an irrevocable mistake.

She turned and lifted her face to his. "Johnny, what are we doing?"

His eyes, dark as rich mahogany, spoke volumes. "We're discovering each other. I thought that's what you wanted." He played with the strap of her sundress.

"I don't know what I want." That wasn't quite true. Scarlett knew exactly what she wanted—a lover, a life-long companion, a best friend, a father to her children—but was it Johnny? "We've known one another for so many years. Are we merely comfortable together?"

Johnny brushed a strand of hair from her cheek. "I've never been so uncomfortable in my life. Scarlett, I think I'm—"

She pressed her fingers against his lips. Swiftly he wrapped his arms around her, enveloping her in such an all-encompassing embrace that the world around them fell away, and it was as if they were the only two souls on earth.

She pressed her cheek to his chest. His heart pulsed in a rapid rhythm, mirroring hers. His cotton shirt smelled of sandalwood, and she ran her fingers over the tight weave, flicking the top button open to explore the warmth of his skin.

"Oh, Scarlett," he murmured. "You're driving me crazy. You always have." He framed her face in his hands and kissed her with such passionate longing that he took her breath away.

Feeling his kiss scorch her body, Scarlett arched her neck, hungry for more, but Johnny pulled away. A smile flickered on his lips. *Those lips.* She blinked and caught her breath. "Wow. Oh. My." No wonder women fell at his feet.

He was smooth. *Did he kiss Carla Ramirez this way?* She shook her head.

Johnny tilted her chin. "My beautiful, brilliant, somewhat naïve Scarlett." His eyes held amusement.

Or is he mocking me? "I'm not that naïve," she huffed, and stepped back.

"Scarlett, please. I find you such an, an oxymoron."

She took another step back. "A *what?*"

"An oxymoron. You know, like jumbo shrimp." He pushed a hand through his hair. "Aw hell, bad choice of words."

"Jumbo shrimp? Well, that's a new one. I don't think any man has ever kissed me and then segued to jumbo shrimp." She crossed her arms and leaned against a column.

Johnny looked oddly flustered. "How about bittersweet? Bitter and sweet." He caught her glare. "Or sweet and bitter. That's kind of what I meant."

"Do me a favor, please don't keep digging. The hole is getting deeper, and I can't stand to see you fall." She swished past him, her skirt whipping against his legs.

Johnny slapped his forehead. "Guess it's time to go."

The Citroën convertible top was down, and Scarlett fastened her loose hair with a clasp against the breeze. It was still siesta time, so there wasn't much traffic.

"We'll make Cádiz by evening," Johnny said, as he steered onto the highway. "Want to make any phone calls while we drive?"

"I should call my mother." Scarlett picked up his phone. "Did you know you had a call from Carla?"

"Carla who?"

"Oh, please. Carla Ramirez. Why is she tracking you down here?" Johnny didn't answer. Mildly annoyed, she tapped her mother's phone number.

Isabel answered right away. "I've been trying to reach you, but your phone goes right to voice-mail. What happened? I thought you were traveling south today."

"We are. I, ah… lost my phone. But take Johnny's number if you need to reach me."

"There's someone who's been calling for you, *nena*."

"Who?"

"A man. He's pleasant, but won't give his name. I don't trust him." She sniffed. "Sounds like an *abogado*." Isabel sucked in a breath. "Aye, *dios mio*. I didn't mean it that way. *Lo siento*."

"Mamá! Even my mother dislikes lawyers?" Scarlett rolled her eyes while Johnny chuckled. Still, her neck bristled at the news.

"This is serious, *nena*. He's not giving up. What should I say to him?"

"Tell him the truth. Tell him you don't trust lawyers." She didn't want to alarm her mother by sharing with her what was happening in Spain. Her mother huffed on the other end of the line. "Just say I can't be reached, which is true, but don't give him any idea where I might be."

"He said he knew you were in Spain."

Of course he does. Scarlett's tension tightened a notch. She reassured her mother and told her she'd call her again when she reached her cousin Teresa's home. She clicked the phone off, her senses on high alert.

Johnny threw her a look. "What did she say?"

"Someone has been calling my mother looking for me."

"Didn't David say something like that at the hotel before he left?"

"Sort of. He started to say something about a call he'd received, but then Lucan came along."

"I don't like this, Scarlett."

"Neither do I." Her neck was crawling with apprehension. She flicked on the radio. "Can't do anything about it until I return, can I?"

Johnny curved one corner of his lips, revealing the fine dimple in his cheek she'd always adored. She stole another look at his profile, at his high cheekbones and dark swath of eyebrows, and the full lips that had threatened to buckle her knees.

She snapped her head back to the passing scenery.

Darkness gathered as they drove, and millions of stars twinkled in the sky, like so many silvery fairy lights illuminating the heavens.

Johnny could smell the damp marine scent of the ocean as they drew nearer the southwestern coast of Spain. In the seat next to him, Scarlett had her head thrown back and was staring at the constellations.

If Scarlett was worried, he was even more so. He'd waited a lifetime to express his feelings to her, and he wouldn't have her threatened or endangered. What kind of people had she been dealing with? Whoever they were, they'd have to get past him first.

He glanced at her well-defined arms, bronze against her tangerine sundress. She might have bested one attacker, but the episode at the Ritz in Madrid had been far too dangerous. Better they stay off the radar.

Scarlett had called her mother's cousin earlier. Teresa wasn't available, but her housekeeper gave Scarlett the address and told her they would be home soon.

As they drove into the coastal community, Johnny heard songs and laughter spilling from the streets.

Scarlett glanced at him, "What do you think that is?"

"Sounds like a party."

The music grew louder. "That's some party. Sounds like the whole town."

Johnny turned a corner onto a small lane, and a group of masked court jesters jogged toward them, singing and dancing. Behind them, musketeers in sherbet shades and towering top hats were playing a kazoo and keeping time with sticks. A woman linked hands with three children dressed as tiny clowns before they crossed the street.

Johnny jerked the steering wheel, swerving to avoid the joyful melee. "What the—"

"Oh, I think I know what this is. I've heard about it from my mother." Scarlett bounced in her seat with excitement.

"Look," she said, pointing to a colorful banner. "It's Los Carnavales, one of the best carnival celebrations in the world. Watch out, there are more coming."

A flatbed truck filled with hay was aiming right toward them. Crammed in the back was another costumed group clutching lutes and guitars. A second gang of gaily festooned revelers were clamoring for a song.

Johnny yanked the wheel. "I think the running of the bulls is safer than this."

"My mother has told me about the satirical *comparsas*, witty performers who compete in the Teatro Falla for the best skits. And the *chirigotas*, the happy minstrels."

They edged closer to the plaza. "I think we should park while we can," Johnny said, easing to the curb. "Ready to have some fun?"

Johnny bought glittery Venetian-style masks from a street vendor, and they quickly got into the spirit. It was a joyous crowd bent on celebrating the last days before Lent, the forty day period of abstinence before Easter.

Tango and flamenco music filled the air, and Johnny and Scarlett were swept into the merriment. Johnny thought he'd never seen Scarlett so carefree. She swirled through the night in her bright tangerine sundress, her coppery blond curls falling in a dazzling riot around her feathered Venetian mask.

"Scarlett, stay with me," Johnny called out, laughing, as a pirate danced her away from him. A woman in a masked Venetian costume of turquoise and coral whirled him around.

"Over here, Johnny." Her bright sundress was a beacon to him, and he led his dance partner through the crowd. When he reached Scarlett, he executed a smooth exchange, and the pirate danced away with the Venetian princess into the merry night.

"Am I glad to see you," Scarlett said, falling into his arms.

"At your service," he replied with a grin, and twirled her into the center of the plaza where the revelry was at its peak. Throngs of performers, groups of students, and families with children were celebrating in the square. A riot of colorful costumes blazed around them.

A long conga line of people shimmied by them, and Johnny and Scarlett were cheerfully pulled into the line. They danced through the avenue and alleys, with everyone chanting, "*Esto es carnaval,*" as they went. Finally, Johnny and Scarlett spun away to catch their breath.

Johnny swept Scarlett off her feet, swirling her in a circle. She dissolved into gales of laughter, and they collapsed on the edge of a fountain. "Something to eat or drink?" Johnny asked. He couldn't remember when they'd laughed so hard.

"Both," Scarlett said, catching her breath. "Oh, let's go there." She leaped to her feet and pulled him into a tapas bar where *jamons* hung from the ceiling.

"Lance would love those hams." Johnny ducked under one on their way to the bar. He wanted to remember every sight and aroma and texture around him, and take the essence of it all back to their restaurant.

"They're Iberian hams, and they're *muy delicioso*." Scarlett's face flushed with joy.

"Are you lapsing into Spanglish, *mi corazon?*" He hugged her neck, thinking she was the most adorable, fearless, fun-loving creature he'd ever laid eyes on. How could he win her heart?

Scarlett pushed her mask over her head. "My papa used to sell a lot of this at his stall at the Farmer's Market."

Johnny remembered tagging along with her brother Franco when they were young. Those were some of the happiest moments of his childhood—because of Escarlata Sandoval and her family. On impulse, he flung an arm around her and kissed her with passion.

Behind them, the bar exploded with cheers for them, and other men slapped him on the back and congratulated him.

"*Su esposa es encantadora,*" a man said to him, and soon all the men in the bar were agreeing that Scarlett was a most enchanting wife, indeed, and began buying him wine.

"No, no, no," Scarlett protested, but soon she found it easier to go along.

A young woman in a glamorous showgirl costume edged closer to Johnny. "*Su marido es guapo,*" she murmured and ran her hand down his arm. A woman next to her playfully smacked the girl's hand. "Please excuse *mi niña*," she said to Scarlett.

"He's very handsome," Scarlett said. "And he knows it,"

she added, laughing. Though he certainly wasn't her husband.

"*Muy guapo, muy guapo,*" waved across the bar.

Johnny ordered Spanish Lanjarón mineral water for Scarlett, and then toasted her with a glass of bubbly rosé cava that was forced into his hand. "Here's to looking at life through pink champagne bubbles."

Scarlett took a sip, and then, with a glint in her eye, she kissed him back, nearly overwhelming him with her passion. "*Ay, mi amor.*" He grinned and kissed her back.

Soon the revelers around them were clapping again. A waiter leaned in. "If you're hungry, order now. This crowd can go on until morning, which isn't that far away."

"We didn't realize it was so late," Johnny said. They'd been having so much fun dancing and watching the performers' witty repartees and songs.

Scarlett and Johnny glanced at the menu scribbled on a chalkboard. They talked about what they wanted, and Johnny ordered. "*Salmorejo, carpaccio de atún rojo, ensalada de langostinos, y alcachofas, por favor. Gracias.*"

The small plates came out one at a time as they were ready. "I thought this would be like gazpacho," Johnny said, tasting the cold *salmorejo.* The creamy soup was made of tomatoes, thickened with olive oil and baguette bread, and served with a traditional side of Iberian ham and hard-boiled eggs. "I have to tell Lance about this."

They devoured the red tuna carpaccio, a prawn salad with mangos and avocado, and a steamed artichoke. More small plates of cheeses, almonds, and olives followed, until they could eat no more. The bartender poured a special sherry for Johnny and toasted with them to their health and children.

Johnny and Scarlett chuckled at the sentiment, though Johnny hoped it might come true.

"How about a walk?" Jonny paid the tab and took Scarlett's hand. "I hear the beach is this way."

"I'd like that," she said.

He encircled her waist with his arm and they strolled toward the water. A few other couples were walking along the water's edge, also tired from the party.

Scarlett kicked off her sandals, and Johnny did the same. Beneath the sun baked crust, the sand was cool and moist. They raced to the shoreline and splashed in ankle-deep water, holding hands.

"Why isn't real life more like this?" Scarlett mused.

"Maybe it can be." He pointed out restaurants that lined the beach. "People do the same things we do here, only at a more leisurely pace. Except for conga lines in the streets."

"That was wild," she agreed. "Wonder how the firm would feel if I closed up shop for the afternoon and took a siesta?"

"Not unless you had your own shop." He squeezed her hand. "You're a smart woman, you can create any kind of life you want for yourself."

Scarlett gave him a curious look, "When I graduated from law school, I thought there was only one path for me.

Land a job at a top firm, word hard, and make partner. I was so focused. Now, I find that life doesn't always turn out the way you've planned."

"Sometimes it might turn out better."

"That's what I love about you, Johnny Silva." She stood on her tiptoes and ruffled his hair. "You're always so positive."

"It's true, Scarlett. You have to have a dream. Lance and I have been talking about our restaurant for a long time."

"I didn't know that," she said quietly. She stooped and picked up a white shell.

"You weren't here. You were in New York." During that time, he'd missed her more than he ever would have imagined. He'd dated a lot, but no one ever measured up to Scarlett in his eyes.

"And we didn't talk much." She tossed the shell into the ocean. "I was always working and traveling, wasn't I?" She gave his a playful punch in the arm. "And you were busy cavorting with celebrities."

"Yeah, like Maude Magillicutty." He chuckled.

"Have you heard anything else from her and her husband?"

"They're studying the plan I gave them. Lance and I will meet with them when I get back."

Scarlett paused and took his hands in hers. "I really hope this works out for you, Johnny."

A gust of sea breeze whipped her hair. Pink tendrils of dawn framed her face, igniting the golden flecks in her arresting green eyes. Johnny reached out to tame her wild mane and smoothed it back from her forehead. He drew her to his chest, feeling the strength in her slender frame. She pressed her cheek to his chest.

Johnny kissed the top of her head and wished he could suspend time. This was the relationship he'd always dreamed of. Scarlett was everything he'd ever wanted. To him, she was the most sensual woman alive. She made him laugh; he loved her stubbornness, her brilliance, her playfulness, and her intelligence. Most of all, he simply loved being with her. She made his life complete.

They stood swaying with the incessant waves that lapped their ankles until the sun burst onto the horizon, cloaking their shoulders with warm golden beams. He wanted to capture this precious feeling, and hold it forever between the two of them. Johnny lifted her chin. "Scarlett, *mi amor.* I have something to tell you."

"Yes?"

Her upturned face was so earnest and serious that it scared him. Why was it he could charm women he cared nothing about, but when it came to Scarlett, sometimes the right words eluded him?

He cleared his throat and grinned. "I have no idea where we parked the car."

13

"WHAT A FUN night that was," Johnny said, rubbing the stubble on his jaw. He was bleary-eyed from being up all night, and Scarlett was, too, but they'd had such a good time that it was well worth it. "I think we both needed that."

"We sure did," Scarlett agreed. She couldn't remember the last time she'd laughed and danced so much.

After Scarlett and Johnny had walked back from the beach, they'd spent half an hour trying to find the car, and finally decided they needed their morning coffee if they were going to have any success.

Johnny reached across the small mosaic table and clasped her hand. "I'm glad we came here together, Scarlett. I like having time to ourselves again."

Though it was never quite like this. "I'm happy, too, Johnny."

They lingered over *café con leche* at a sidewalk café,

watching the groggy city awaken around them. Scarlett hadn't seen her cousin Teresa in twenty years; she certainly hadn't wanted to wake her at daybreak.

After they found the car, they started off in the direction of the address her mother had given her. Scarlett peered at the crumpled map. "We're almost there. Teresa should be in the next building." They were driving parallel to the ocean, and the sound of breaking waves was a pleasant constant. Condominium and apartment buildings rose along the strand, their balconies open to the sea.

"Here it is," Scarlett said, pointing to a stately white building. Johnny parked, and they made their way up to the penthouse unit.

A housekeeper answered the door. Scarlett introduced them and asked for Teresa.

"The family is not here," the housekeeper told them. "They left for the horse farm late yesterday."

Scarlett was disappointed. "We were told to come by yesterday."

"*Sí, sí,* they were here then." The older woman looked flustered. She asked them to come in, and said she would call La Señora for them.

Scarlett and Johnny stepped inside. From the expansive glass windows and doors, the view of the ocean was astounding. The living room was furnished with casual white sofas and chairs, accented with marine blue pillows and hand-painted pottery. Colorful abstract paintings covered the walls. Even at this height, the sounds of the ocean filtered in, and the breeze carried the scent of the sea.

"Senorita, La Señora would like to speak to you."

Scarlett picked up the phone. Her cousin was excited, and invited them to stay with them on the farm. "We'd love to, but we've been celebrating Carnaval all night," Scarlett explained. "We thought we'd find a pensione to catch a few hours of sleep."

Johnny grinned at her, and Scarlett felt herself flush.

"No, no, no, you'll stay at the condo," Teresa said. "Come to the farm whenever you want. I'll have the casita prepared for you. We dine late here, so there's no hurry." Teresa gave her directions, and then told her housekeeper to show them to the guest rooms where they could rest before making the drive.

Johnny went to the car to retrieve their bags, while the housekeeper showed Scarlett to one of two rooms that also opened onto balconies overlooking the ocean. Scarlett peeled off her sundress, and nestled into a downy soft bed, grateful for a place to lay her head. She was so tired the *café con leche* hadn't had much effect on her.

The sliding glass door was open to the sea, and the sound of the ocean waves was mesmerizing. Scarlett felt safe here, especially after she heard Johnny arrive in the room next to her. The breeze rippled the curtains, and the squawk of gliding shore birds punctuated the quiet tranquility.

A few minutes later, her door creaked open, and Johnny shut it quietly behind him. He slid under the covers and curled his body around hers.

"Let's sleep, *mi amor*," Johnny murmured.

She snuggled into the curve of his body. She couldn't remember the last time she'd felt so relaxed. No phone, no email, no schedule. No one except her mother knew where she was. The incident at the Ritz receded from her mind, and before long she drifted into a deep, satisfied slumber.

After sleeping for several hours, Scarlett and Johnny rose to the aroma of baking bread. The housekeeper had prepared a fresh seafood salad with warm bread slathered with butter.

After eating, they freshened up, thanked the housekeeper, and soon they were on the road again, heading into the countryside of Andalusia.

Scarlett watched the scenery change to green pastures lined with olive trees. "We're definitely in horse country," she said. They passed several horse farms. Through open-sided arenas she could see riders practicing dressage, the balletic performance of horse and rider.

Johnny rested his hand on hers as they drove, and Scarlett felt reassured. Occasionally she checked the rear view mirror, but no one followed them. They were alone. Out here, with clear blue skies above, the world seemed brighter and finer than it had in Madrid. She'd almost convinced herself her attack had been a random occurrence. Maybe it was someone who'd sat next to her in a restaurant, or overheard a conversation. Crazed people often looked like everyone else, didn't they?

She glanced at Johnny as he navigated the twists and turns of the narrow country roads. The wind tousled his glossy black curls, and his bronzed cheekbones gleamed in the sunlight.

She was well aware of Johnny's reputation as a ladies' man; more than a few Hollywood stars lusted after him. She'd known him for so many years. What had shifted in their relationship? she wondered. *Is it real and true?*

They turned into a long driveway, passing pastures on either side. Johnny eased the Citroën convertible to a stop in front of a sprawling, white stucco home topped with a tile roof. "This is an amazing property," he said, swinging around to take it all in.

Scarlett looked out. Palm trees soared above an enormous trickling fountain. Red bougainvillea grew in profusion, and bright green ferns sprawled with abandon. Behind the house and beyond the pastures, purple mountains rose to frame the verdant valley.

A trim, dark-haired woman of her mother's age strode from the house. She wore a white shirt, beige pants, and black riding boots. "You must be Scarlett," she said, a broad smile lighting her face. "I'm Teresa."

The last time Scarlett had seen her cousin, she'd been a little girl leaving Spain for America.

Scarlett introduced Johnny and they greeted each other with warm embraces. They followed her into the main house, and Scarlett felt the immediate warmth of family. Photos of their children and prized horses lined the walls. Wood-beamed ceilings soared overhead, cool tiles paved the floors, and comfortable groupings of sofas and chairs filled the room.

"It's wonderful to have you," Teresa said. "My children are away at university, so our home is quieter than usual." She continued through the house and out onto a covered courtyard filled with potted plants. "This is where we have our morning coffee, and on the other side is the casita where I thought you'd be comfortable."

Scarlett threw a look at Johnny. Teresa had assumed they were a couple. Was it obvious? In such a short time she'd grown to love the intimacy of Johnny's arms around her. Teresa swung the door open.

Scarlett caught her breath. "It's lovely."

"I've been redecorating," Teresa said. The casita was a smaller version of the main house and consisted of a living room, a small kitchen, a bathroom, and two bedrooms. "The workmen installed the new whirlpool tub a few days ago. It's large enough for two," she added, arching an eyebrow. She opened a pair of French doors. "Here is the pool, and over there are the horse stables. I'll show you our Andalusian horses tomorrow."

"As we drove in, we saw a lot of magnificent horses," Johnny said. "What an incredible place. You might never get rid of us."

"I like having company," Teresa said. "I love our horses, but as you can see, our neighbors aren't very close. Fortunately, we have many friends who visit us here. So make yourself at home. *Mi casa es su casa.*"

Teresa had left a bottle of Spanish Rioja wine in the

casita. Johnny poured a glass for himself and opened a ginger ale for Scarlett.

Scarlett swung open French doors to the gathering dusk. "Let's watch the sunset." The patio was paved with terra cotta tiles that felt cool beneath her bare feet. She'd changed into gauzy, airy white cotton pants and a matching loose shirt. She brought a light jacket to ward against the encroaching evening chill, though the temperature was moderate, much like southern California. Feeling relaxed, she sank into a tufted cushion on a loveseat to watch the sunset.

"Look what else Teresa left for us." Johnny appeared behind her. "Blanched marcona almonds with sea salt and olive oil, Iberian ham, and Spanish olives." He placed the tray on table and sat next to her.

Scarlett sipped her bubbly tonic. "What a wonderful way to live."

"Here's to enjoying life, Scarlett." Johnny raised his glass. "You should do it more often."

"And here's to the success of your new restaurant." She clinked her glass with his. "Do you have a name yet?"

"We're still searching for inspiration."

Scarlett slipped her hand into his. It was a movement that felt natural to her. In years past, how many times had he held her hand in comfort following the deaths of Franco and her father? And yet tonight, it was different. The connection between them was charged with new energy.

They watched the sun slip beneath the horizon and sat talking and laughing until Teresa called them for dinner.

She'd set the table on the covered patio that stretched across the rear of the house, and introduced her husband, Miguel, who looked a little like the actor Antonio Banderas, Scarlett thought. Miguel was a well-built man of about fifty, with a healthy outdoors glow and salt-and-pepper hair.

"I hope you like paella." Teresa spooned aromatic saffron rice and seafood onto bright earthenware plates.

Scarlett sat down near a crackling outdoor fireplace that took the light chill from the air. "I love it. My mother still makes it quite often."

Miguel poured wine, and Johnny asked about their Andalusian horses. Scarlett could tell that Teresa and Miguel were passionate about what they did. She loved seeing such passion in people, and thought about the love that Johnny had for food and entertaining. Was she still as fervent about her work? For her profession, yes, but for Marsh & Gold, she had to admit her devotion was waning.

Teresa asked about Isabel and expressed her condolences for Scarlett's brother and father. They caught up on family connections, and Teresa assured them they could stay as long as they wished.

They dined at a leisurely pace in the cozy warmth of the patio, talking and laughing for hours over some of the best food Scarlett had ever tasted. She sipped fine local mineral water while the others shared excellent wine from a friend's vineyard. "This is the way life should be," she told Johnny, who agreed with her.

After dinner, Scarlett and Johnny retired to the casita.

As before, Johnny joined Scarlett, nuzzled her neck, and promptly fell asleep.

Scarlett reached behind her and ran her hand over his powerfully built leg. She wondered where their relationship was really going.

The next morning after breakfast, Scarlett and Johnny joined Teresa and Miguel at the riding arena on the property. In the ring was Teresa in her riding gear, astride an elegant grey horse. The horse was compact, yet amazingly agile.

They stood to the side, watching Teresa work with the horse. Classical music filled the air, and Scarlett was amazed at the seamless combination of dexterity and strength.

"Have you ever seen dressage?"

"Not since I was very young," Scarlett said. "And I don't remember much."

"Dressage is the highest form of horse training," Miguel said. "It's a centuries-old, baroque tradition of Spanish horsemanship. It's performed to a musical score, and movements performed are a result of many hours of exacting training."

"It's a very competitive equestrian sport," Johnny said. "I've watched events in California. Your horses are pure Spanish horses, *pura raza Española,* right?"

"That's right, known as P.R.E." Miguel smiled at Johnny. "Then you're familiar with what we do."

Johnny gave a modest shrug. "A little. I appreciate the artistry and beauty of it. The Andalusian horses are such noble animals. They're highly intelligent, graceful, and strong."

Scarlett was surprised. She didn't know Johnny, child of the barrio, had an interest in such things. There was a lot more to him, she realized. "Tell me more."

Miguel went on. "Many of our Andalusian horses are this light grey color, and they are among the finest for this type of competition. Dressage is a French word that means training. Through intense training, the horse is taught to hone its natural athletic ability. As you can see, Teresa gives few cues. Both horse and rider perform a routine mostly from memory."

Johnny watched with obvious admiration. "The Andalusian horse is particularly suited to these ballet-like movements."

"Would you like to ride?" Miguel asked. "I can have two riding horses prepared if you'd like, and we have plenty of extra gear."

Scarlett, not to be outdone by Johnny, immediately accepted, though she'd only been on a horse once before. Johnny grinned at her and looked impressed.

Scarlett changed into an outfit of Teresa's, and she and Johnny found riding boots in the barn that fit them. Scarlett's horse was a light grey mare with a thick white mane. She had the most soulful eyes Scarlett had ever seen. She stroked her horse's fine head. "Hope you take care of me, girl," she whispered. The horse flapped her ear as if in answer.

Johnny spoke to the groom and approached two fine

horses he'd readied for them. From the corner of her eye, Scarlett watched everything Johnny did, and emulated his actions.

Johnny double checked the girth, adjusted her stirrups, and gave her a leg up to mount her horse. Once they were ready, they started off at a trot across a broad pasture.

Scarlett was impressed at Johnny's experienced handling of his horse. She had trouble adapting to her horse's rhythmic walk, and knew she'd feel it tomorrow. She called after him. "Where'd you learn that?"

Johnny slowed, turned, and grinned at her. "I *do* work at the Polo Lounge." The sunlight shone on his dark eyes, illuminating golden flecks.

"That's not fair. Come on."

He shook his hair back, clearly enjoying himself. "Maude and her husband have a ranch near Santa Barbara. I've ridden there a few times. Among other places."

"Looks like more than a few," Scarlett muttered. "I must've been gone longer than I realized."

"What?" Johnny slowed his horse.

"Nothing. Just admiring your horsemanship." She definitely needed to get out more.

"Thanks, *chica*. Hey, are you okay there?" Johnny's horse was prancing now, and he was handling it with ease.

"Absolutely. No problem." One of her boots was stuck in a stirrup and her hair had whipped into her eyes, but she was terrified to let go of her horse.

"All right then, I'll race you to the ridge."

Johnny surged ahead with the wind in his hair, while Scarlett labored to keep up.

After a while, Scarlett began to imitate Johnny's motions on the horse and found a rhythm that, thankfully, seemed to work better. When they reached the ridge top, the valley stretched before them. Horse farms, vineyards, and rural hamlets dotted the landscape.

"This view is breathtaking." Johnny raised a hand and tented his eyes. "Just look at you. I never thought I'd see you on a horse, lawyer lady. You're a good sport."

Scarlett heard the chiding in his voice. "You mean you *knew* I didn't ride? How dare you, racing me to the ridge like that."

"Whoa, you were the one who jumped at the chance to ride, *mi amor.*"

He had a point. Scarlett scowled at him.

"Had enough?"

"Now that I've nearly got the hang of it, we can keep going." Scarlett brushed her hair over her shoulder with mock indifference, clucked her tongue, and shook the reins. Her horse tossed its mane and began trotting faster than she'd anticipated.

"Oh, damn it!" Scarlett lost her balance and hung on for dear life. Behind her, she could hear Johnny laughing.

After they returned, Johnny helped remove her boots, and Scarlett flopped onto the bed, entirely spent. Every bone in her body ached, though once she'd learned some basics, she'd enjoyed the ride.

Johnny dropped her boots onto the floor with a thud. "I'll shower and then run a hot bath for you. Wait here."

Scarlett groaned.

Johnny showered in the separate glass enclosure. He returned to Scarlett, his hair wet and smelling of lavender soap. He wore a towel around his hips, and water droplets glistened on his bare chest.

Bending over her, he kissed her on the forehead. "You'll feel better after a long soak. I poured in bath salts and bubbles for you. And started the whirlpool jets."

"You dear, sweet man, thank you." Scarlett slid her hand around his neck and yanked him onto the bed.

"Hey, watch the towel," Johnny said, falling onto her.

"Oh, I am," she said, teasing him. In a quick movement, she wrapped her leg around him and rolled over on top of him, pinning his arms to the bed.

"Uh, nice move," he said. "Now what are you going to do with me?"

Scarlett leaned in and met his lips in a feathery kiss. "I haven't decided."

"Really? Well, I have a few suggestions." Johnny's eyes sparkled with pleasure.

They kissed for a while, and then Scarlett thrust herself off him and strolled to the bathroom, seductively peeling off her shirt as she went. As she tossed it aside, she glanced over her shoulder, blew him a kiss, and shut the door behind her.

"Oh, no!" She shrieked and started laughing. With the whirlpool on high speed, the jets were manufacturing massive mountains of bubbles that reached halfway up the wall. They were billowing from the tub and spilling across the floor, but the aroma was heavenly. The entire bathroom smelled like fresh orange blossoms. He'd also turned off the lights and lit candles that sat on the tile vanity. She tore off the rest of her clothes and started digging through the bubbles to find the whirlpool controls.

Johnny pushed through the door. "What's the matt—uh-oh, too many bubbles?"

"Where are the controls?" Scarlett's voice was muffled in the bubbles. She couldn't see Johnny at all.

"Over here," he called. "Teresa must have installed the industrial strength whirlpool."

"I think it's jet propelled. I can't see anything. Where are you?" She stumbled and splashed into the water.

"Careful, there. Can you find my hand? Oh, no—"

Johnny fell into the tub after her, and a tsunami wave enveloped her face and hair. Sputtering, she flailed to the surface, spitting bubbles and clinging to Johnny.

"There you are," he said, wiping foam from his face. They dissolved into gales of laughter amid mounds of fragrant froth.

Finally, Scarlett leaned back in the tub, relishing the warmth.

"Believe it or not, I left a bottle of bubbly in here for you. Just have to find it." He whisked away a giant bubble formation that looked like a whale's tale, and triumphantly produced a bottle of sparkling water. He shook foam from the glass and poured. "For you, *mi alma, mi corazon.*"

She sipped the cool *aqua con gas*, the fizz tickling her nose, her eyes never leaving his. She couldn't remember when she'd had so much fun with a man. She held the glass to him. "We can share."

After he drank, he said, "Turn around, I'm sure your shoulders are sore."

She slicked her wet hair back and turned. Johnny began to knead her shoulders and neck, massaging sore muscles and working out the tension that had been lingering for weeks. "Mmm, I think I've died and gone to heaven."

He continued until all the stress she'd carried had melted into the warm sudsy water. She turned back to him and brought his face to hers. "*Mi cariño,*" she murmured. "Come to me, *mi amor.*"

Johnny's face lit with passion, and he pulled her to him, their slippery bodies melding together as one. She found his lips, and the heat of his skin spread through her.

They kissed for what seemed like an endless time, yielding to their pent up desire. Though she'd known him for most of her life, she still felt a little nervous, but her excitement soon supplanted her reticence. *This is how love is meant to feel.*

They explored each other's body, and their senses took flight as they made love.

Johnny vowed his love for her, over and over. "*Te amo, te deseo, te quiero, mi amor.*" She loved the rich throatiness of his voice. *I love you, I desire you, I want you.* Scarlett felt as though she could soar in his arms.

Afterward, Scarlett lay sated in the warm water, every inch of her skin alive for what seemed like the first time in her life. The candles flickered on the walls, dancing in unison with the swaying bubbles. She raised her eyes to Johnny, gasped in mock horror, and suppressed a giggle.

"Now what, *mi amor?*" Johnny tickled her under the water.

She screeched, and brushed bubbles from his hair. "You had bubble horns, you devil, you."

"What am I going to do with you?" Johnny grinned.

Scarlett wiggled her eyebrows and slid under the water. She had a fairly good idea.

14

AS THE ELEVATOR climbed high in the glass office building, Scarlett looked down at her conservative navy blue suit with dismay. Though she and Johnny had returned to Los Angles together, she was already having withdrawals. From him, from Spain, and from the joy they'd discovered. She remembered the warmth of his kiss under the Andalusian sun.

She sighed as the doors slid open, and then squared her shoulders and marched forward into the Marsh & Gold office. *All I need is another cup of coffee*, she told herself.

The blond receptionist glanced up with her usual bored expression, and then gasped. "Scarlett, what are you doing here?"

"And a good morning to you, too. I've been on vacation." She strode past her, firmly clutching her weighty briefcase.

"You can't go in there."

Scarlett stopped. "And why not?" She drew her words out. "I work here, remember?"

"Wait, wait right here." The receptionist raced back to her desk and punched an intercom button. "Scarlett Sandoval is here. Is Lucan there?" A pause. "Ok, I'll try."

Scarlett turned on her heel. She'd been on vacation for a week, and surely there was a pile of work waiting for her. And she had to arrange to replace her cell phone today.

Walking through the office, she nodded to her colleagues. "Hello John. Hi Martha." They stared at her as if she had two heads, and mumbled greetings in response. The skin on the back of her neck crawled.

Her assistant was not at her desk. She arrived at her office and turned the knob. "Why is my door locked?" she mumbled. She never locked it. Exasperated, she headed for Lucan's office.

A flurry of activity was going on in Lucan's glass walled office. Scarlett's assistant, the receptionist, and David were gesturing to Lucan, whose face was so red it looked like he was about to blow a gasket. *What on earth?* She slowed down. Mental alarms were clanging in her head.

Hector Gonzales, the security guard from downstairs, was striding toward her. She'd known him for years. In her book, he was a big old teddy bear of a man.

Scarlett held up a hand. "Look, Hector, I appreciate it, but I don't need protection here." She was not going to walk around with a guard, no matter what had happened in

Madrid. She'd convinced herself the attack was a fluke. Even so, she'd slept at Johnny's garage apartment last night.

The guard stopped in front of her. "Ms. Sandoval, I'm going to have to escort you from the building."

She hadn't heard him correctly. "No, I plan to work here today."

Hector lowered his voice. "Come on, Scarlett, don't make a scene. Your employment has been terminated. What are you doing here?"

Scarlett stepped back. She felt like she'd been socked in the gut. *What is he talking about?* She blinked. Hector was looking at her with sad eyes, like people do when someone has lost their mind.

She had *not* lost her mind. Not yet, anyway.

"I've been on vacation." She put a hand on her hip. "What's going on, Hector?"

"Please, Scarlett." He looked like he was fighting tears, but he still blocked her way to Lucan's office.

Scarlett fought the panic rising within her. She held up a hand to steady her thoughts. "Hector, I'm not dangerous. But someone needs to answer some questions for me. Like, why is my office locked?"

"Surely they told you, Scarlett."

"Nothing, Hector. I swear." Watching him waffle, Scarlett touched his shoulder with compassion. "God strike me dead if I'm lying."

Hector nodded and cast his eyes down. "*Gracias*, Hector. Can you hold my briefcase?"

Her heart pounding, Scarlett hurried to Lucan's office and burst in. The door banged against the wall, rattling the glass mineral water bottles she knew were filled with vodka on his built-in bar.

Despite her growing anger, she steadied her voice. "Someone want to fill me in?"

"David." Lucan turned his back to her, while David's eyes grew wide.

Scarlett shot a glare at her assistant and the receptionist. "You two, out. This is between me and the partners."

The two young women scurried out. David approached her, his hands held out in a reconciliatory manner. "Look, Scarlett, let's be reasonable."

Scarlett leaned in, jabbing a finger at him. "Reasonable? I'd sure like to hear some reasons first. Like, why is my office locked? Why did someone call the security guard on me?"

"Didn't you receive the email?"

"What email? I lost my phone a week ago. And you carried my laptop back to the office, remember?"

"Yeah, Lucan wanted it." David passed a hand over his forehead as if he were the one in agony, not her. "Lucan, you want to tell her?"

Her laptop. An email. Things were adding up, and she didn't like the math. She swallowed her fear.

"Sure." Now Lucan was eerily calm, his silver hair icy under fluorescent lights. "Scarlett, you're fired."

"Hector just told me." She jerked her thumb over her shoulder. "Care to tell me why?"

"A box containing your personal belongings has been delivered to your residence."

She hadn't been home yet. "That's not an answer, Lucan. I'm the best damn associate here and you know it. It's one thing to pass over me for partnership, but this is low, Lucan. Even for you."

"Scarlett, please, just go," David said, his voice a whimper behind her.

She whirled around. "What have you become, David? Lucan's lap dog?"

David clutched her sleeve. "Scarlett—"

"Oh, get a spine, David." She shook off his grasp. "I know who makes the decisions around here."

"No, you don't—" Lucan blurted out, and then stopped himself.

Scarlett's mouth opened, but she was so struck by his comment she couldn't speak. *What did that mean?*

Lucan balanced his fingertips on his sleek glass desk and composed himself. "In your absence, the partners reconsidered your employment and determined your services were no longer necessary. As long as you were on vacation, it was thought best to make the cut so you wouldn't have to return to the office."

Scarlett shook her head. "In my absence. Right. And how was I notified again?"

Lucan cleared his throat. "By email."

"And you had my laptop."

"It also went to your phone. You had it at the Ritz."

Lucan said this with such certainty that she fought the urge to scream. *How was he so sure?* She hadn't checked her phone the next morning because she was with Johnny, and her phone had died overnight. As she almost had. She narrowed her eyes, and measured her words. "You insipid jerk. You don't fire people by email."

"No, you're right. We shouldn't have." Lucan curled his lip in displeasure. "Because we need you to sign these final documents."

Scarlett scanned the paper; she didn't like what she read. Lucan plucked his gold fountain pen from his jacket and offered it to her. It was a collector's pen he used to ink important deals.

Scarlett's eyes fixated on the shiny black-and-red writing instrument, recalling what he'd once told her. *Montegrappa. Invito a Rigoletto. A rare, collectible pen named for an Italian opera by Verdi.* Not that Lucan even appreciated opera. He simply endured it to reel in business. *Pretentious jerk.* She snatched the pen, jabbed the 18-karat gold nib onto the paper, and ground it as hard as she could.

"Scarlett!" Lucan's face turned devil red.

Furious, she ripped the documents in half and tossed them onto the floor. "You haven't heard the last of me, Lucan Blackstone."

David yelled, "Scarlett, don't do anything you might regret!"

She whirled around and headed for the door.

"Scarlett, drop that pen," Lucan bellowed.

"Oh, surely you jest." She paused by the bar, dropped the harlequin patterned pen into the sink, and flicked the garbage disposal switch.

The metallic grinding noise was deafening.

Who needs a thirty thousand dollar pen anyway?

Lucan exploded as Scarlett pushed through the door and waved to Hector. "Shall we?" she said sweetly, hitching up her briefcase. As she stormed from the office to her car, Hector hurried behind her.

Driving home, her head pounded in agony. *Fired.* She couldn't believe it.

Fired.

She wrapped a trembling hand around her sore neck and rubbed it as she drove. Thoughts swirled through her mind. *Lucan, the Ritz, the laptop, Fleur, the stock fluctuations.*

Now, more than ever, Scarlett didn't believe in coincidences.

Johnny was at his post at the entry to the Polo Lounge checking lunch reservations when he saw Scarlett rushing toward him. Her lips were white with fury. "Scarlett, what happened?"

"I was fired." Her voice was trembling.

He encircled her with his arms. "I'm so sorry, *mi amor.*" He nodded to his assistant. "Let's get out of here."

Johnny cut through the kitchen, and guided Scarlett into Lance's office. He knew Lance would be out, making lunch preparations with his crew.

"Sit here," he said, pulling out Lance's chair for her. She looked like she was about to explode. He spied a box of tissues on the shelf and grabbed it for her. "I'll get water for you."

He rushed through the kitchen, got a bottle of cold water, and ran a clean towel under the faucet. "Here's a cool cloth for your forehead. Your face is beet red."

Scarlett took a slug of water and burst into tears. "Oh, Johnny, I'm so angry. They had the nerve to fire me by email. Can you imagine?"

Johnny wrapped his arms around her and held her as she ranted against the company. She alternated between anger and hurt, and he ached for her.

"Just let it out, *mi amor.*" He swept her hair back and feathered kisses on her cheek, wishing he could vanquish her pain.

Becoming a partner in a law firm had been Scarlett's dream ever since high school, when she participated in moot court, an exercise in oral advocacy. She lived to champion cases and help people.

Scarlett dabbed her eyes. She told him about what she'd done to Lucan's precious pen.

Johnny chuckled. "What else happened, *chica?*"

"Lucan said something strange." She shook her head. "When I said I knew who made the decisions—meaning him—he contradicted me. He said 'no, you don't.' The partners make decisions as a committee, but it was the *way* he said it. I think someone else is pulling Lucan's strings."

"Any idea who?"

Scarlett thought for a few moments. "I don't know, but David looked scared to death. I think he's involved in something way over his head. David's a sweet guy."

"Careful, Scarlett. David is playing on Lucan's team now."

Scarlett sniffled. "Lucan said they boxed up my personal effects and sent them to my home. A box must be sitting outside."

"I'll have someone pick it up. You're not going back there, Scarlett. Not after that episode at the Ritz. No such thing as a coincidence, remember? You're staying with me."

She managed a half-smile through her tears. "You're beginning to sound like me."

"That's not so bad. You're one smart cookie, Scarlett." He kissed her forehead and hugged her. "But I smell a giant rat in this whole mess. Is there anyone you can talk to?"

Scarlett nodded. "I need to see Zelda Robinson." She blew her nose and dried her eyes.

Johnny grinned. "Want to borrow my phone?"

15

"I'M NOT SURPRISED to see you again," Zelda said. "Please sit down. It's not that I'm a prognosticator, I've simply seen too many of these cases, unfortunately."

"And there's more I have to report." Scarlett eased into a tapestry wingback chair in front of Zelda's antique desk and crossed her legs. She'd shed her conservative black corporate suit as soon as she'd returned to Johnny's, opting for pencil thin black pants and a supple white jersey blouse, which was casual, yet stylish. After spending time in Spain with Johnny, her view of the world and her place in it was shifting.

Scarlett went on to tell Zelda about returning to the office after vacation and discovering she'd been fired by email.

Zelda brushed her short, sophisticated grey hair over her ear as she made notes. "Did they give you a reason or reasons for your termination?

"No, only that the partners determined my services were no longer necessary," Scarlett replied.

"Did you sign anything upon your exit?"

"They wanted me to sign a final document, but I refused. When I glanced at it, the point that caught my eye was that if I signed it, I would have resolved Marsh & Gold of all liability, and my future business activities would have been restricted for a period of five years."

"That's hard to enforce in California, which is a right-to-work state. Many people move here to work for that reason. Did it include an offer of severance pay?"

"No."

"Idiots." Zelda made a note.

Scarlett clasped her hands. "I'm afraid I destroyed some of the partner's personal property before I left."

Zelda snapped her head up. "Such as?"

"A fountain pen. Rather expensive." Scarlett wasn't proud of what she'd done, and it was certainly out of character for her. But neither was she accustomed to dodging snipers at luxury hotels. And she'd bet money Lucan had been behind it.

"What else?" Zelda adjusted her red reading glasses.

Scarlett told her about the attack at the Ritz Hotel, and Zelda's eyebrows shot up.

"You could have been killed. As nefarious as they are, that's not how they usually conclude employment agreements." Zelda shook her head. "When did the trouble begin?"

"When I began to represent Fleur of London to High Gloss Cosmetics." Scarlett leaned forward, her elbows on her knees. She told her about the news clip Fleur had recorded, which was picked up on CNBC, and the news anchor's comments. "When Fleur reneged on the deal with High Gloss, their stock plummeted. Then she announced a deal with Color Color, and their stock shot through the roof. Supposedly, the deal was done after she returned to London, but the tape had been prerecorded."

Zelda leaned back in her chair and tapped her manicured nails on the desk in thought. "How do you know?"

"Fleur had a nasty lump and cut on her face when I picked her up. Everyone could see it. But there was no hint of an injury on the taped piece that CNBC aired. I had technical analysis done on it."

"Smart. You suspect insider trading?"

"Absolutely. I'd bet fortunes were made on that deal." Scarlett had had a lot of time in Spain to think about the turn of events. *And I will not pass quietly into the shadows.* She'd worked far too hard and paid her dues.

"Did you tell anyone about this?"

"David Baylor, my colleague at the firm. He and I were both up for partner, but he won it."

"Qualified?"

"Not so much. Even he admitted that."

Zelda made another note. "Did you see him again?"

"He was at my exit meeting." She'd never seen David look so spooked. He knew more than he was letting on. "He's definitely in on it. He's worried about something."

Zelda took her glasses off. "We have more than enough to pursue a case. Wrongful termination is just the tip of the iceberg. Attempted murder, insider trading, and a few other juicy tidbits, I'm sure. Should we go forward, you'll begin by producing documents and giving a deposition. I can represent you on the wrongful termination, sexual harassment, and promotion pass-over issues."

"I'd like to see Lucan Blackstone and his partners, if they're involved, stopped."

"If there's proof of insider trading—and by insider, I mean anyone who gives or trades stocks on information that undermines the level playing field required for the capital markets to function in a fair and equitable manner—then they could be looking at significant time behind bars. The Securities and Exchange Commission will be mighty interested in this."

"And the near miss in Spain?" Recalling that horrific night, Scarlett shuddered.

"That depends on the Spanish authorities. But it sounds like there's a lot of circumstantial evidence."

"A wise law professor once told me there are no such things as coincidences."

Zelda smiled. "Glad you were listening. That looks like the case here. Lucan made sure you stayed in the hotel after they left. He probably had David take your laptop, or paid a hotel employee to snatch it from your room. Your photo printout from the firm's website, though tenuous, does add to the confluence of evidence. More details would probably surface if you kept digging. However, attempted murder on foreign soil adds a great deal of complexity to the case."

Scarlett sighed. As an attorney, she knew more about lengthy depositions, the tedious discovery process, and trial preparation than most people. This would disrupt her life, and become an emotional rollercoaster. But then, the partners at the firm had already disrupted her carefully planned life, hadn't they?

Zelda folded her hands on the desk. "What do you want, Scarlett?"

Scarlett thought about the outcome she wanted to achieve. On a basic level, she wanted Lucan and his cohorts to pay for their transgressions. She wanted her safety and her life back. And she needed to earn an income to support herself and her mother.

Scarlett lifted her chin. "Let's bury the bastards."

Later that afternoon, Scarlett parked in back of Sunset Plaza on Sunset Boulevard and hurried up the back stairs at Le Petit Four, one of her favorite casual bistros. It was situated at the fork in Sunset Plaza, where part of the attraction was the people watching.

Scarlett cut through the crowd queued up for a table. "Hi Verena, sorry I'm late. My meeting with Zelda Robinson ran over."

"No problem." Verena greeted her with a kiss on each cheek. "They're holding a table for us." The hostess showed them to a table on the crowded sidewalk seating area.

"This area reminds me a little of Madrid," Scarlett said as she sat down. She pushed her sunglasses up on her head.

"It's very European. It reminds me of Paris," Verena said. "How was your trip?"

"Most of it was amazing." Scarlett was glad to see Verena. So were other men at the café, who kept glancing at the svelte blonde in the ivory silk dress and matching buttery leather jacket. "Love your outfit, by the way. It's really fabulous on you."

"Thanks, it's from Fianna's latest collection. I fell in love with it right away. The photographer thought it would be perfect for headshots for the new skincare line."

"I'm so proud of you, and how you came out of that disaster with Herringbone Capital. And how is Skinsense doing?"

"The infomercial began running on television last week, and everyone looked gorgeous on camera. We're doing a soft launch to work out the kinks, followed by a huge debut promotion next month. This first week, sales are exceeding projections by three hundred percent. And Penelope is really pitching in on the publicity. She's such as sweetheart."

The server stopped by their table to share daily specials, and they placed their drink orders. Just then, a well-known Hollywood powerhouse couple walked by, with bags from Armani, Boss, and Ole Henriksen dangling from their toned arms. Unlike in Hollywood, the crowd around them was far too cool to show much notice.

Verena went on. "Johnny told us about your scare at the Ritz Hotel. I'm so glad he was there, that must have been horrible." Verena grimaced. "Do you think you're safe here?"

"That's why I'm staying with Johnny," Scarlett said. "He's living in a large apartment above a four-car garage on a huge property that's under renovation. There's a security gate, and now that they're delivering expensive building materials, there's a security guard, too." Scarlett picked up the menu. "The seared ahi tuna looks good. What are you having?"

"The duck confit salad." Verena lowered her menu and looked amused. "But don't you dare change the subject. We're just getting to the good part."

"What's that?"

Verena made a face. "You and Johnny, of course. Lance said he's completely smitten. What about you?"

Scarlett raked her teeth over her bottom lip and smiled. "I've known him most of my life, but I have to admit, he's really changed, and for the better. We had a wonderful time in Spain."

"So Lance said." Verena winked. "Is Johnny the one?"

"It's a little too early to tell." Scarlett rested her chin in her hand. Should she trust her passion? She had in Spain, but once she'd returned to Los Angeles, her analytical side took charge again.

"Come on, you just said you've known him forever."

"Maybe that's the problem."

"Oh, I see. No mystery in the relationship?" A young

actress waved at Verena from across the patio. She waved back. "One of my former salon clients. I'll have to give her a new card before I leave. Now, where were we? Oh yes, mystery."

"Actually, there's so much I didn't know about him. Did you know he's an expert horseman?" Scarlett thought about their race to the ridge, and remembered the look of joy on his face as he rode.

Verena suppressed a smile. "Are you holding that against him?"

"No, what I mean is that the Johnny I once knew has undergone a metamorphosis. He's no longer Johnny from the barrio."

"Any more than you're Escarlata from the barrio." Verena flagged the waiter and they ordered their food.

Scarlett passed her menu to the server. "No, but I went to college and law school. There's a difference. He might resent it later. Some men do."

Verena raised an eyebrow. "Well, lucky you. Like Johnny, I didn't have the chance to continue my education. Don't hold it against him."

"But you're different, Verena. Your family is from Switzerland, and you ran a successful company."

"Which I learned from the ground up, just like Johnny is doing." Verena crossed her arms. "Don't be a snob, Scarlett. Johnny's a good man. He's ambitious, he's smart, and he adores you."

"I'm not a snob," Scarlett said, surprised that her friend

would think that. She felt her cheeks color.

An older woman with an impeccable complexion stopped by the table. "Why Verena, I thought that was you." She was a former client of Verena's.

While they spoke, Scarlett thought about her friend's words. She had to admit that Johnny's apartment was bursting with books, from philosophy to business and everything in between. He was a voracious reader, and could speak intelligently on almost any topic. She'd witnessed that in Spain. Johnny had held his own with Teresa's husband, Miguel, as they spoke about horses, wine, investments, and politics.

Scarlett picked at a thread on her napkin. Not only did Johnny mix easily with people from all walks of life, he knew when—and how—to take charge of a situation. *Even in his underwear*, she acknowledged, recalling his cool head and hot boxer briefs at the Ritz Hotel.

Verena said good-bye to the woman who'd stopped by the table and returned her attention to Scarlett. "Now, where was I? Oh yes, I believe I was calling you a snob, right?" She grinned.

Scarlett took her sunglasses from atop her head and put them on the table. "Maybe I am guilty of that, and I apologize. There's so much going on right now. I'm unemployed, and I've just decided to sue my old law firm."

"Don't doubt yourself, Scarlett." Verena gave her a warm smile. "When I let Lance into my heart, my entire world changed. He came along at the worst imaginable time in my life. Now I don't know what I'd do without him."

Scarlett studied a speck on the white tablecloth, ruminating over her relationship with Johnny. They had been so perfect together in Spain. Why was she questioning what they had now? Verena was right; she should listen to her heart. "It's easy to say, but my life is really a mess, Verena."

"You're not the only one at this table to have been fired from a job."

Scarlett nodded, remembering Verena's trials. She'd represented Verena through one of the worst debacles she'd ever seen. "It's tough to start over, especially when you've been on one path for so many years. I've had blinders on. I'm not sure what to do next, but I have to make a decision soon. I have a little money set aside, but between student loans and my mother's support, it won't last long."

"I understand. Sometimes you have to eat pasta and tuna for a while. You can always camp on my couch, or Dahlia's or Fianna's, if you need to. Though Johnny's place sounds much more exciting. I hear he has a thing for bubble baths."

Scarlett laughed. "I think the guys gossip more than we do."

"It's good to hear you laugh," Verena said, touching Scarlett's hand. "I have to tell you, I never really saw you as a law firm partner. I'm sure you would have been brilliant, but was it really you?"

"I thought so at the time." Scarlett passed a hand over her forehead. "The problem is that I don't think other firms will hire me after I bring suit against Marsh & Gold."

Verena frowned. "Are you sure about doing that?"

"Absolutely." Scarlett pressed her lips together. "I couldn't, in good conscience, let those jerks get away with what they did to me. What woman would be next on their hit list?" Scarlett smacked her fist as she spoke. "What they did is against the law, against everything I vowed to uphold." *How dare they?* She took her dedication to her profession seriously.

Verena grinned. "There's the passion I love in you. What else are you passionate about?"

"That's what Johnny and I talked about in Spain. Maybe it's time I hung out my own shingle."

"That's a great idea. You're good at what you do, and you know dozens of people in the beauty industry." Verena gazed into space and held her hands up like a mock plaque. "I can see it now: Scarlett Sandoval, Esquire."

Scarlett could see it, too. At once she saw her life unfolding before her, as if she were standing at a crossroad watching previews of coming attractions. "That's exactly what I'd like to do. But I have no idea where I'll find the clients, or the money to hang up that shingle."

"Just begin and believe," Verena said, placing her hand over Scarlett's. "My grandmother calls it kismet."

"So I've heard."

Later, after they finished lunch and got up to leave, Scarlett hugged Verena. "Thanks for meeting me for lunch today. I really needed to speak to someone who's been where I am."

"Hang in there, Scarlett. Never give up." Verena picked up her purse. "And don't forget about the 10k walk I told you about next weekend. It's a fundraiser for breast cancer. I'm trying to get the whole gang together."

"Thanks for reminding me. I'd almost forgotten." Scarlett waved good-bye. Strolling along Sunset Boulevard, she paused at the colorful resort-style window displays at Calypso St. Barth, which reminded her of the shops on the beach in Spain. Here it was, a sunny afternoon, when she should be toiling away in a high-rise building in Century City advancing her career. Instead, she was wandering past boutiques and thinking about what to do with her life.

When Verena was going through her difficult times, Scarlett found it easy to advise her, yet her own troubles weren't as clear or straightforward when it came to weighing and making decisions.

Scarlett walked on, considering the undertaking with Zelda she was about to embark upon. The road ahead would be fraught with turmoil. Scarlett was a transactional intellectual property attorney, not a trial attorney. That meant depositions, discovery, and trial preparation. She was more accustomed to researching trademarks, drawing up licensing agreements, and assisting clients in making deals.

She didn't particularly care for the amount of work it would take, but it was necessary.

No one was going to get away with attempted murder if she could help it.

16

THIN RAYS OF morning sunshine slanted across Johnny's face. He blinked and rolled over on his side. There beside him was the most beautiful woman he'd ever known. "Good morning, *mi corazon.*"

He loved waking up with Scarlett.

"Mmm, good morning yourself." She stretched her warm, toned body in a sensual feline fashion that never failed to arouse him. Her golden hair was strewn across the pillow, and her peridot green cat eyes blinked lazily at him.

He arched over her and nuzzled her neck. "Stay here, *mi amor*, I'll get the coffee brewing."

Johnny padded across the wooden floor. He made his way into the traditional black-and-white, hexagonal-tiled kitchen. As he filled the coffee carafe, he looked out the window and watched the craftsmen arriving to work at the main house. Mexican music blared from their radio, and laughter rose in the air.

While the coffee brewed, Johnny leaned against the cool counter and went over the tasks on his mental to-do list. Today was his day off from the Polo Lounge. The first item on his list was to meet Lance, as well as Maude and her husband, Patrick, at the restaurant.

Since Johnny had returned from Spain, he'd spent time refining the business plan with Lance, drilling down to the exact amount of funds they'd need to open and operate until they began to realize a profit. Maude and Patrick had submitted the proposal to their business team. Johnny had fielded several calls from their accountant, attorney, and investment advisor.

Maude had already seen the restaurant, but now that Patrick had returned from Shanghai, he was interested in inspecting it, too. This would be the last step in the process. It was a vitally important meeting. The one thing they still lacked was a name. Nothing they'd thought of had been quite right.

In the meantime, Lance had been working on the eclectic menu, and he'd added a number of tapas and dessert items Johnny had discovered in Spain. Lance was preparing a menu sampling for Maude and Patrick. Johnny blew out a breath. He and Lance had been working hard for this day. Their entire future hung on this meeting.

Johnny also had a special surprise planned for Scarlett. He grinned as he thought of it.

He was glad she was no longer with the law firm, but he

was still worried about her. She'd been spending hours with Zelda Robinson working on their case. He fully supported her in her decision, but he could see that it was draining her. She had to revisit all the horrible events in excruciating detail.

Every chance he got, he thought of ways to lift her spirits and brighten her mood. Last night he'd taken her out dancing at new salsa club. She had great rhythm, and she'd really let loose. He smiled. He loved seeing her laugh.

The coffee machine beeped, and Johnny poured the steaming liquid into deep blue Talavera pottery mugs. Balancing the cups, he returned to the bedroom.

"Java time," he said, putting the mugs on the shabby chic nightstands he'd found at a thrift store.

Scarlett reached up and pulled him down onto the bed. "Oh, I don't think so, *mi cariño.*" She wrapped a leg around him and rolled on top of him, smothering him in kisses. "Not yet, anyway."

Johnny sank into the downy bed beneath her, savoring every moment of his sweet capture.

When Johnny and Scarlett arrived at the cottage restaurant in Beverly Hills, Lance was already there. The landlord had opened the restaurant early, allowing Lance to test the kitchen equipment. Johnny was relieved that the landlord had been so accommodating.

He glanced at Scarlett. He was awfully glad she was here with him for moral support. She wore a short white lace dress, which made her tanned skin gleam in contrast. Strappy heels made her legs look even longer. *What a lucky guy I am.*

Johnny took Scarlett's hand and led her to the kitchen, where Lance was at work. He wore a white chef jacket and checked pants, and he was intently focused on preparing an array of small plates to his exacting standards. A sous chef worked behind him on other plates.

"Hey, chef," Johnny said, giving him a brotherly hug. "Smells fantastic. What have you got here?"

"Check it out," Lance said. "Hello Scarlett, great to see you. I think some of these might remind you of your trip to Spain."

Salmorejo, carpaccio de atún rojo, ensalada de langostinos,

"Is that salmorejo?" she asked.

"Sure is," Lance said. "There's a lot of gazpacho around, but I like this better. It had a nice, creamy consistency, with the hard-boiled egg and Iberian ham as side garnishes."

Maude and her husband appeared at the kitchen entry. "Hello, darlings," Maude said, air kissing each one of them in turn. "I can't wait for Patrick to see everything." She glanced at Johnny and smiled. "I do believe that's Gregory Peck's bow-tie, isn't it?"

Johnny touched the fine vintage silk. "Indeed it is." That morning Scarlett had suggested he wear it for luck.

Maude held up a bottle. "Lance, when Johnny told me you were preparing selections from the new menu for us, I thought we should at least supply the wine. Here's a special bottle that's been resting in our cellar for some time."

Lance peered at the dusty bottle. "Château Rothschild. An excellent wine, thank you."

Johnny busied himself with opening the wine, while Scarlett spoke to Maude and Patrick. Lance and his sous chef turned their attention back to food preparation.

Once he'd removed the cork, Johnny tasted the wine. "While that's breathing, and the chef is putting the finishing touches on our treats, I'd like to take you on a tour and share our vision for the new restaurant."

With Scarlett by his side, Johnny led Maude and Patrick through the vintage cottage restaurant. This was the most import meeting of his life, and he'd spent days preparing for this. Having Scarlett there meant a lot to him; her presence gave him confidence. This was their future.

"In the front we have the dining and lounge patio, which will be the most popular place for lunch." Johnny went on to guide them through the space, pointing out cozy fireplaces and the bar area, and tallying the number of tables and guests they could accommodate.

When they returned to the kitchen, Lance served the small plates and described each dish. Maude and Patrick enjoyed each sample, exclaiming how delicious they were.

Johnny added, "Lance recently won an award in Paris for his crab dish, which will be a main feature on our menu."

"And this dish," Lance said, taking another plate from the sous chef, "is one we call Isabel's Paella, a specialty of Spain."

Johnny watched Scarlett's face as the surprise registered.

Lance went on. "We have Scarlett's mother to thank for this old family recipe." At his cue, Isabel stepped inside the kitchen and executed a little bow.

"Bravo," Johnny said, giving her hug.

"Why didn't I know anything about this?" Scarlett asked.

Isabel began distributing small plates of Spanish paella to the guests. "It was a surprise, *nena*. Johnny called from Spain, and asked me to work with Lance on a recipe for the new restaurant. He took our family recipe, and standardized it for a commercial kitchen. What do you think?"

Maude and Patrick tasted it and exclaimed over the blend of seafood, saffron, and other spices.

"It's perfect, Mamá," Scarlett said, hugging her mother. She blew a kiss to Johnny.

As they were concluding the tasting, Maude and Patrick shared a look. "I suggest we raise our glasses in a toast," Maude said. "Here's to the success of the new restaurant, and a long run with our new partners, Johnny and Lance. Congratulations, gentlemen. We're in."

Johnny and Lance thanked Maude and Patrick, and then Johnny picked up Scarlett and whirled her around. "We've done it, *chica!*"

Lance raised his glass. "Now all we need it a name."

Scarlett threw her head back and laughed. "I've got an idea. How about Bow-Tie?"

"Bow-Tie." Maude raised an eyebrow. "It's classy, retro, and clever."

"Vintage cool," Lance added.

They all looked at each another and began to nod.

Johnny grinned and raised his glass. "By Gregory, I think we have a name."

After everyone else left the restaurant, Scarlett stayed behind with Johnny to tidy and lock up. Scarlett was so pleased and relieved for him. She curved her arms around him as he was turning the key in the cottage door lock. People were strolling along the Beverly Hills sidewalk behind them.

"Congratulations, *mi cariño*, you're on your way with your restaurant. Your dream." Scarlett laughed at the irony of the situation as she recalled her conversation with Verena. Now Johnny was pulling ahead of her, professionally speaking. And she was unemployed.

But was it really a race between them? Maybe she'd been too competitive with Johnny. A relationship shouldn't be a contest.

He turned around in her arms. "You're my dream, Scarlett. The restaurant, as much as I've worked for this moment, is just business." He kissed her forehead. "The last week in Spain, that's the sort of life I want to spend with you. That's my dream."

"Without that nasty bit at the Ritz Hotel, please."

"Never again." Johnny released her and pocketed the key. "I'll return this to the landlord and tell him we've got a partner. We'll work on the lease this week. I can't wait until we open the doors."

"Johnny, wait up!"

Scarlett turned around, and her heart sank. It was Carla Ramirez. She was strutting toward them in a red spandex dress with matching high heels. She had a curvy figure to show off, but in Scarlett's opinion, it was far too obvious. Carla reeked of fresh perfume, too. Scarlett knew Carla lived nearby. Had she driven by, seen the cottage lights, and raced home to change? She wouldn't put it past her.

"Johnny, I left you a couple of messages. Didn't you get them?"

"Um, yeah, I did. Things have been pretty hectic, Carla."

Scarlett folded her arms. *Is that what this is called?*

"Johnny, I've spent hours collecting pictures for the interior of your new restaurant. I really want you to see them and decide which design you'd like me to do. Like I said before, I can start right away."

Scarlett wiggled her fingers in a wave. "Hello, Carla. I'm here, too."

Carla flipped her curly dark hair over her shoulder. "I see that. Hi." She turned back to Johnny and put her hand on his arm.

Johnny smiled at her. "Lance is my partner, Carla, and we'll make those decisions together."

Scarlett was fuming. Why didn't he remove Carla's hand? Why did he stand there with a silly smile on his face? And why was he talking to Carla about restaurant design?

"Perfect," Carla said. "You can decide which ones you

like and then we'll show those to Lance."

"Okay, sure. Why don't you bring them to the Polo Lounge and I'll have a look."

Scarlett spoke up. "I'd like to see them, too, Carla." She might as well have been invisible. Carla didn't even acknowledge her. Nor did Johnny. Was a clingy red dress all it took to capture his attention?

Carla slid her hand up his shoulder. "I can't bring them in, Johnny. I have far too much to carry. I have it all set up in my dining room at the house. Why don't you come by? I have the evening free. Or tomorrow."

"He's busy, Carla." Scarlett hooked her arm in Johnny's. "Ready to go?"

"Johnny can make his own decisions," Carla said. "I might even invest in the restaurant, too. Come on, Johnny, I've been working so hard for you."

Scarlett gave a sarcastic laugh. "That's pretty obvious." She remembered what her mother had told her about Carla's plan for hooking Johnny.

Carla shot her a sizzling look.

"Hey, you two," Johnny said. "Carla, I'll be happy to look at your work, but Scarlett and I have dinner plans tonight. We're dating."

"Tomorrow, then?" Carla pouted.

Scarlett couldn't believe Carla's brazen behavior. *Does this actually work with men?* She was embarrassed for Johnny.

"I'll call you, Carla," Johnny said, his voice edging on

exasperation. "It was good to see you."

"Always good to see you, Johnny." In a flash, Carla kissed him on both cheeks, tossing her hair into Scarlett's face as she did.

I'm too old for this. Scarlett started counting in order to control her anger. Carla Ramirez wasn't worth it. She knew she could trust Johnny.

Couldn't she?

17

SCARLETT SAT FACING the window in a downtown Los Angeles skyscraper. The grey smog was especially thick this Monday morning, obscuring the San Bernardino mountain range that rimmed the city. Dark, tempestuous storm clouds threatened rainfall, and a hail line was forming low in the sky. Scarlett shuddered in her light wool suit jacket. Everything about the day was foreboding.

"State your name for the record, please." Peering at her from under bushy eyebrows, the attorney for the defense began his line of questioning for the deposition.

"Escarlata Sandoval."

A court reporter sat at the end of the long conference table in the defense counsel's office. Her job was to type everything that was said.

"Occupation."

"Unemployed." She shot a sharp glance at Lucan and

David, who were sitting beside the bald-headed attorney facing her. A line of men in dark suits sat on the side of the defense, while Scarlett, Zelda, and an associate, Lori, sat on the opposing side. It was so clichéd in today's integrated world of business, Scarlett thought wryly. A classic men-versus-women scenario. Clearly she'd gone to work for the wrong firm.

The attorney droned on, asking questions, laying the foundation, and probing to discover additional information.

Zelda had prepared her for these questions. Scarlett recalled her advice and kept her answers succinct and on topic, reserving her energy.

"Did you ever feel physically threatened by anyone who worked for Marsh & Gold?"

"Yes." Scarlett braced herself against a surge of emotional memories. Zelda sat beside her, making notes.

"Who?"

"Lucan Blackstone." *Here we go.* Scarlett paced her breath, remaining calm. Zelda had warned her; the questions would become increasingly detailed.

"Anyone else?"

"No."

The attorney made a check mark on his yellow notepad. Lucan rolled his eyes and shook his impeccable silver-haired head, leaned over to the attorney, and whispered in his ear. The attorney made a note.

Zelda had alerted her about such actions, too. Scarlett understood that Lucan's behavior was meant to torment her into withdrawing the action against the firm, or to make errors in deposition to shred her claim at trial. It was part of the defense strategy.

"And when did this occur the first time?"

Scarlett gave the date. She stared at Lucan. She would not be intimidated, though her recollections were painful. *The attack in the garage, the terror at the Ritz.*

"And where did this occur?"

"On the corporate airplane in route from London to Los Angeles." Another look.

"Was anyone else on board the plane?"

"Yes."

"State their names."

Scarlett gave the full names of David, Fleur, the pilot, and the flight attendant, Lavender.

"Was anyone present in the cabin with you when the incident occurred?"

"Yes."

"Who?"

"David and Lavender." The questioning continued in excruciating detail. The attorney asked where each person was, what they saw, how Lucan approached her, where his left hand was, where his right hand was, how she responded, and every other detail imaginable. As Lucan made faces, opening his mouth in surprise at her comments, Scarlett struggled to keep her cool.

Zelda scrawled a note. *Will Lavender corroborate your account?*

Scarlett nodded, took a breath, and continued. Perspiration gathered around her torso.

"And did you enjoy his attention?"

"No." *What nerve.* However, Scarlett knew it was part of the attorney's job to discover details, make her flustered, and hope she'd slip up or contradict herself.

"How were you dressed?"

"Business suit."

"Describe it."

The questioning continued until lunch, when they took a short break. Most depositions might only take a few hours, but Zelda had prepared her for a long, arduous process.

Zelda was right. By the time they broke for the evening, they had barely scratched the surface of her employment history, and were only halfway through Lucan's attack on the airplane.

The following day, the parties took their places again, and the opposing counsel began.

"Tell me why you stayed on at the Ritz Hotel in Madrid after Lucan left."

"Because he told me to."

"Any witness to the conversation?"

"David Baylor." Scarlett looked at David, who averted his gaze.

"And what is his position?"

"Partner." Scarlett wanted to scream at the slow, deliberate pace, but she maintained a calm demeanor. The questions continued.

Lucan scratched a note on his pad and swung it around so his attorney could read it. The lawyer nodded, and ran his hand over his bald spot. He cleared his throat and began to ask questions about the sniper incident.

Scarlett blinked. She could still hear gunshots in her ears and feel the fear that seized her chest. She remembered thinking she would die alone, but when Johnny arrived outside her door, his presence gave her the strength to get through it. Just thinking about it increased her heart rate.

Scarlett took a swig of water from a bottle. As she relived the terrifying ordeal though the lawyer's questions, her throat tightened.

"Ms. Sandoval. Did you attempt to buy illegal drugs in Madrid?"

Where did that come from? Scarlett's lips parted in astonishment.

"Objection." Zelda cut in, stated her objection, and the opposing counsel restated the question. Zelda strenuously objected again. Scarlett sat quietly, listening to the heated exchange, while the court reporter recorded every word. The record could be referenced in trial. The whole process was exhausting.

By Friday afternoon, Scarlett was worn out. She and Zelda waited at the elevator to leave the building.

"A week of deposition questioning is unusually long," Zelda said. "They're trying to wear us down. But you did a good job. These cases are tough on plaintiffs. The deposition is often as troubling as when incidents initially occurred."

Scarlett nodded. She hadn't slept well all week, reliving events in her mind. Johnny had taken good care of her, bringing dinner home and drawing hot baths, but between working at the Polo Lounge and making plans for the new Bow-Tie, he was working nonstop, too. After last weekend, she'd put Carla out of her mind. She hoped he hadn't seen her.

"Zelda, I forgot to mention something. My mother has been receiving calls from a man who won't identify himself. She won't give him my phone number. Should she?"

"Do you have any idea who it might be?"

"None." The elevator doors opened and they stepped inside. With a subtle swoosh, the cage began its descent.

Zelda leaned against the wood paneled interior. "You don't think it's a salesperson?"

"No, he seems to know too much about me. But my mother is very protective, and she refuses to give out information. Especially after the incident at the Ritz Hotel."

"I don't blame her." Zelda thought for a moment. "If the calls occur at a certain time, try to be there and take the call. It won't hurt to listen."

"Thanks, I'll do that." She could go to her mother's tonight. Johnny was working the Friday night shift at the Polo Lounge.

The elevator doors slid open and they stepped out. Zelda said, "Scarlett, try to get some rest this weekend."

"I plan to burn off some anger at a 10k walk tomorrow."

"That's a great idea. I'll be reviewing your notes." Zelda

grinned. "Because next week I'm going to nail Lucan at his deposition."

Scarlett got into her car, steered out of the garage, and started in the direction of her mother's home. The Friday afternoon traffic was snarled on the I405 highway, so she opted for Wilshire Boulevard. However, the usual half hour trip still took more than an hour on rain slicked streets.

As she stopped and started in heavy traffic, her thoughts drifted to Spain, and the serene Andalusian countryside. The memory of the wind in her face and the sun on her shoulders was awfully appealing right now. Someday she'd like to return and learn the proper way to ride a horse.

No longer did she want to spend her days cooped up inside tall office buildings. She was ready for a change. Where were the husband and family she thought she'd have by now?

"*Hola, Mamá,*" she called, as she let herself into her mother's condominium.

"*Hola, nena.* How was your day?" Isabel emerged from the kitchen. From the delicious aromas wafting through the house, she'd clearly been preparing more of her Spanish dishes.

"Don't ask." Scarlett moved a half-knitted yellow baby blanket from an overstuffed chair and sank into it.

"My poor child. I wish you didn't have to go through this." Isabel wiped her hands on her apron. "Stay there, I have something for you." She returned with a plate of hot empanadas.

"These smell delicious," Scarlett said. She picked up a

folded pastry pouch, which had just come out of the deep fryer, and bit into it. "Delicious. Pork, yes?"

"That's right. With oregano and roasted red *piquillo* peppers. I was on the phone with Lance earlier today, and I was telling him about these. He's planning quite the menu. He asked me to make some for him. Do you think these are good enough to serve at Bow-Tie?"

"Absolutely. No one serves empanadas like these in restaurants. At least, not in Beverly Hills." Scarlett licked her fingers and smiled at her mother. She'd had no idea Isabel would embrace the restaurant as she had.

Excitement lit Isabel's face. "I've always cooked by memory, but now I'm writing down recipes for Lance. Guess what? He asked if I'd like to cook part-time at the restaurant."

Scarlett couldn't believe what she'd heard. *Her mother, a restaurant cook?* "Is that something you *want* to do, Mamá?"

Isabel put a hand on her hip. "You're not the only one in the family with talents." She gestured toward her knitting. "How many more baby blankets can I make? Besides, I'm not *that* old, *nena*."

Scarlett shook her head in amazement. Yet her mother looked happy and engaged, more so than she'd seen her in years. "Then I think working will be a good thing for you."

Isabel perched on the arm of the sofa. "It's been a long time since your papa and Franco died. I let you take care of me because it was easy, and you were so good at it. I kept telling myself that grandbabies would be coming soon, but now I know my attitude must have put tremendous pressure on you."

"It's not for my lack of wanting, too, Mamá."

"I know. Love happens when it happens. And if grandbabies never come, I want you to know that's all right, too. Not that I wouldn't adore them, mind you. But it's time I did something other than knit and watch television. My brain was turning to mush."

Scarlett had to laugh. "I'll be honest, this was the last thing I expected to hear from you, but I'm happy for you."

Isabel stood and placed her arm around Scarlett's shoulder. "When you lost your job, it made me reconsider my life. I want you to have the ability to make choices that are good for you, not because you feel you have to support me. At least, not yet." She mussed Scarlett's hair with love. "I've got to get back to my cooking now."

Her mother's revelation did take some of the pressure off, but Scarlett knew she'd still have to support Isabel when she was older. She'd accepted that long ago.

"I'll join you in the kitchen," Scarlett said, rising from her chair. As she did, the phone next to her rang. "I'll get it." She picked up the receiver. "Hello?"

"I'm calling for Scarlett Sandoval."

Scarlett pressed a hand to her chest. Was this the man who'd been trying to reach her? "Who's calling please?"

"Is this Ms. Sandoval?"

"That depends on who you are."

The man was quiet for a moment. "This isn't Mrs. Isabel

Sandoval, is it?"

"No, it isn't."

The man on the other end of the line drew a breath. "If this is Scarlett Sandoval, I want you to know I've been trying to reach you for some time. This is Finnegan Smith, with the United States Securities and Exchange Commission."

The SEC. Just who she wanted to speak to. "Yes, how might I help you?" she said pleasantly.

"We're investigating some stock trades made by Lucan Blackstone and other partners at your former place of employment. Do you have a moment to speak?"

Scarlett couldn't be happier. "I'd be delighted, but I'd rather speak to you with my attorney present."

"That's fine. Tell me when, and where."

Scarlett gave him Zelda's office address. When she hung up the phone, a smile crept across her face. She might be out of a job, but Lucan Blackstone was about to get his just dues.

"Over here, Scarlett." Verena was waving to her near the starting line.

"I had no idea there'd be so many people here." Scarlett peeled the backing off her entry number label and stuck it to her sleeveless racer back shirt. She'd brushed her hair into a ponytail and laced up her best walking shoes. After a spending a week in an office building in depositions, she was itching to tackle the beach course.

The weather had been rainy all week, but this morning the sun had finally burst through the clouds over Santa

Monica. The waves were good, too, so morning surfers in wetsuits dotted the water, floating on their boards and catching waves when they could.

"There's Dahlia and Fianna." Verena waved again. "And Penelope and Elena."

They greeted each other with laughter and hugs. The atmosphere was cheerful, and Scarlett appreciated the positive energy around her. She and her friends stretched before the walk began. They passed around the sunscreen and opened bottles of water. They listened to the announcer and her instructions, and then the two-hour walk commenced.

Scarlett fell in rhythm with Verena, and they quickly worked up to a brisk pace. Behind them, Penelope and Dahlia matched their speed, followed by Fianna and Elena. Scarlett looked back and waved at her friends, pleased to see them all here.

"How was your week?" Verena set her digital meter to measure her number of footsteps.

"Tough," Scarlett replied. "The deposition lasted all week. But there was an interesting development last night. Seems the SEC is looking into potential insider trading at Marsh & Gold, by none other than my old boss, Lucan." She grimaced. Couldn't happen to a more appropriate person.

"I have no doubt he'll get what's coming to him," Verena said, pumping her arms. "But what about you? Have you given any more thought to your future?"

"I'd like to start my own practice. But I'm afraid I might have trouble attracting clients because of my termination. I really need to support myself again soon, Verena."

Penelope jogged up to join them, her long legs covering the short distance in just a few strides. "Did I hear you say you're starting your own practice?"

"Hi, Penelope." Scarlett nodded. "As soon as everything settles down." Her eyes travelled up to Penelope's ruby-colored hair. "I almost didn't recognize you with your new henna red hair this morning."

"And next week, I'll be raven-haired." Penelope ruffled her short style. "Say, ever since I heard about Fleur reneging on the agreement with High Gloss Cosmetics, I've been thinking about it. My last cosmetics endorsement expired a few months ago, but I didn't know if it would be a conflict for you to bring me into the picture. Now that you've left Marsh & Gold, do you think Olga Kaminsky would be interested in me for the gig? If so, I'd love for you to negotiate the deal."

Scarlett grinned. "I think you'd be absolutely perfect as the new High Gloss spokesperson. And now, there's no conflict. I'll be happy to make the call."

Verena winked at her. "See? I told you clients would come running once you hung out your shingle."

"Do you have an office?" Penelope asked.

"Are you kidding? I haven't even had a chance to replace my mobile phone yet." Scarlett thought about everything she'd need to do if—no, when—she went into business for herself. Buy a new phone and laptop, set up email, have business cards printed. Get clients. *Correction.* Get more clients. As of now, she *was* in business.

Scarlett picked up her pace. The brisk morning breeze felt good on her face.

"Hey, did I hear you say you're representing Penelope?" Fianna hurried along beside Scarlett. Her flaming red hair was pinned up in a messy bun that looked cute on her. "I'd still like you to look over my licensing agreement. Verena read it, but I'd really like your input. I have a large retailer interested in my line, and a couple of manufacturers interested in producing branded items for me."

"Why Fianna, that's fantastic. I promise I'll look at it this time," Scarlett said.

"I've been working hard, Scarlett. I know my little line wasn't large enough for your old law firm, but I'd still like your help."

"I appreciate your understanding, Fianna. I was worried you were still upset with me over that."

"Two clients," Verena said, casting a grin her way.

"Not only us," Fianna said, growing excited. "Elena was just telling me she wants to trademark her jewelry line, too. Nordstrom is interested in it." She motioned to Elena to join them.

"Three clients." Verena poked Scarlett in the ribs.

"Wow, is this what you call kismet?" Scarlett asked her.

"You bet it is," Verena answered. "We good ol' girls stick together. Because sometimes, you have to make your own kismet."

18

ON MONDAY MORNING after Johnny left for work, Scarlett visited her bank on Wilshire Boulevard. Despite having limited funds in her savings account, she stepped out on faith and withdrew money to buy a new phone and laptop, and ordered business cards that read, *Scarlett Sandoval, Esquire. Intellectual Property Attorney.*

Two hours later, Scarlett was officially in business. She emerged from the store feeling incredibly happy, with a vision of racing into the middle of Rodeo Drive, throwing up her hat, and spinning around, just like actress Marlo Thomas did in the old reruns of *That Girl* her mother used to watch on television.

She smiled to herself at the silly thought. But she had no hat, traffic was heavy, and then she'd need a good personal injury attorney, so she decided against it.

Instead, she drove back to Johnny's apartment. Unlike

her sparely furnished townhouse, his apartment had such an inviting atmosphere she never wanted to leave. Built over four garages, the spacious residential apartment was level with surrounding trees, so she could watch and listen to birds nesting in flowering boughs outside the windows.

His furniture was covered in sturdy white cotton and colorful paintings lined the walls. Johnny told her Lance had painted many of them and needed a place to store them. Johnny's guitar was in a case in back of the sofa. Late at night, he'd starting taking it out and strumming for her. He hadn't played since Franco had died.

In the kitchen, black-and-white hexagonal tiles created a charming, 1930s vintage ambiance. Herbs of basil, oregano, and rosemary grew in terra cotta pots in the bay window. Fireplaces in the living room and bedroom were decorated with period hand-painted tiles from California pottery artists.

Scarlett sat down at Johnny's desk and corralled her nerves. This was the critical moment of her first phone call. She dialed Olga Kaminsky's direct line at High Gloss Cosmetics.

"Hello, Olga? It's Scarlett Sandoval. I've started my own practice now, and I have a great idea for you. Do you have a few minutes to talk?"

An hour later, Scarlett hung up the phone and did a little happy dance, pumping her fist in the air. At this moment she knew her life was headed in the right direction again. It felt good to be back in the game without abusive partners breathing down her neck. Once she finished her private celebration, she made a call to her first client.

"Hi, Penelope. I just got off the phone with Olga. She's definitely interested in you for their new line and wants to meet later this week. Since Fleur failed to honor the agreement, she was very excited to hear of your interest."

She and Penelope chatted about strategy, and then they agreed on a time to meet. She clicked the phone off and leaned back in the chair, her hands laced behind her head. She was back in business, and on her own terms.

Next, Scarlett made a few phones calls related to the lawsuit. Then she set appointments with Fianna and Elena, and checked in with Zelda.

She caught a glimpse of the time. It was still early afternoon, yet she'd accomplished so much. And she had just enough time to make it to the Van Nuys airport.

After making record time to the private airport, Scarlett stood in the terminal watching corporate jets taxi, take off, and land.

It had only been a few weeks since she'd been part of this world of corporate jet travel. She'd thought she would miss it, but now she saw the real opportunity in her life lay in her own entrepreneurial efforts, not in vying for an elusive partnership in a male-dominated firm with partners who didn't really want her to be part of their club.

All she'd ever been to them was a hired hand. As soon as she'd outlived her usefulness, she'd been kicked to the curb, like so many other women before her had been. It was ludicrous, especially now that half of law school graduates were women.

She'd clearly chosen the wrong firm. Women were certainly advancing at competing firms.

Scarlett pulled her shoulders back. *Not anymore.* Now she was in charge of her destiny. She turned around. A dark-haired woman in a flight attendant's uniform walked toward her.

"Hi Lavender, thanks for agreeing to talk to me."

"I've been thinking about you, Scarlett." Lavender greeted her with a firm handshake. "Since I hadn't seen you aboard the aircraft, I was worried something might have happened to you. I'm glad you're okay."

They found a couple of seats near a window and sat down. Scarlett explained what she needed, and Lavender listened.

"I think you'll be surprised." With a mysterious smile on her lips, Lavender quirked an eyebrow and nodded.

The next afternoon, Scarlett met Finnegan Smith, the investigator from the SEC, at Zelda's office. Scarlett placed her large purse on the floor close to her chair. She couldn't wait to share what she had with her.

Zelda adjusted her crimson red reading glasses. "Tell us why you're here, Mr. Smith. Why do you wish to speak to my client?"

"Call me Finn," the angular, thirty-ish man in a navy blazer said. He flipped open a notebook. "At the Securities and Exchange Commission, we take insider trading very seriously. It's not limited to those inside publicly traded companies, but also includes those who have access to private information that impacts the fairness of public stock markets. Consultants, lawyers, and bankers are often privy to such details. Trading on this information is illegal."

Scarlett listened. This was the government office that had put Martha Stewart and others behind bars.

Finn began by asking questions about Lucan and other partners at Marsh & Gold. Scarlett told him what she knew and what she suspected.

"When did you become suspicious?" he asked.

"The day I took Fleur to a meeting with Olga Kaminsky at High Gloss Cosmetics," Scarlett said.

Finn scratched a note on his pad. "And why was that?"

"It was a little thing, really. When I picked Fleur up at the Chateau Marmont, she had a nasty swollen cut on her lip. She said she'd slipped in the shower. I didn't think any more about it until I saw a clip of her on CNBC a couple of days later. She had no visible signs of injury, which I thought was strange. I recorded it with the video on my phone and had technical analysis done on it. There was no discernible injury."

"Could she have been wearing makeup?"

Scarlett shook her head. "I've done a lot of work in the beauty industry. Some of my closest friends manufacture cosmetics and skincare. No way could makeup have covered an injury like that. Furthermore, the investigator found another video online of Fleur at a live awards show that same evening."

Scarlett reached into her bag and gave Finn an envelope. "Here are the videos and photos made from them." She removed some pictures. "As you can see, Fleur tried to cover her injury with makeup, but she couldn't hide the swelling. Plus, here's a paparazzi photo from the morning I picked her up at the Chateau Marmont." She pointed to Fleur's lip. "She tried to angle her head, but this photographer caught it."

As he inspected the photos, Finn whistled. "That was a real bruiser." He made a note. "How would you describe the relationship between Lucan and Fleur?"

"Personal and intimate. The aircraft has a stateroom, and they both disappeared into it when the flight took off from London. Fleur didn't come out until we landed in Van Nuys. Lucan was with her most of the time."

With a little smile, Scarlett drew a package Lavender had given her that morning from her purse. "This is a statement from the attendant on the flight. Along with video from the aircraft cabin security cameras. Lucan removed the video and threw it in the trash at the airport after that flight. As luck would have it, the flight attendant saw him toss it out."

"Amazing." Finn took the package and scribbled more notes. "So how did you put it all together?"

Scarlett nodded and went on. "After Fleur backed out of the High Gloss agreement, I heard a CNBC reporter discussing the stock price fluctuations of High Gloss and Color Color. Then they played Fleur's video clip. When I saw her perfectly smooth face, I figured it had been prerecorded. If so, that meant something was rotten. And it usually tracks back to money." Scarlett glanced at Zelda. "There were too many coincidences."

"You're right." Finn rubbed his jaw. "Anything else you can think of?"

"I shared this with a colleague at Marsh & Gold, David Baylor. I believe someone at the firm might have been listening to our conversation, because shortly after that, I survived a sniper attack in my hotel room—through the balcony door—at the Ritz Hotel in Madrid. And I was attacked in the parking garage at my office building."

"Good Lord," Finn said, alarmed. "Did the police have any suspects?"

She shook her head. She pulled out several documents she'd just received by fax. "Here's the Spanish police report and here's the Ritz Hotel manager's statement. That confirms Lucan asked him to extend my stay two days *before* Lucan suggested it to me. And insisted upon it."

"So Lucan Blackstone set you up." Finn whistled. "You've conducted quite the investigation. Sure you don't want to come to work for us?"

"No, I only want to see justice done." Scarlett sat back in her chair, satisfied. Lucan would soon get his payback.

Half an hour later Scarlett opened the door to Johnny's apartment, dropped her bag by the door, and kicked her shoes off.

"Is that you, Scarlett?" Johnny emerged from the kitchen. "You've had it tough lately," he said, kissing her. He wrapped his arms around her, and she rested her head on his shoulder. She loved coming home to him.

"What smells so good?"

"I'm making shrimp Veracruz and chile rellenos."

Scarlett smiled with pleasure. "Another hidden talent, I see."

Johnny unbuttoned her blouse and ran his lips along the upper curve of her breast. "Go change and get comfortable. Dinner will be ready soon. And after that, I'm going to draw a bath for you and serenade you on the guitar while you relax in the tub."

"Mmm, I'd like that." Just hearing his warm loving voice, tension melted from her shoulders. Scarlett smiled as she thought of the last time he'd drawn a bath for her. "More bubbles, too, please."

Johnny laughed. "We'll never forget that night, will we?"

The following day, Zelda called Lucan for his deposition. Scarlett joined her in the conference room in her Beverly Hills office, and put her notes and binder on the table. At least they didn't have to trek to downtown Los Angeles.

Lucan arrived with the bald-headed lawyer who had deposed Scarlett. David Baylor followed behind them, looking nearly as haggard as Lucan. He needed a haircut, and he'd missed a few spots in what looked like a harried shaving job. David's grooming was usually impeccable.

Zelda acknowledged the court reporter, and folded her

hands on the conference table. "State your name for the record."

Lucan smirked. "Lucan Blackstone."

Scarlett took pleasure in seeing Lucan on the hot seat, though not as much as she'd thought she would. His charm had vanished, and he looked like hell—even worse than the last time she'd seen him. His normally tanned skin was sallow, his eyes were sunken, and his hands were trembling. Lucan was a seasoned attorney with years of trial work under his belt. Clearly something was troubling him more than this deposition.

Her eyes slid across to David, who was chewing his nails. *And David as well.*

Zelda continued her line of questioning. After a couple of hours, she came to the event on board the corporate jet, where Lucan had attacked Scarlett.

Lucan vehemently denied it. His eyes darted around the room as if he were looking for an escape route. Perspiration gathered on his brow, and his face grew white. "I need to make a piss," he mumbled.

Zelda arched a brow and shot a look at the Lucan's attorney. "That's fine."

While the men were out of the room, Zelda said to Scarlett, "I think he's going to break."

"Sure looks like it." Scarlett wondered what she could to hasten his demise.

"Actually, it looks like he's going through withdrawals. Does he have a drug or alcohol problem?"

"I'd say so. I don't think a day went by that he didn't have a few cocktails. He had a bar full of designer water bottles. One summer night we were working late and I was parched. When he went to the bathroom, I grabbed a bottle from the bar, opened it, and took a drink. What I thought was water was pure vodka instead. I nearly choked. I don't drink." She paused, recalling Lucan's asinine reaction. "Lucan thought it was hilarious."

"Interesting." Zelda made a note on her pad. "Anything else?"

"He offered me a white powder on the flight back from London."

"Did you take it?"

"Of course not."

Zelda beamed her approval. "I imagine this might be on the video from the cabin."

Scarlett nodded. "That, too."

"Anything else you can think of?"

Scarlett considered her words. *What might make Lucan flip?* "I have an idea. I'll be right back," she said. She hurried downstairs to the gift shop next door. A few days ago she'd been shopping for a thank-you gift to send to Teresa and Miguel and remembered seeing something that jogged her memory.

Twenty minutes later, Scarlett was back in the conference room when Lucan, David, and their lawyer trooped in.

"Ask me for a pen in a few minutes," she whispered to

Zelda. She closed her binder and waited.

Zelda nodded and continued her line of questioning. Lucan dodged questions, gave partial answers, and flat-out lied under oath.

Scarlett knew she should be used to Lucan's lies, but she was still appalled at the level of his dishonesty.

Several more exchanges ensued. Zelda had been making notes, but she stopped to shake her pen. "Excuse me. My pen is not working. Scarlett, do you have an extra one on you?"

Scarlett grinned. "Surely you jest," she said, repeating the words she'd uttered to Lucan before the unfortunate demise of his beloved pen. She pulled out a pen with a red-and-black diamond-shaped design. A harlequin pen inspired by Rigoletto, the court jester. She handed it to Zelda and braced herself.

Lucan's eyes dropped to the pen. As he stared at it, his eyes widened and his nostrils flared. He leaped to his feet and pointed at Scarlett. "You! This is *your* fault!"

This time, Scarlett was ready for the onslaught.

"Lucan, settle down." David jumped up and grabbed Lucan's arm in an attempt to restrain him, but Lucan thrashed him aside. He reached into his suit jacket and whipped out something that glinted under the fluorescent lights overhead.

The court reporter and the bald attorney dove for the floor. Scarlett realized with horror what Lucan held in his hand.

A gun.

The terror she'd known at the Ritz Hotel came crashing back to her. She'd meant to break his façade, but how could she have known he was armed? For a moment, she was paralyzed with fear.

David tried to wrestle the handgun away from Lucan, while the court reporter dialed for the police on her cell phone.

Zelda crouched and tugged Scarlett's jacket. "Get down!" Scarlett tucked beside her.

As David and Lucan struggled, a shot rang out, and the window to the street shattered in a shower of glass. "Where's Scarlett?" Lucan yelled. "Come out, come out."

How dare he intimidate me again? Scarlett leapt up, picked up her binder and flung it at his throat. Lucan choked and grabbed his neck. The gun clattered to the floor, and Zelda snatched it away.

Lucan lunged across the table for her, but Scarlett scrambled up and slid across, kneeing him in the groin as she did, and finished him off with a stiletto heel to his instep.

Bellowing in agony, Lucan doubled over and rolled onto the floor, ranting and spewing choice words. "You bitch, you should've died in Madrid."

David and the other attorney restrained Lucan on the floor.

"You're a sorry excuse for a human being." Scarlett glared down at him in disgust. "You'll get your justice." She was shaking from the ordeal, but now she was the one in control.

The building security guard appeared and took over from David and the other attorney, restraining Lucan in a chair. The Beverly Hills police station was a few blocks away; officers arrived in minutes.

After Lucan was arrested, David turned to Scarlett. He was breathing heavily from the exertion and wore a tired expression on his face. "Nice move with the pen, Scarlett."

She raised her brow. "I don't know what you're talking about." She turned to watch Lucan being taken away in handcuffs. "But something sure got into your partner." She breathed out a long sigh of relief. With Lucan in custody, she'd rest easier.

David shoved his hands into his pockets. "This morning he got a call from a guy named Finn at the SEC. Same one who's been trying to reach me."

"Really? Sounds like a coincidence to me." Scarlett shot a look at Zelda, who pursed her lips and nodded. "You should probably return his call."

Lucan's attorney brushed himself off and turned to Zelda. "We'll have a settlement offer to you later today."

"I'm sure the partners at Marsh & Gold wouldn't want this case to go to trial." Zelda smoothed her short hair and picked up her glasses from the floor. "So it had better be a damn good offer."

The opposing lawyer heaved a deep sigh. "No doubt it will be."

19

A FEW DAYS later, Scarlett met Penelope for lunch in the fashionable Melrose area. As they ate, they caught up and discussed the final points of the licensing agreement Scarlett had prepared between Penelope and High Gloss Cosmetics for a new high fashion color cosmetics line to rival MAC Cosmetics. *Fashion News Daily,* the beauty industry trade paper, called it the deal of the decade.

Due to Fleur's withdrawal and the ensuing time crunch, Olga Kaminsky had hired Penelope on a contract basis to collaborate on the new line while the formal licensing agreement was being finalized. It wasn't an ideal situation, but all parties were in agreement and wanted to move forward.

After lunch, Scarlett and Penelope started back to the nearby High Gloss offices. It was a sunny day for a walk.

"I think Olga will be fine with your request," Scarlett

said. "I'll add that to the contract, and then it will be ready for final signatures."

"These agreements always take twice as long as I imagine they will," Penelope replied. "I appreciate your work, Scarlett."

As Penelope glided along the sidewalk in her short, sapphire blue, silk shift dress, Scarlett saw heads turning in her wake. Penelope was one of the most stunning faces on the runway. And today her hair was dark indigo blue. Scarlett suppressed a giggle when one teenaged boy stumbled into a fire hydrant as he was checking out Penelope's endless legs.

"Watch out there, sugar." Penelope waved at the teenager, who blushed furiously.

Penelope was a dream client. She was so gorgeous, nice, and down to earth, unlike some other famous people she had worked with, such as Fleur. Penelope modestly credited it to her upbringing in Denmark, which she told Scarlett had the distinction of being rated one of the happiest country in the world.

"This has been a year of launches," Scarlett said. "Verena launched Skinsense, I started my new practice, and you're next with Penelope of Denmark for High Gloss."

"Don't forget Bow-Tie," Penelope said. "What are you wearing to the restaurant opening?"

"I have no idea. I've been so busy." Whatever she wore, she wanted to look fabulous. She'd just seen the guest list, and she wasn't happy to see Carla's name on it.

"Fianna has some incredible pieces in her upcoming

summer line. This is one of them. You should stop by the boutique."

Scarlett loved Penelope's dress. "Maybe I will." She'd been conserving cash because of her new practice. Everything cost more than she'd anticipated, but that was the price of starting a business. Johnny was working late, so she could call Fianna tonight.

Over the past couple of months, Johnny had been working double schedules. Between their jobs at the Beverly Hills Hotel, and getting the new restaurant ready, both of them were stretched thin.

Penelope opened the front door to High Gloss. "Would you like to see the new color palettes? We can have you made over, too, if you don't mind."

"I'd like that. I need a new look."

Penelope sauntered over to a makeup station, where a black-clad makeup artist was tidying her studio section. "Hi Joanie. I'd like to try the new colors on Scarlett. Do you have some time?"

"Absolutely." Joanie took a fresh set of brushes from her apron pocket. "Have a seat, Scarlett. You're not wearing much makeup. Mind if I remove it?"

"Go ahead. I'm in your hands." Scarlett closed her eyes. It felt good to be pampered. "Work your magic on me."

Joanie cleansed her face. "Your skin is utter perfection. What kind of skincare are you using?"

Scarlett opened her eyes and traded a look with Penelope. High Gloss was strictly a color cosmetic company.

"Skinsense. Verena Valent's new line."

"Oh, right. I've heard wonders about her restorative serum. I'm going to have to try it." She touched the delicate skin around her eyes. "I'm afraid my laugh lines are showing."

"I can't see a thing," Penelope said. "But Verena is a friend of ours. I'll bring some product to you."

Joanie pulled out a tray of new color palettes. "Let's see. With your green eyes and golden hair, I'm going to use complementary colors on your eyes, and shades of coral on your lips and cheeks. First, I'll contour your cheeks and nose, and then we'll apply color." She dabbed her brushes and went to work.

Penelope stood by, watching Joanie work and making suggestions. From her years of modeling, Penelope had a good eye for makeup. She also had a degree in fine arts, and in her free time she dabbled in oils and watercolors.

When Joanie was finished, she stepped back. "What do you think?" She held up a hand mirror.

"Wow, what a difference," Scarlett said, touching her cheek.

"The colors are excellent on you. I love the consistency of the products. They blend so well." Penelope angled Scarlett's chin and inspected her from each side. "Sensational. Your coloring is perfect for this color palette. And you look so natural."

After Scarlett left Penelope and Joanie, she called Fianna. "Hi, I've just had a makeover at High Gloss with Penelope,

JAN MORAN

and she gushed over your new summer line. Can I get a preview?"

"Absolutely," Fianna replied. "I haven't seen you here in forever."

Scarlett laughed. "There's a reason for that. I'm self-employed now."

"Like the rest of us. Let's complete that makeover. Don't worry, this one is on me. I can't have my attorney looking dowdy. Not when you're representing me and my line. Come on over, let's play dress-up."

A few minutes later, Scarlett arrived at Fianna's boutique on Robertson Boulevard, where hordes of famous people strolled after lunch at The Ivy restaurant.

"Hi, love," Fianna said, looking breezy in a white shirt and a bright yellow, six-gore skirt that fell to her knees and flared flirtatiously. Her red tresses were piled high on her head. "What divine makeup. We can definitely work with this new look. I know just what to do."

Fianna had already pulled several dresses of her own design for her to try on, and they were hanging in the dressing room.

She flitted to another rack and chose a sexy, sage green dress that set off Scarlett's eyes and natural highlights. "This is so elegant. Try it on. I think it's you."

Scarlett went into a large mirrored dressing room, which Fianna had designed to showcase every angle of a garment. She slithered into the dress and stepped onto a raised platform.

She caught her breath. Fianna was right. The dress skimmed her figure and transformed her into a better version of herself. It was understated, yet sensual, and sexy without being too obvious. It oozed sophistication.

Something Carla Ramirez could never manage.

Scarlett winced. She wasn't usually the jealous type. What was it about Carla that irked her so?

Fianna let herself into the fitting room. "That dress looks great on you, though it needs proper fitting in the back." She stuffed straight pins in her mouth, clenching them between her lips as she pinned extra fullness to fit Scarlett's slim figure. "Last one…there, that's it. Now look."

"Even better." Scarlett held her hair up in the back and turned from one side to another.

She felt renewed. Fianna's styles were much more *her* than the oppressive suits she'd lived in for years at Marsh & Gold. Now that she had her own firm, she could dress more stylishly, unless she went to court, which, as a transactional intellectual property attorney, she seldom did.

"My seamstress can whip this up in no time. You have to wear this to the opening of Bow-Tie." She snapped her fingers. "I should make Johnny a matching bow-tie, with a little extra pizzazz."

"That would be fantastic," Scarlett agreed.

"Before the party, we should all get dressed here," Fianna said. "Maybe you can get that makeup artist magician to come in, too. Wouldn't that be fun?"

"I'll ask Penelope if Joanie will do that." Scarlett tried on several other outfits, and Fianna insisted she take three that were perfect on her. Scarlett hated taking the clothes, but promised she'd pay her when she could.

Fianna waved Scarlett's pledges away. "I'm your client now, Scarlett. You're going to put together some great licensing deals for me, I just know it."

Scarlett laughed. Except for the tight cash flow, she was enjoying having her own business. Every day when she rose from bed, she looked forward to working. Even Johnny had noticed the change in her demeanor. "You look happier, *mi amor*," he'd told her. And it was true.

"Are you meeting Johnny tonight?" Fianna gathered Scarlett's outfits and hung them with care for her to take.

"I am. He wants to show me the new barstools and chairs that were delivered to the restaurant today."

Fianna plucked a flowing, coral and turquoise blouse from the rack. "Then wear this," Fianna said, blowing a wayward strand of red curls from her freckled face. "It will look great with your pants and heels. Simple, yet sexy." She scooped up a stack of bangle bracelets in an array of metallic tones. "Pile these on these, too. I showed them at a charity event yesterday, and the women loved them. There. See if Carla Ramirez can match your class."

Scarlett turned. "You know about Carla and Johnny?"

"Where've you been? The whole town knows she's after him. But my bet is on you."

Scarlett narrowed her eyes. Love wasn't a competition. Why was Carla making it one?

Fianna leaned over the counter and rested her chin in her hands, clearly pleased at Scarlett's new look. Her mismatched blue and brown eyes sparkled with pride.

Scarlett changed her blouse and slipped on the bracelets. She caught a glimpse of herself in the mirror. Fianna was right, this was a great look for her. She picked up her packages. "Love you, Fianna. And we'll get some licensing deals for you, mark my words."

"That would be great. Love you, too, sweetie. Have fun tonight."

"Think we'll make the opening date?" Johnny stood in a T-shirt and jeans with his hands on his hips, surveying the restaurant. The gleaming stainless steel kitchen was a mess. Cartons of dishes, silverware, utensils, pots, and skillets had arrived earlier, and Lance and his team were unpacking. Boxes and packing material were strewn across the floor, and clanging noises filled the air.

"We have to, buddy, we're committed," Lance said, brushing packing particles from his chef jacket. "We've already put in our notices of resignation at the hotel." He opened another box. "Ah, great. My immersion blender."

Johnny squinted at the contraption. "What's that for?"

"It's for emulsifying things like sauces. Makes it a snap to puree, or make vinaigrette dressing."

They'd bought a lot of equipment at a restaurant auction house at great prices. But where it counted, they didn't scrimp. Lance insisted on the proper tools in the kitchen, just as Johnny made sure the interiors were stylish and comfortable.

Johnny was relieved that Maude and Patrick backed them on this one hundred percent. They had a discriminating clientele in Beverly Hills. Everything had to be flawless, from the food and service to the ambiance.

Johnny and Lance had a devoted following from the hotel, but friendships would carry them only so far. In Beverly Hills, everyone rushed to visit a hot new restaurant, but they wouldn't return unless it was unique.

"How's the patio and the bar coming together?" As he spoke, Lance organized an area of the kitchen for efficiency.

"The chairs and barstools came in today, but the patio furniture got backordered. And now it's stuck at U.S. Customs in the Long Beach harbor." Johnny shook his head. "Those were the only things I ordered through Carla. Scarlett is going to hit the ceiling when she learns about it."

Johnny knew he shouldn't have succumbed to Carla, but she'd been so insistent on showing him her ideas for the restaurant. He hadn't told Scarlett because he'd felt embarrassed about it, and he knew Scarlett didn't like Carla.

Lance rubbed his stubbled chin. "You're right, bud. Watch out."

When Johnny had arrived at Carla's home, she had lit candles, turned the lights down low, and practically attacked him.

"Come on, Carla, you know I'm seeing Scarlett," he'd told her.

She'd slid her hands across his chest and murmured, "Johnny, don't be shy. Come on, I know what you really want."

"Patio furniture," he'd blurted out. "That's what I came here for." *So much for being nice.*

Lance grinned. "So what's your plan?"

Johnny pushed a hand through his thick hair. "I'll rent outside tables and chairs for the opening if I have to. Or, if the furniture clears customs in time, I'll send someone to pick it up."

"You'll figure it out." Lance slit open another carton. "Have the invitations been mailed?"

"Yesterday. Also lined up the food critics. A different one every night. Didn't want to overwhelm you."

"Thanks, but that's what I do, buddy. Perfection. Every dish, every table, every time."

"Hello, where is everyone?" Scarlett's voice rang out.

"In the kitchen, *chica.*" Johnny opened the swinging door for her. "Hey, new outfit? You look fantastic." He wrapped his arms around Scarlett and kissed her. They'd both been so swamped with their new ventures they'd hardly had time to see each other.

He pulled back and brushed a wisp of hair from her cheek. She looked even more beautiful than usual today. "Something is different about you, *mi amor.* Your face is glowing."

"I went to see Penelope at the High Gloss offices. The new color palettes are ready, and the makeup artist did a trial run on me." She held her arms up and executed a perfect pirouette. "And the outfit is courtesy of Fianna."

Lance came out of the kitchen. "Hi, Scarlett. Good to see you. Did you know we're serving Isabel's empanadas and paella at the grand opening?"

"No, in fact, I've been trying to reach my mom."

"I've been here, *nena*." Isabel poked her head around the corner. "I'm organizing the pantry."

"It's all hands on deck," Lance said. "We're training everyone this week, too."

"Anything I can do to help?" Scarlett asked. "The patio seemed awfully bare when I came in. What can I do there?"

Johnny shot Lance a warning look. "We're expecting the furniture any day now," Johnny said, grimacing. "Let me show you around."

Johnny had worked with one of Maude's designers to create a sleek, stylish scene inside. Taking his cue from the name, Bow-Tie, he'd envisioned a 1920s jazz bar inside, and conversation pits on the patio with casual groupings, sofas, umbrellas, and fire pits.

However, only the umbrellas and fire pits were in place. Johnny chided himself again.

The dining room was an eclectic mixture of sumptuous fabrics and furniture, combined in a casual, artistic manner.

"It's really come together well. The chairs are perfect," Scarlett said.

Johnny looked around, satisfied. This was his dream. He ran his fingers along the small curve in Scarlett's back, which caused a frisson of excitement in him. Scarlett was his true dream.

"Come on into the bar," he said, encircling her waist and guiding her with him through the restaurant.

Scarlett paused at the door, taking in all the different textures and silky colors in the room. "I love these exotic pillows," Scarlett said, running her hand along an assortment of vivid silk pillows from Shanghai Tang. "They look so inviting on the eggplant banquettes."

"Then you should try them out," Johnny said.

Scarlett gazed at him with a playful glint in her eye. "Maybe I will." She wrapped her hand around his shoulders and pulled him down onto the leather banquette with her. They crashed onto the pillows, laughing. As Johnny touched his lips to hers, he felt every dream he'd ever had was coming true.

If only he could manage to keep his life just like this.

20

JOHNNY AND LANCE'S last day had turned into a party at the Beverly Hills Hotel. All their regular customers had heard about their planned departure and the opening of their new restaurant, Bow-Tie.

Johnny watched as familiar faces poured through the entryway. Lance emerged from the kitchen wearing his Beverly Hills Hotel chef jacket for the last time. "What a turn out tonight."

"I hope we see them all again soon at our new place," Johnny said. And that was the day after tomorrow.

"*Hola, mi amor.*"

Johnny turned. "Carla, nice to see you." She wore a strappy white dress that left little to the imagination. He plastered on a professional smile. He'd really had just about all he could take of her.

"Wow." Lance raised his eyebrows. "That's quite a, ah,

dress you have on."

Carla twirled around, obviously enjoying the attention she was attracting. All around them, men's eyes roamed over her nearly bare limbs.

"The designer calls it a band-aid dress." Carla shimmied her shoulders.

"Careful with that move," Johnny said.

Lance's eyes widened. He excused himself to return to the kitchen.

Carla giggled in Johnny's ear. "Oh, come on, Johnny, you'll take care of me if I have a little dress mishap, won't you?"

"Please don't let that happen," Johnny said with a grimace. Eager to change the subject, he said, "What have you heard about the furniture for the patio?"

"I called my customs broker this morning. Relax, *mi amor*, it will be there. I'm a professional designer."

"Carla, this is your first job." Johnny's patience was wearing thin. "If you want to work, I suggest you spend less time shopping and more time making sure you order goods in time to have them delivered." He paused. "I saw the purchase order, remember? I have no problem paying you, but we needed that furniture by now. I can't replace it because the order clearly states that it's nonreturnable."

"Okay, okay, I'll call the customs broker tomorrow. I'll wait there all day for you if I have to." Carla stuck out her lower lip. "Don't be mad at me, Johnny. It's my first job. I'm not a workhorse like Scarlett. But I do have other talents," she added with a wink.

On the day of Bow-Tie's grand opening, Scarlett stood next to Verena in the new kitchen, enjoying the aroma of her mother's fresh empanadas, hot from the fryer. The scent of food rose in the air, making Scarlett remember she'd skipped lunch. Her stomach growled in complaint.

"I'm so proud of them, I'm bursting," Scarlett whispered.

"Is that what that sound is?" Verena chuckled. "I'm starving, too."

Johnny and Lance were opening their new restaurant tonight. As Johnny walked by, Scarlett gave him a kiss for luck. This was a night she would never forget.

Johnny and Lance had been at the restaurant all day to make sure everything ran smoothly tonight. During the day, Scarlett and Verena had pitched in, too, before they left to get ready.

Verena leaned over to Scarlett. "What a great idea to get ready at Fianna's boutique. That was so much fun."

Scarlett had asked Joanie, the makeup artist from High Gloss, to go to Fianna's boutique on Robertson. Fianna had set up a special table and mirror, and they all had their makeup done before they dressed. It caused quite a scene, and attracted lots of curious shoppers, especially when people recognized Penelope Plessen from the covers of *Vogue* and *Harper's Bazaar*. It turned out to be an excellent day for Fianna in terms of sales, and Scarlett was pleased for her.

"You look marvelous," Verena said.

"So do you, especially in that white silk." Scarlett wore the sage green dress that Fianna had fitted to her, and she felt fantastic. All her close friends were here: Verena, Fianna, Dahlia, Penelope, and Elena. Scarlett was so glad to have their support for Johnny and Lance. Zelda, Lavender, Olga, and a host of former clients had told her they'd stop by, too.

Johnny and Lance were nearly ready to open their new restaurant. They gathered their kitchen staff, servers, and hosts to say a few words.

"Thank you all for being part of our launch team," Johnny said, straightening the new sage green and purple print bow-tie Fianna had made for him. He'd supplied colorful bow-ties to all the servers to wear, too.

Lance stood next to him in a new white chef's jacket with the words *Lance Martel, Executive Chef* and *Bow-Tie* embroidered on the front.

Johnny slung his arm across Lance's shoulder. "This is the best partner I could've asked for, and we want to thank each of you for being part of our dream."

Everyone started clapping, while small glasses of champagne were passed around to toast to their success.

Johnny went on. "And special appreciation to Maude Magillicutty and her husband Patrick for sharing our vision and allowing us to realize this dream. Whenever they come in, always give them the best table in the house."

More cheers rang out. "Finally, to our girlfriends, Scarlett and Verena, for putting up with our absences while we worked to bring Bow-Tie to fruition. And to Scarlett, without whose help the patio would be bare."

Johnny kissed Scarlett, and Lance pecked Verena, amid catcalls from the staff.

Scarlett saw Isabel with the rest of the kitchen team, looking so proud and happy, too.

Scarlett and Johnny had dashed around this morning, renting furniture and gathering accessories when his designer hadn't delivered the furnishing for the patio.

"And now, places everyone. It's show time!" Johnny walked to the front and cued the jazz musicians.

He and Lance made a big show of unlocking the door and cutting the ribbon they'd draped across the entryway earlier. Maude had tipped the paparazzi, so flashbulbs popped and people cheered. Within moments the excited crowd filtered in, exclaiming over the unique interior.

"Hey, *chica*, we did it!" Johnny exclaimed, lifting Scarlett off her feet in triumphant celebration. His face was flushed with excitement. She thought she'd never seen him look more handsome. The golden flecks in his dark eyes glittered and the dimple in his cheek winked as he grinned. He'd slicked his black hair back in a 1920s style, and it curled around his collar.

Scarlett hugged his neck. She was so happy for him, and she just knew a fabulous evening lay ahead.

"If you're hungry, you'd better eat now," Johnny said. "Isabel's empanadas are going to be a big hit. They might not last long." He flagged a server, who scooped up a few for

Scarlett.

She bit into one. "Mmm, these are even better than I recalled."

"Lance tweaked the recipe and added more spices." Johnny signaled the bartender, who sent a sparkling water with lime for Scarlett.

"Johnny, my good man!"

Johnny turned around. A large group of his regular customers from the Beverly Hills Hotel had arrived. The men shook his hand and slapped him on the back, while the women double kissed his cheeks in the European fashion.

He's in his element, Scarlett thought as Johnny was whisked into the middle of the group. She wiggled her fingers in a wave, realizing it was going to be like this all evening. She was fine with that. It was his dream, his business, and at the end of the night, he was hers. She blew him a kiss across the crowd, and he turned his palms up in a helpless manner.

"Go have fun," Scarlett called to him across the cheerful throng. She cut through the growing mob and returned to the kitchen, where Lance was leading his kitchen team like a general. *He's in his element, too.*

She saw Verena watching him, and the two woman traded smiles. They were both so proud of their men.

Isabel glanced up from her post, and Scarlett lifted her chin in acknowledgement. Her mother wore kitchen whites with her grey hair in a bun. She looked radiant and happy with her new colleagues.

Food orders were coming out of the kitchen now, and

Scarlett recognized adaptations of a few meals they'd had in Spain, though the menu included other global fusion dishes, too.

She walked through the dining room, eavesdropping to learn what people thought of their meals and greeting friends who'd come in. The impressions were overwhelmingly positive.

As Scarlett was looking for Johnny, Fianna stopped her and touched her arm. "Look who just walked in," Fianna said.

Scarlett turned.

Carla stood in the entryway, her annoying laughter jangling across the crowd. She wore a sultry black dress cut low on her bosom and slit high on her thigh.

Fianna whistled. "Wow, she's sure on the prowl. Better lock up Johnny."

Scarlett huffed and turned away. "This is not a competition. Johnny and I have a great relationship." Still, she couldn't help but be on her guard.

Fianna moved on and Scarlett made her way to the patio. When the furniture Johnny had ordered hadn't arrived, they had thrown the patio together that morning with furniture from a rental agency and decorations from Pier 1.

The crowd was buzzing out here, too, with couples and friends relaxing around the fire pits, talking and laughing, and nibbling small tapas plates from the menu.

Scarlett glanced around and was pleased to recognize someone she knew.

"Scarlett, what a success this is." Outside her office, Zelda looked more relaxed.

"Thanks for coming," Scarlett said.

"Wouldn't have missed it for the world."

Scarlett spied Johnny across the patio and waved. Fortunately, Carla was nowhere in sight.

"What a handsome young man your Johnny is."

Scarlett sat down with her and they chatted for a while. She really admired Zelda, and had from the first time she'd taken a class from her in law school.

Presently, Zelda leaned in and lowered her voice. "By the way, I have great news for you. Before I left the office I received another settlement offer from the lawyer representing Marsh & Gold. I won't tell you what it is now, but I think you'll like it. Call me tomorrow and come by."

"I sure will." Scarlett blew out a breath of relief and thanked Zelda. This was the best news she'd heard in a long, long time.

After what she'd experienced at the law firm, and then in the lawsuit she'd brought against them, she was often near exhaustion. Only Johnny, her mother, her friends, and now her desire to build her own practice, had kept her going through it all.

Feeling lighter, Scarlett moved on, alternatively stopping to speak to Dahlia and Elena, as well as Olga, Penelope and Joanie. Everyone was in great spirits and loved Bow-Tie. They all promised to bring their friends, too.

Scarlett stopped to say hello to Dahlia's glamorous

grandmother, Camille, who was there with Verena's equally elegant grandmother, Mia. They were well-known in the beauty industry and no strangers to the pages of *Fashion News Daily*. Camille had founded the perfumery Dahlia ran today, and Mia had created the serum Verena built Skinsense around.

With them were Verena's teenaged twin sisters, Anika and Bella, who were growing up to look like Verena, with her porcelain skin and fair blond hair. "Are you the next generation of skincare entrepreneurs?" Scarlett asked them.

The girls laughed. Bella said, "I'd rather work in fashion with Fianna."

"Already planning your career? Good for you. Maybe you'll be my next clients," Scarlett said, but she was only half-kidding.

The jazz group took a break, and the noise level receded. Scarlett was walking back into the restaurant when she heard a familiar voice coming from the side of the cottage just off the patio. She started to pop her head around the corner and say hello to Johnny when she heard a second voice.

Scarlett froze, hardly daring to believe who it was.

Carla.

She clenched her fists.

"I waited all day," Carla said, on the verge of wailing.

"I don't believe you," Johnny said. "I called and you were nowhere to be found."

Carla was sniffling. "I swear I waited all day for you. But you didn't even call me. I thought this meant a lot to you. I was only doing it for you."

Doing what? Scarlett wondered. She leaned closer.

Johnny was clearly angry. "You should have told me sooner. Then I could have done something about it. You don't understand. This is *my baby*, Carla."

Scarlett couldn't believe what she was hearing. *Baby?*

Carla was crying now. "I only wanted to do this for you."

"It's not like this is something that could be returned like a new dress." Johnny's voice was hushed, yet harsh. "You're unbelievable."

"I can make it right, just give me another chance."

"Carla, it's done."

Scarlett stepped around the corner.

Johnny looked up with a guilty expression on his face. "Scarlett, I didn't see you. How long have you been there?"

She folded her arms. "Long enough."

Carla sniffled again, and ran a finger under her eyes. "I need a handkerchief, Johnny. My makeup—"

Johnny cut her off. "There are tissues in the bathroom. Run along, Carla. I need to talk to Scarlett."

Scarlett pursed her lips. "You sure do. A baby?" She didn't know whether to be angry at or feel sorry for Carla.

"What?" Johnny scratched his head.

"Oh, don't act dumb with me. I overheard everything."

Johnny spread is hands. "Carla ordered the patio furniture for me. That's why it didn't arrive in time."

"That's not the conversation I just heard."

"Look, I don't know what you think you heard, but I'm

telling you the truth."

Scarlett jabbed her finger in the air. "You never told me you were working with Carla. You said a decorator had ordered the furniture."

Johnny looked sheepish. "It was Carla."

Scarlett stared at him. "I don't know what to believe. But I *know* what I heard."

"That was a coincidence. I was calling the restaurant my baby."

"Nice try. There is no such thing as a coincidence." Scarlet whipped around. She couldn't believe such a wonderful evening—and her relationship with Johnny—was ending like this.

Her mother was right. Carla had snagged her next man, the old-fashioned way.

Struggling to maintain her composure, she stormed from the restaurant to her car, her heels clicking the pavement like firecrackers.

Johnny raced after her into the parking lot behind the restaurant. "Please stop, *chica*. You don't understand."

"I understand more than you know. I watched my father treat my mother that way for years. She was a fool for putting up with that, and his drinking, but she loved him." Scarlett choked at the memory. She cleared her throat, forcing herself to push on through her pain. "I'm not going to make the same mistake. If the lies start now, they will only get worse later. *Adiós*, Johnny."

She swung into her car, tossed her purse onto the seat,

and screeched away. In her rearview mirror she could see Johnny standing there, still pleading for her to return.

Scarlett was devastated over what she'd heard. *How could he?* She wiped tears from her eyes as she drove, and when she arrived at her townhouse, she fell fully clothed into bed.

It was times like this when a margarita would taste so good, but she wouldn't squander her sobriety on the likes of Johnny Silva. She was stronger than that.

21

SCARLETT HADN'T SLEPT well after she'd returned home from the party at Bow-Tie. She'd finally rolled out of bed at five in the morning, peeled off the beautiful dress Fianna had given her, and sat in her empty living room, staring at the walls.

What a devastating end to a nearly life-long relationship. This was exactly what she'd feared would happen when she began dating Johnny. Not only had she lost the love of her life, but she'd also lost her best friend, as well as cherished memories linked to her brother Franco.

But Johnny was a womanizer, and that's all there was to it.

When sunlight streamed onto the bare walls, Scarlett rose to her feet with a heavy heart. She showered and dressed, and then met Zelda at her office, anxious to her what she had to say.

"What a grand party that was last night," Zelda said. "The food, the décor, the people. Johnny and Lance are destined for success."

"I'm sure they're glad you came." Scarlett quickly changed the subject. "Tell me about the latest offer."

"It's not often I get a solid seven-figure settlement offer in a case like this," Zelda said, leaning back in her chair. "But you earned every penny of it—the hard way. I'm sorry you had to go through what you did, Scarlett. You might have been killed, not once or twice, but three times."

That much was true. *In the garage, at the Ritz, and in the deposition.* Scarlett sat in Zelda's office, hardly believing the sum they'd offered. Never had she imagined such a large settlement. But it had not come without a price.

Lucan, Fleur, and two top partners at Marsh & Gold had been indicted for insider trading based on findings by the Securities and Exchange Commission. The scandal had made headlines in the *Wall Street Journal.* All of which meant she was virtually unemployable at any major law firm now. It was a classic case of guilt by association. At least she'd decided to hang out her shingle for her own law practice.

"I'll miss you, Zelda, but I'm relieved it's over," Scarlett said, though she would still have to testify at the upcoming SEC trial.

David had been given immunity for his part in exchange for his testimony. After the trial, he and his fiancé planned to go to Africa with the Peace Corps. David wasn't a bad guy;

he'd simply been in the wrong place at the wrong time. Just as she'd been.

"And that's not all," Zelda said, adjusting her stylish reading glasses. "Marsh & Gold is transferring female partners from New York to Los Angeles."

"That's good. Then we effected change in the west coast office culture." Scarlett was pleased her former female colleagues would have a better working environment and opportunities for advancement. It was too late for her, but not for them.

"What are your plans now?" Zelda asked.

"I'm going to continue building my practice in the beauty and fashion industry. And maybe take a vacation." She'd always dreamed of taking her mother to Spain. Would Isabel break away from the restaurant now? If not, she could plan a local spa trip.

Zelda got up and walked with her to the door. "You're still a young woman. Invest these settlement funds well, and you'll be set for life. Then you can do whatever you please."

Scarlett thought about that. The first thing she'd do would be to write Fianna a check for her new clothes.

Knowing she had that sum of money coming in felt great, but it was also a little frightening. Overnight she would go from watching pennies to investing seven figures. She'd have to find professional guidance for that.

She could also establish a retirement fund for Isabel and one for herself. And when her babies came along—*if* they ever came along—she could choose to spend time with them.

Until she'd seen Johnny with Carla last night, she'd thought Johnny was the man she was going to spend her life with. Now, she was still seething as his lame excuse rang in her ears. She was having serious second thoughts.

It seemed Carla had won the competition after all. And Scarlett certainly wasn't getting any younger.

Maybe it's time to move on.

The luxury coach wound through arid mountains studded with natural desert plants that were one stiff breeze away from being rambling tumbleweeds.

With the restaurant a success, Isabel hadn't wanted to leave Bow-Tie for an extended trip to Spain, but Scarlett managed to talk her into a week at a spa to celebrate the conclusion of the lawsuit and her financial settlement. Rancho La Puerta was in Tecate, Mexico, just three miles south of the border between the U.S. and Mexico.

Scarlett was working through her breakup with Johnny, so it would be a bittersweet celebration for her.

Early Saturday morning she and her mother had driven from Los Angeles to San Diego and left the car at a long-term parking lot at the airport, where they met spa representatives and fellow spa-goers.

As the bus whisked them away for the hour drive to the secluded spa and wellness resort, a party atmosphere prevailed. But instead of toasting the holiday with alcoholic drinks, guests clinked bottles of water, and passed around bags of homemade organic granola.

Isabel made friends quickly, and when other guests asked what she did, she told everyone about her new career cooking at Bow-Tie, which was quickly becoming the hottest restaurant in town. Her empanadas were the most popular appetizer. Lance had hated to part with her, even for a short trip.

However, as proud as Scarlett was of her mother, that was the last subject she wanted to hear about.

But that didn't stop Isabel from talking about it. "What happened with Johnny, *nena*? I thought everything was fine between you two until the evening of the grand opening."

Scarlett settled back in the plush seat and crossed her arms. "He made his decision, Mamá."

"What decision?"

"I overhead him talking to Carla at the party. He said something about a baby. You were right. She trapped him the old-fashioned way, just like her last husband." Scarlett took a swig of water. "I hope they'll be very happy. As far as I'm concerned, they deserve each other."

Isabel frowned. "Oh, *nena*, I don't think that's the case at all. He misses you. All he does is mope around the restaurant when he thinks no one is watching."

"He's probably regretting his involvement with Carla," Scarlett said with sarcasm. "I sure would."

"Hmm, I see." Isabel grew quiet.

When they arrived at the border crossing, they disembarked.

Isabel's mobile phone rang. She looked at it and

frowned. "I'd better take this before we cross into Mexico," she said to Scarlett. "It might be hard to get service there."

"Who is it?" Scarlett asked.

"Must be the sous chef at Bow-Tie. I'll call him back right away." Isabel strolled off to the curb to speak in private.

Scarlett sighed. She was glad her mother had found a fulfilling new career, but she dreaded having to hear the name Bow-Tie whenever she spoke to her mother. And Scarlett had named the restaurant. Her heart ached every time she thought of Johnny.

Does Johnny have similar regrets? She wondered if he even thought of her.

She stopped and waited for her mother outside of the border entry office. Closing her eyes, she imagined the sun burning away the tension she carried in her shoulders. She couldn't wait to arrive at the spa and have a massage.

A few minutes later, Isabel returned. "Let's go," she said brightly. She tucked her phone into her purse.

Scarlett followed her into the little border crossing, where they were asked to show their passports and answer questions.

Massage, facial, swim. Scarlett kept thinking about how much she needed to de-stress. Receiving a generous settlement alleviated her financial worries, but it did nothing to ease the pain in her heart.

When they arrived at the sprawling property, they were shown to a charming red brick casita at the base of the mystical Mount Kuchumaa, a rugged mountain that rose behind the property.

"How lovely," Isabel said, exclaiming over the furnishings. Terra cotta pavers lined the floor, and hand-painted Mexican tiles covered the bathroom counters and walls. Hand-carved furniture filled the living area and two bedrooms. A fireplace stood ready to warm the cool desert evenings.

Scarlett opened the doors to the patio, where lush red bougainvillea flowers brightened the area. She could see a circular meditation maze not far away. Chameleons skittered across sun-warmed stone pavers, and birds sang in fragrant eucalyptus trees above. She sighed. It would be the perfect place to stay with someone she loved—besides her mother.

"They're having an orientation meeting before lunch," Isabel said. "Let's go."

Her mother tugged her from the patio. Begrudgingly, Scarlett went along. They wound down stone paths to the main area, and joined many of the same newcomers they'd met on the bus.

Without Johnny by her side, Scarlett found she was merely going through the motions. Although the property boasted pools, fitness bungalows, spa facilities, tennis courts, dining rooms, and meditation areas, nothing seemed to excite her as she'd thought it would. Even the flowers seemed duller to her.

They ate in the main dining pavilion, and then Scarlett had a massage, followed by a manicure and pedicure. She had a list of fitness classes she planned to attend tomorrow.

Maybe that would reinvigorate her and lift her depression.

Though she knew it wouldn't.

Her mother had scheduled a massage and planned to attend an author lecture that evening, so Scarlett would be alone with her thoughts tonight.

There were no televisions in the bungalows, the spa director had told them, in order to allow mental space for peaceful reflection during the visit. Scarlett thought miserably that she'd had enough reflection since the opening party to last a lifetime.

As the sun sank in the sky and the evening breeze cooled the warm climate, Scarlett hiked the rosemary-lined path back to the casita. She shivered, pulling her light exercise jacket around her. After everything she had been through, would she ever feel any joy in her life again?

When she opened the door, she noticed the fireplace was crackling with a newly laid fire. "Oh, good," she said to herself, and hurried to warm her hands, glad the service was excellent here.

However, as she stood there, the back of her neck prickled and she had the unsettled feeling that she was not alone.

And then she heard the patio door slide open. Her heart palpitating, she spun around.

It was Johnny.

"What are *you* doing here?" She backed away from him, but as she did, she stumbled against a step to the bedrooms, lost her balance, and fell backward.

"Are you okay?" Johnny rushed to kneel by her side.

"No, it's my ankle. Now look what you've done." Tears sprang to her eyes. She didn't know if they were tears derived from pain or anger—or both—but she hastily brushed them away.

"Can you move it?" He took her ankle and gently rotated it.

"No, that hurts." She covered her face with her hands. *Of all people, why is he here?*

"I think you've sprained it." He brushed a strand of hair from her cheek like he used to do.

"Is there ice in the little refrigerator?"

"I have no idea." Her ankle was really throbbing now. She didn't know how she was going to stand up and put any weight on it. *What a great way to start a week at the spa,* she thought. And it's his fault. *Damn him.*

She heard a clattering sound in the kitchen, and flung herself onto the cool tile in exasperation. Why wasn't life fair?

Johnny hurried from the kitchenette with ice cubes wrapped in a dishtowel. "Here, keep this on your ankle. It will keep it from swelling so much."

"It's cold."

"Sit up." Johnny shrugged out of his fleece jacket, helped her raise herself from the floor, and placed his jacket over her shoulders. "Better?"

His jacket held the heat of his body, and the fibers retained his unique masculine scent. She looked up at him. His brow was furrowed with concern. Gazing into his dark brown, gold-flecked eyes melted her glacial heart, and she had to look away to protect herself.

"My mother called you." It didn't take a law degree for her to figure that out. She'd have to talk with Isabel.

"She's concerned about you." Johnny drew a breath. "She thinks you have the story wrong."

"I doubt that." She shifted on the floor. "Ow, that's painful."

"Don't try to get up." Johnny grabbed a blanket and pillows from the bedroom and made a nest on the floor in front of the fireplace. "I'm going to lift you onto this. Put your arms around my neck and I'll lift you."

She hesitated, afraid to touch his skin, but at the same time, longing to.

"Come on, *chica*. Don't hate me until you know the whole story. Isn't that what lawyers do? Try to get at the truth?"

"Oh, all right." Scarlett placed her arms tenuously around his neck. A shiver coursed through her.

Johnny lifted her and moved her to the mound of pillows. He elevated her ankle and reapplied ice.

Scarlett groaned. "I feel like we're on a Mexican camping trip. But a really luxurious one." The dancing flames warmed her face and scented the air with the smell of autumn.

Johnny got up and returned with a glass of lime-infused water for her. He gave it to her, and then stretched his muscular frame beside her on the blanket. "Now that I have a captive audience, please listen to me."

Scarlett pursed her lips. She'd already heard his lies, but she couldn't exactly run away. "Go ahead. Say what you came to say, and then you can leave."

"I should have told you that Carla had ordered the furniture for the patio."

"I don't care about furniture," she snapped.

"Scarlett. Listen." Johnny went on to tell her what had happened.

He sounded remorseful when he admitted that he'd gone to her house, and Scarlett almost fell for his explanation. "Go on."

"When Carla came to the opening party, I lost my cool with her. She couldn't understand how much Bow-Tie meant to me, and to Lance. This was our baby. *My baby.* That's what I said, and that's what you heard."

"You said something about getting rid of it."

"Returning it. The furniture was nonreturnable." Johnny smoothed her hair and kissed the top of head. "I love you, Scarlett. That was a stupid mistake on my part. Please don't throw away our life over this." He took her hand and pressed it to his heart. "We belong together, *mi amor.*"

Tears gathered in her eyes again and she lowered her lids. Everything he said made sense. What an idiot she'd been, jumping to a conclusion. She'd been trained to be better than that in law school. But in matters of the heart, she'd had little experience. Her mother knew the signs, though. She was glad now that Isabel had called Johnny.

Feeling embarrassed by her misconception, Scarlett

raised her eyes and saw moisture skimming Johnny's cheeks.

She laced her hands around his neck, threading her fingers through his thick dark curls, and drew him toward her. She touched her lips to his. The warmth of his mouth spread like wildfire through her.

Afterward, Scarlett ran her finger over her lower lip. "There's still one thing I need to know, *mi cariño*. Is this how you knock all women off their feet?"

He grinned and smothered her with kisses. "You know what I'd like, *chica?*"

"I can just imagine."

Johnny lifted himself up. "Alrighty then, two hot chocolates coming right up. I brought churros, too."

Scarlett laughed. "Just like old times."

The End

In memory of my brother Frank,
who was my real life Franco.

To hear about Jan's new books first and get special offers, join Jan's VIP Readers Club at www.JanMoran.com.

Read on for an excerpt from *Runway*, the next novel in the *Love, California* series by Jan Moran.

Runway

CAMERA FLASHES EXPLODED on the red carpet just ten feet from Fianna. She blinked against brilliant blue-white auras blurring her vision, straining to see the media's reaction. Amid the lights and the flicking whir of digital cameras, a slender young actress swirled and posed in Fianna's platinum evening dress, the silk rippling around her legs. *Snap, snap, snap.* Spearheaded by a top entertainment attorney and his wife, an A-list talent agent who probably out-earned him, The Pink Ball to benefit The Women in Pink cancer foundation was one of the most well attended charity functions. *Snap, snap.*

Fianna breathed a sigh of relief. Her evening design shone to perfection now, but an hour ago, she'd been taking in the side seams for the Best Supporting Actress Oscar nominee, who was so nervous she hadn't eaten much in days and had lost weight.

Fianna leaned toward Penelope. "I'll never know how Giselle keeps her composure through such intense media scrutiny. But she seems to come alive under pressure." Fianna hoped she could do the same tonight.

"It's the adrenaline rush. She's doing great." Penelope touched Fianna's arm in support. "And so are you. Glad you could fill in at the last minute."

"Thanks again for pitching me." Fianna watched as Giselle swirled and posed once more, dazzling the media that lined the entrance to the grand tented affair on the grounds of a private estate in Malibu, where the ocean lapped just outside the power couple's home. They'd bought the house next door for double digit millions and demolished it, just so they'd have privacy and room to entertain.

"We have about two hours…cocktails, introductions, dinner, closing speech, and then we're on." Penelope raised a dark, high arched brow, a striking contrast to her spiky pink cut, dyed especially for the event. With her high cheekbones and expressive eyes, she carried it off with aplomb, lending elegance to the avant-garde color. "Nervous?"

Fianna realized she was chewing on a freshly manicured nail. "You know I am." She shoved her hands into the sleek black knit jumpsuit she'd chosen to wear backstage.

Penelope was an internationally known Danish model who walked the runways of the world's top fashion designers from New York to Paris, London to Milan. When the fashion designer who had been scheduled for the runway show had been found dead in a hotel room in Las Vegas, his family had cancelled their involvement. Penelope was one of the models cast to walk, so she'd immediately pitched Fianna as a replacement. No other designers could act as quickly as Fianna could, so she'd won the opportunity.

"I still have a lot of staging to do," Fianna said. Giselle moved on to give an interview to a television reporter, and Fianna could hear her talk about her dress, which the reporter gushed over. *So far, so good.* Connected to the elaborate main tent was another tented dressing area that had been erected for the models. The whole gilded affair had cost a fortune and looked like something from The Arabian Nights. But it was worth it; millions would be raised tonight for a good cause.

Penelope nodded toward a photographer. "I'll come with you. I have to get in makeup."

Mounting a runway show was a costly endeavor, and the fashion media was ruthless. As a relative newcomer to the fashion scene, Fianna hadn't yet planned a Fashion Week show of her collection. However, several months ago her aunt Davina had asked her to give a show in Dublin, the timing of which coincided with her cousins wedding, so Fianna already had a small collection prepared. Her friends had urged her on, calling it kismet. So she'd swung into action at her tiny Robertson Boulevard shop, which she'd opened with a loan from her aunt.

When they reached the backstage area, Fianna stepped inside. To the outsider, it looked like chaos, but Fianna was in her element. The colorful, gauzy, romantic clothes she'd designed were arranged like a rainbow on racks, shoes and accessories were neatly organized to accompany each outfit, and notes and sketches detailed each look. At a bank of mirrors, makeup artists and hair stylists were working on models, highlighting and contouring, spiking and fluffing. Lanky young women waited their turn, chatting, flipping through *Vogue*, or swaying to music piped through headphones.

Penelope pulled her shirt off over her head, and then slipped into a thin wrap. She eased her slender, well-toned frame into a director's chair.

Laughter bubbled from one corner, and Fianna frowned at a man wearing dark smoky sunglasses and high-tech earbuds seated next to a model. His long, dark blond hair was brushed from his forehead, grazing his white linen shirt in the back. He stretched out his lengthy legs and laced his fingers behind his neck. "Who's that?"

"Must be her boyfriend."

The backstage area was crowded as it was, and she didn't need some creepy guy ogling the models as they raced to change. She made her way to them. "Hi, Kaitlin. Sorry, but I have to ask your guest to leave. No backstage passes tonight, this is business." She pressed her lips together. This young model was a last minute addition after others had dropped out. Fianna had chosen her based on her model card. She made a note to be more careful in the future.

"Oh, sure," Kaitlin replied. "Niall was just leaving."

The man removed an earbud from his ear. "Your music

is all wrong."

Fianna glared at him. "What?"

He waved a hand toward the rack of clothing. "It doesn't fit with your clothes."

She immediately recognized his trace Irish accent. It smacked of the city. Dublin, she'd bet. "Look Niall, I'm not changing it now. And how do you know about the music I chose?"

"I talked to the sound engineer."

Growing even more irritated, Fianna folded her arms. "Why would you do that? This is *my* show." Finding the right music had taken a long time, and it was far too late to start over.

"Sure, and I figured you've worked hard. So your show should be the best it can be." He held the earbuds to her. "I gave your engineer this music. If you like it, use it."

The nerve of this guy. "I don't have time for this. I don't know who you think you are, but I don't appreciate you going behind my back." She shot a look at Kaitlin, who was suppressing a smile.

She wouldn't hire her again.

His lips curved into a grin, further infuriating her. And he still hadn't removed his sunglasses. Why did people wear sunglasses at night? It was so pretentious. Who did he think he was, Brad Pitt? Or some wanna-be rocker? LA was full of those types, and she steered clear of them. All they wanted were groupies and invitations to the Playboy mansion. And what was with the ridiculous full-sleeved poet's shirt he wore?

"Come on, just listen."

"Get out now." She pointed toward the exit, her finger wavering with anger.

He shook his head, sliding a lock of hair behind an ear. "You can't tell me you're happy with that music. Not until you hear this, anyway." He unplugged a cord from his phone and tapped the screen.

"That's it. I'm calling security." She turned to leave, but a haunting, lilting melody filled the air, and she hesitated, her feet inextricably rooted to the ground.

She lowered her eyelids. At once the music transported her to Ireland; in her mind's eye she saw rolling emerald hills and smelled the sweet scent of peat logs spiraling from country cottage chimneys. She shuddered as the mesmerizing melody increased in intensity, serenading her Celtic soul. Artistic passion awakened and bloomed within her, and she felt herself sway in rhythm to the melody.

Niall's deep voice rumbled behind her. "It's perfect, isn't it?"

Her eyes flew open. *How arrogant of him.* She whirled around, ready to kick him out. But the room had fallen quiet, and others were also transfixed by the magical score. A flash of inspiration soared through her, and she glanced at the designs she'd created. She pressed a hand to her chest, as if to stem the tide of anger washing from her. She had every right to be furious, but she'd never heard anything like this before.

"The engineer has this music?"

Niall nodded.

She lifted her chin and flipped her fiery red mane over her shoulder. "Then I'll have him use it."

"That's a grand decision." Another grin spread across his face. "If you don't mind, I'll see to it for you."

Fianna shrugged her acceptance, though she was inwardly thrilled. The music set the mood she'd envisioned. "Whose work is it?"

"Just some lad's." He rose and sauntered toward the exit. With his broad shoulders, lean waist, and shoulder length hair, he could've been a male model, or a nineteenth-century artist. The sleeves of his shirt were turned back, and dark trousers skimmed his hips.

Fianna stared after him. There was something familiar in the way he moved, though if she'd ever met him before she would have remembered. She dragged her attention away from him and twisted her thick hair into a messy bun to cool her neck against the sudden heat that surged through her. And she'd taken such pains to have her curls blown into a sleek style for the show. She clapped her hands. "Come on, everyone, back to work."

A makeup artist called out. "Who's next?"

Penelope caught Fianna's gaze. "What about your makeup, Fianna? You'll have to take a bow, too." A team of makeup artists from High Gloss, the cosmetics company for which Penelope served as a spokesperson, was cycling the models through. "You'd look great in these new colors." Penelope had helped the company create the new line that carried her name.

"Five minutes, that's all I can spare." Fianna sat next to Penelope, watching her friend's transformation in the mirror as the makeup artist went to work. Her artist touched Fianna's chin to scrutinize her face, and the woman's mouthed formed an "O" in surprise. Fianna blinked and quirked a corner of her mouth. "It's a condition called *heterochromia iridium*." She had one slate blue eye, and the other was hazelnut brown. It was always a challenge at the makeup counter.

The makeup artist twisted her mouth to one side in thought. "For your eyes I'll try purple, no, maybe green. Or cognac brown..."

Penelope winked at her in the mirror.

Fianna closed her eyes as the High Gloss artist selected her brushed and colors and went to work. A five-minute respite, that's what she needed.

Fianna stood by the entrance to the runway with her list, checking each model before she strutted onto the runway. The gorgeous young women were lined up like gazelles, some fussing with their outfits, others jiggling a leg or clicking fingernails in anticipation. Even though they were professionals, they were still young and excited.

A stylist twisted hair and sprayed tendrils, while another wielded a lipstick brush, touching up glossy lips. The magical melody flooded the night and spotlights blinked on. The time had come.

"Are you ready?" Fianna asked Penelope, her voice

wavering with nerves.

"Relax, I've got this." Penelope winked, then her expression changed as she got ready to lead off the show. "And your designs are fabulous."

Would the critics think so, too?

Looking slightly haughty with a sensual pout, Penelope took to the runway with an experienced step, prancing in rhythm with the soulful music that filled the night. The layered silk skirt she wore flowed behind her. After an expert swish and turn, applause thundered through the room.

Fianna smiled with relief. Penelope could make a Hefty bag look like a million dollars. The next model stepped up. Fianna adjusted a sleeve and sent her out.

"You're an absolute goddess, Penelope." Fianna blew a kiss to her friend as Penelope glided off the stage and hurried to change. Kaitlin was next in line.

"Dip your chin a little, Kaitlin. There, that's it." Fianna whispered, fluffing the romantic lace ruffles that flowed around a deep neckline, framing the young model's face and shoulders. She was lovely; no wonder Niall couldn't keep away from her. Fianna waited for a beat in the music. "Now go."

Glancing out, Fianna watched Kaitlin strut down the runway and pause. She had to admit, she was good.

Fianna glanced out and was pleased to see her friends at a nearby table. Verena Valent, who ran a skincare company, Scarlett Sandoval, an intellectual property attorney who specialized in fashion and beauty, and Dahlia Dubois, whose family ran one of the oldest perfume companies in the U.S. She had dressed them all, too, eager to showcase as many of her designs tonight as she could.

Kaitlin turned and applause rippled across the room again.

"Let's keep it going, ladies." Fianna snapped her fingers above her head and turned her attention to the next model. This was all she'd ever dreamed of—a runway show of her own to introduce her designs.

One after another, Fianna sent the models out in rapid succession. And each one met with applause and approval, and until finally, she sent her evening gown selections out, with Penelope leading the way once again.

Fianna looked out. Not even her closest friends had seen these. Judging from their expressions, as well as those on the faces of fashion buyers, members of the press, and high profile charity donors, everyone loved them.

"Hurry, hurry," she said to the models. "Now, everyone out again, all together." All the girls returned to the runway for a final walk and a storm of applause.

"Bravo, bravo," she heard from the audience. Fianna drew a hand through her bright auburn mane. It was over, and she'd survived.

"Come out and take your bow," Penelope said, taking her hand and pulling her onto the runway.

Fianna paused for a moment, drinking in the sight to remember. *My first show.* A smile spread across her face as she raised her hands in acknowledgement of the audience and then applauded her models. She bowed, blew kisses, and bowed again.

Penelope took Fianna's hand again and led her offstage. "Everyone loved it," she said, and hugged Fianna as soon as they were backstage. "You did it, Fianna! How does it feel?"

"Honestly, my head is still spinning. It moved so fast."

"It sure does," Penelope said, laughing with her. "But you did a great job. You're a real pro. You were the calmest new designer I think I've ever seen. Most of them are half crazed or half blitzed."

"I was more like scared stiff," Fianna added, grinning.

"That's because you're a sane one. Genius doesn't always reside with sanity. When it does, the stage for greatness is set."

All the models hugged Fianna or kissed her cheek as they filed back, and crystal champagne flutes were quickly passed around. "Here's to an incredible show, thank you all for a fantastic job out there. You made my designs look amazing."

"That was easy enough, because they are," Kaitlin said, raising her glass. "And here's to you, Fianna."

Fianna smiled. Kaitlin's expression was genuine, and she seemed like a sweet young woman. She was probably the youngest of the group. Niall and Kaitlin were certainly an attractive couple.

Niall. Why was she still thinking of him? But she had to find him and thank him for the music. With its evocative melody, it had really helped make the show. Everything had synergy—from the models to her clothes, from the music to the lighting. If anything was out of sync, the show would suffer. Tonight, as if by magic, all the elements had coalesced, and all the stars had lined up in the celestial heavens for her.

Tonight was her night.

All Fianna needed was someone to celebrate with. She sipped her champagne, crinkling her nose at the bubbles. She loved her friends, but she wished she had someone special in her life.

Her mother often told her she had made a huge mistake leaving behind the man who loved her in Ireland. Was that true? A demanding man might get in the way of her aspirations, of the passion for her craft that many could not understand. Especially her mother. And yet, as much as she loved what she did, she missed having someone with whom she could confide her deepest thoughts and desires. She often stole glances at Verena and Lance, or Scarlett and Johnny. They seemed so happy together.

"Kaitlin, do you know where I can find Niall?" Fianna asked. "I'd like to thank him again for the music."

"He said he was joining some of his friends." Kaitlin giggled. "Look for a group of handsome guys, and you'll find him." She lowered her voice. "But I think they're all taken."

"Well, Niall is certainly taken with you." Before Kaitlin could say anything else, Fianna excused herself. She gave instructions to her assistant and the interns who were helping her organize clothes and accessories, and then decided to look for Niall.

As she pushed the door to the event space open, she

wished Davina were here. Only her aunt understood how much tonight meant to her. The youngest of her mother's sisters, Davina had been like an older sister to her at first, and later, more like a surrogate mother. Davina had been one of the most popular runway models of her day before she retired.

Watching her aunt on the runway had sparked Fianna's passion for fashion design. Davina had helped her with her application to FIDM, the Fashion Institute for Design and Merchandising in Los Angeles.

Her mother had refused to condone such "nonsense," as she called her daughter's creative ambitions, saying it was much more sensible to find a man, marry, and begin a family, since that's what she would do anyway. Why run away to America to study when one had no intention of ever using that knowledge?

And then Fianna had opened her boutique on Robertson Boulevard, and her mother had stopped talking to her. So much for being proud of her daughter.

At least her sister Lizzie was getting married soon. That would alleviate some of the pressure.

Fianna paused and looked around. The crowd showed no signs of thinning out, and a singer was setting up on another stage. No doubt the party would last long into the night.

"Fianna, come join us." Verena was waving to her from the table where her friends were seated. "You should have seen it from out here. It was the best runway show I've ever seen. And the crowd loved it. Imagine, even Greta Hicks had a smile on her face."

"That's a good sign." The *Fashion News Daily* reporter was not one to conceal what she thought.

"I bet you'll have great coverage in the media. And I heard this event raised the most money ever for the Women in Pink Foundation, even topping last year." Verena had been honored the prior year at the foundation's fundraiser at the Beverly Hills Hotel.

A well-built athletic man in a tuxedo seated next to Verena leaned toward them, draping his arm around Verena. With a tender movement, he straightened the thin strap of the romantic, flowing dress in rosy pink Fianna had picked out for Verena to wear, which was perfect with her alabaster skin and fair blond hair. "Nothing could top that night," Lance said. "That's the night Verena and I met. This is our one year anniversary."

Verena laughed. "And what a year it's been." She clasped Fianna's hand. "For all of us. This is your dream, Fianna. I'm so happy we're all here tonight."

"Who's at the restaurant?" Lance and his partner, Johnny, had opened a restaurant called Bow-Tie a few months ago.

"We have an assistant manager now," Lance said. "Since it's a weeknight, it's not too crowded."

Fianna winked at him. "You mean, only a dozen or two people waiting to get in, as opposed to the line down the block on the weekends? I'm awfully glad I know you guys or

I'd never set foot inside."

A dark-haired man with a red bow-tie leaned over and pecked her on the cheek. "That's what friends are for, *mi amiga*."

"Johnny, it's so good to see you. Where's Scarlett?"

A smile lit his face as looked past her. "My lovely lady is coming this way. She stopped to talk to Greta." He held a hand out to a coppery blonde woman wearing one of Fianna's designs, a ruby red gown. She moved through the crowd with calm assurance.

"Scarlett, what did you think?"

"I think I've got a licensing deal in the works for you. That was a magnificent show." Scarlett Sandoval was an intellectual property attorney, and since she'd opened her own practice she'd promised to help Fianna secure licensing agreements for accessories such as purses and sunglasses.

"This is certainly your night, Fianna," Verena said. "The Saks west coast divisional manager for fashion just left, but she told me she's going to contact you about your line."

Fianna let out a little squeal. "And where's Dahlia? I can smell her fabulous perfume lingering here at the table."

Scarlett laughed. "I think we're all wearing one of her perfumes tonight. And Verena's skincare. Last I saw, Dahlia was going to the dance floor."

Fianna turned in her chair. The music had started again, and the dance floor was filling fast. She saw a petite, dark haired woman wearing the black evening gown she'd designed with her in mind. It was reminiscent of the classic dress in artist John Singer Sargent's portrait of Madame X. Fianna tilted her head, apprising the look. The sweetheart neckline and nipped waist was perfect on Dahlia.

Scarlett shot a look at Verena. "What do you think of her date?"

"We don't really know him," Verena said, seeming to choose her words with care.

Fianna was intrigued. "What's he like?"

Scarlett twisted her mouth to one side, and Verena threw her a *be nice* glance. "What I meant was that it's probably a little daunting meeting your date's friends all at once," Scarlett said.

"How diplomatic." Fianna grinned. "But Scarlett, that's what I love about you. You always tell it like it is."

"That's the attorney in her." Verena sighed. "Scarlett, the poor guy's not on trial tonight. You've been going after him like you're interrogating him."

"So? I look after my friends." Scarlett winked. "But I got some good information, didn't I?"

Fianna shook her head, amused. She was sure she'd hear the whole story later. "I'd love to stay with you, but I'm looking for someone, and I want to catch him before he leaves."

Johnny waggled his eyebrows. "And who's the lucky guy?"

"Just one of the model's dates. He gave me the music to use. His name is Niall."

"Niall's here?" Johnny shot a look at Lance. "I thought I

recognized that music."

"Oh, you know who he is?" Fianna rose from the table, craning her neck. She thought she caught a glimpse of him striding toward an exit.

Johnny raised his brow. "You're kidding, right?"

"I nearly threw him out for hanging around backstage. But he turned out to be really helpful. Excuse me, I think I see him." Fianna darted through the crowd after him. She felt curiously drawn to him. He was Kaitlin's boyfriend, but she had to speak to him.

She reached the exit and stepped from the red carpet onto the soft sand. She reached down and slipped off her black heels. Shoes dangling in her hand, she started for the shoreline.

At once she saw him, and her heart quickened. The moonlight illuminated his broad silhouette. He jerked his arm and threw something into the water.

Fianna was suddenly incensed. Having grown up on the island of Ireland, she was protective of the ocean. She marched toward him. What was he throwing into the sea?

To continue reading *Runway*, visit your favorite retailer.

About the Author

JAN MORAN IS a writer living in sunny southern California. She writes contemporary and historical fiction, and nonfiction. Keep up with her latest blog posts at JanMoran.com.

A few of Jan's favorite things include a fine cup of coffee, dark chocolate, fresh flowers, and music that touches her soul. She loves to travel just about anywhere, though her favorite places for inspiration are those rich with history and mystery and set against snowy mountains, palm-treed beaches, or sparkly city lights. Jan is originally from Austin, Texas, and a trace of a drawl still survives to this day, although she has lived in California for years.

Her books are available as audiobooks, and her historical fiction has been widely translated into German, Italian, Polish, Turkish, Russian, and Lithuanian, among other languages.

Jan has been featured in and written for many

prestigious media outlets, including *CNN, Wall Street Journal, Women's Wear Daily, Allure, InStyle, O Magazine, Cosmopolitan, Elle,* and *Costco Connection,* and has spoken before numerous groups about writing and entrepreneurship, such as San Diego State University, Fashion Group International, The Fragrance Foundation, and The American Society of Perfumers.

She is a graduate of the Harvard Business School, the University of Texas at Austin, and the UCLA Writers Program.

To hear about Jan's new books first and get special offers, join Jan's VIP Readers Club at www.JanMoran.com and get a free download. If you enjoyed this book, please consider leaving a brief review online for your fellow readers.

Made in the USA
Coppell, TX
28 September 2020